P9-CTA-213

Praise for **Starship: Mutiny**

"Resnick's reputation for writing two-fisted adventure has already been established, and *Starship: Mutiny* doesn't change that. Once again, the author demonstrates his ability to create characters several shades above stereotype, as well as fit them into a carefully conceived universe. Readers looking for an old-fashioned yarn will find this novel an auspicious start to a promising series."

—Starlog

"Resnick's writing is effortless, full of snappy dialogue and a fast-moving plot. The real delight to reading this novel is the banter and jokes in the conversations between Cole and the crewmates he does get on with, the insults and sarcastic comments with those he doesn't get on with, and the real feeling of camaraderie and society it creates. It's very easy to imagine this as a real world and setting because the characters act so naturally together. . . . This was my first time at a Resnick book, so I had no expectation coming in. Needless to say, I was impressed. This is high-quality work. . . . There's a veneer of quality and above all believability that makes this heads above many space operas. . . . It's damn good fun."

—SF Crowsnest

"[F]ew writers have Resnick's gift for pace and momentum, . . . his talent for producing a fast, smooth, utterly effortless read."

—Analog Science Fiction and Fact

Praise for **Starship: Pirate**

"One of the characters in this sequel to *Starship: Mutiny* asks, 'Whatever happened to heroes who didn't think everything through, but just walked in with weapons blazing?' The answer is 'They're buried in graveyards all across the galaxy.' This sums up nicely Hugo-winner Resnick's approach to military SF, which isn't so much about fighting and hardware as it is about strategy and leadership. . . . Readers craving intelligent, character-driven SF need look no further."

—*Publishers Weekly*

"Mike Resnick is one of the finest writers the science fiction field has ever produced, and *Starship: Pirate* is one of his very best works. A wonderful book."

—Robert J. Sawyer
Hugo Award–winning
author of *Hominids*

"This sequel to *Starship: Mutiny*, set in Resnick's Birthright Universe, . . . shows the author's genuine flair for spinning a good yarn. Snappy dialogue, intriguing human and alien characters, and a keen sense of dramatic focus make this a strong addition to most SF collections, with particular appeal to the SF action-adventure readership."

—*Library Journal*

Praise for **Starship: Mercenary**

"The ability to write good space opera is increasingly a misplaced, if not lost, art, but Resnick knows how to draw on a hidden lode of it. . . . Genuine fun."

—*Critical Mass*

"This is classic space opera at its best with plenty of rapid-fire action, quick wit, and fast thinking that will leave readers cheering for an honorable man who, although wronged by the system, continues to behave with dignity. The well-conceived characters continue to expand and develop with each installment, making for great escapist reading with enough humor to maintain a light feel."

—Monsters and Critics

"As ever, Resnick is effortlessly readable. The plot feels under control at all times and yet many of the events feel spontaneous and random. The characters are funny, eclectic, and engaging and the action thrills. This is a writer at the top of his game, writing extremely enjoyable space opera."

—*SF Crowsnest*

"While the novel is fast paced and entertaining, Copperfield's character adds a great deal of humor and comedic relief to the story and grows into more than strictly comic relief by the novel's end. I'm still enjoying this series and am interested to see where Resnick is going to take the *Teddy R* and its crew. So the bottom line is this: if you've enjoyed the first two *Starship* novels, there is no reason not to continue on with the story."

—*SFF World*

Praise for **Starship: Rebel**

"If you haven't read books one through three yet, you are missing out on some great science fiction. And if you've never read Mike Resnick's works before, you really should. . . . They are great reading."

—Intercontinental
Ballistic Discourse blog

"If you accept *Starship: Rebel* for what it is (fast paced and entertaining), then I think you'll have just as much fun with it as I did. I'm looking forward to seeing where this series goes next. Eight out of Ten."

—*Graeme's Fantasy
Book Review*

"Resnick's quality never falters throughout the first four books: they maintain a consistent level of enjoyment, which is to say that if you like one you'll like them all."

—*SF Signal*

STARSHIP: FLAGSHIP

ALSO AVAILABLE BY MIKE RESNICK

IVORY

NEW DREAMS FOR OLD

STARSHIP: MUTINY
BOOK ONE

STARSHIP: PIRATE
BOOK TWO

STARSHIP: MERCENARY
BOOK THREE

STARSHIP: REBEL
BOOK FOUR

MIKE RESNICK

STARSHIP:
FLAGSHIP

BOOK FIVE

an imprint of **Prometheus Books**
Amherst, NY

Published 2009 by Pyr®, an imprint of Prometheus Books

Inquiries should be addressed to
Pyr
59 John Glenn Drive
Amherst, New York 14228–2119
VOICE: 716–691–0133
FAX: 716–691–0137
WWW.PYRSF.COM

13 12 11 10 09   5 4 3 2 1

Library of Congress Cataloging-in-Publication Data

Resnick, Michael D.
    Starship—flagship / by Mike Resnick.
        p. cm.
    ISBN: 978–1–59102–788–1 (acid-free paper)
    1. Space warfare—Fiction. I. Title. II. Title: Flagship.

PS3568.E698S733 2009
813'.54—dc22

2009033113

Printed in the United States on acid-free paper

To Carol, as always

And to Blarney, who knows why

Singapore Station—oddly shaped, built of dozens of disparate pieces, close to seven miles long—moved almost imperceptibly through space at the heart of the Inner Frontier. It was not a world but merely a structure. It possessed no government yet was home to almost twenty thousand permanent residents and a quarter million transients. A dozen mile-long docking arms shot out from its core, giving it the appearance of a gigantic, shining, mutated spider.

The most important location on the three oxygen levels of the station was Duke's Place, a casino run by the once-human individual known as the Platinum Duke. It attracted humans and aliens for its gaming tables, its drinks, and its willingness to look the other way when black marketeers gathered to do their business. But on this particular day, more important things were transpiring than simply the winning and losing of money. To the men, women, and aliens gathered in the Platinum Duke's back room, the stakes were a lot higher than that.

Wilson Cole faced the assemblage. He was a nondescript man, an inch or two below normal height, a few pounds overweight, his brown hair starting to turn gray. There was nothing in his appearance to suggest that he had been the most decorated member of the Republic's vast military machine, or that for the past four years he had been that same military's most wanted outlaw.

"It's time," he said. "We leave tomorrow."

"Tomorrow?" exclaimed a few surprised voices.

"I've received word that the Navy has dispatched a fleet of eight hundred ships, and they should reach Singapore Station in two days' time. So like it or not, we're in a state of war."

"We always were," snorted an extremely tall, statuesque redhead.

"Not until last month, Val," Cole corrected her.

"Okay," said the woman named Val. "*You* weren't at war with the Republic. *I* was."

"It makes no difference," he replied. "Right now we all are."

"You can't say this was unanticipated," said a man whose face and limbs, indeed everything but his eyes and tongue, seemed to be made of platinum.

"Of course it wasn't," answered Cole. "But it means that it's time to go on the offensive."

"Are you sure we're ready?" asked a short blonde woman.

"I don't think it matters," said Cole. "It's been forced on us." He paused. "Look, the Navy tortured two of our officers and then destroyed an entire planet for harboring them. So we declared the Inner Frontier off-limits, and began picking off Navy ships one at a time whenever they'd cross the border. It was only a matter of time before they responded in force. They did that last month, and we beat them—at a cost of half our fleet. This time they're coming with more than twice as many ships. What will it cost us to beat them again— and if we do, how many ships do you think they'll send the next time? They've got three million to choose from, and four worlds devoted to doing nothing but building more. We have less than a thousand, and most of them have no defenses against the kind of weaponry they'll have to face."

"If we can't hold off eight hundred ships, or fifteen hundred, or two thousand, on our own home ground, how the hell do you plan to conquer the Republic?" demanded the Platinum Duke. "I trusted you, Wilson. Now you tell me you can't defend Singapore Station."

"I *can* defend it," said Cole. "I'm telling you I *won't* defend it. We can't stay here. It just wouldn't be worth the cost in ships and lives. If we lose, it's over; and if we win, then we'll lose the next time, or the time after that."

"So instead you're going to conquer the Republic, with its sixty thousand worlds and three million military ships?" persisted the Duke sarcastically. "I'll tell you something, Wilson: if you promote God to Gunnery Officer of the *Teddy R*, I'll still put my money on the Republic."

"Wars are like safaris," answered Cole calmly. "The best ones are where you only have to fire one or two shots."

"Spare me your platitudes!" snapped the Duke. "Eight hundred ships are coming out here for blood. They don't know that you've teamed up with the Octopus. They don't know about the few hundred ships you recruited from the Republic itself. They don't even know if the *Theodore Roosevelt* still exists. All they know is that we annihilated their last force at Singapore Station, and that's what they're coming to destroy."

"They're not coming to destroy Singapore Station," chimed in the Octopus, a huge man who stood out even among the more bizarre aliens in the room. He wore no shirt and had six misshapen hands projecting, armless, from his rib cage, three on each side. "Use your brain, Duke. Just make it clear that you're doing business as usual, have your girls greet them with open arms, and keep your casinos and bars and drug dens running around the clock. They know that Singapore Station doesn't have motive power. Until last month they never lost a ship anywhere near the station. The only reason they came here is because they were tipped that Cole was here. They don't want your station. They want *him*—and, in all immodesty, me."

"Fine!" snarled the Duke. "So they're not going to blow it away; they're just going to appropriate everything I own. That makes it all okay."

"Shut up!" said Val irritably. "If we win, we'll take it back. If we lose, you won't be around to worry about it."

"How comforting," growled the Duke.

"Come off it," said Val. "You spent a good twenty years running rigged games and serving watered whiskey. It's time you paid your dues."

"I thought that was what I was doing when I let you draw them to the station last month."

"Hey, Cole!" said Val, getting to her feet. "What say I make him the first casualty of the war?"

"Just calm down, Val," said Cole. "We've got serious things to talk about."

"Yeah? Well, I am seriously offering to coldcock him."

Cole smiled and turned to the Duke. "You have to forgive the Valkyrie. Sometimes she forgets who the enemy is."

"Then get on with it!" muttered Val.

"Sometimes she forgets who the boss is, too," continued Cole. "All right, to repeat: at last count we have eight hundred and four ships, including those that Lafferty can make available to us. The computer can't give us an exact total for the Navy, but it estimates three million four hundred seventeen thousand two hundred eighty-nine as of an hour ago."

"Where *is* this Lafferty?" asked one of the men at the back of the room.

"I notice that nobody minded accepting his help last month," said Cole with a smile. The smile vanished. "He's our contact within the Republic, and he's staying there. They're watching any ship that approaches Singapore Station, so why let them know they have a turncoat—actually, a few hundred turncoats—in their midst?" He paused. "Now, even someone as bloodthirsty as Val can't really want to take on three and a half million ships with a force of eight hundred—"

"Three million four hundred thousand," she interrupted him.

"I stand corrected. If you find those odds considerably more favorable, I'm going to have the computer give you a course in remedial mathematics." There were a few chuckles; the Valkyrie wasn't laughing. "Not only can't we go up against them, but it would be foolhardy to travel in any discernible formation, or even in any proximity to each other. We're fighting a guerrilla war, and it's a big galaxy. If we do it right, finding us should be even harder than finding needles in a haystack."

"That's going to make it damnably hard to coordinate any action at all," offered another man.

"We're working on that," answered Cole. "Christine Mboya and Malcolm Briggs are our two computer experts. They're on the *Teddy R* right now, working on a code we can use that—"

"There's never been a code that couldn't be broken," interrupted an alien.

"You didn't let me finish," said Cole, just the slightest hint of steel beneath the mild response. "As I was saying, they're working on a code that will be keyed in only to those ships that are meant to receive it, and will instantly vanish should any other ship or computer try to decipher it."

"It'll never work."

Cole indicated a humanoid alien seated in the first row. "Commander Jacovic?"

The alien stood up and turned to face the room. "The Teroni Federation has been using such codes for four years. They exist, and they work."

"One of the advantages we have," said Cole, "is that most of the Republic's military assets and forces will be occupied by the Teroni Federation. It's true that they have three and a half million ships, but about three million are engaged in this interminable war against the Teronis."

"So it's only half a million to eight hundred," said the Platinum Duke. "That makes it all okay."

Val glared at him until he lowered his gaze.

"Another advantage we have is that my First Officer"—Cole nodded toward Jacovic—"is the former Commander of the Fifth Teroni Fleet. Should we inadvertently come into contact with them, he will be our spokesman."

"He's their version of *you*," said the Duke. "They'll blow him away the second they identify him."

Cole shook his head. "He resigned in disgust. I mutinied. There's a difference—perhaps not to the ruling parties, but to the officers he may have to contact." He turned to face the Platinum Duke. "Now, as to your last bit of arithmetic: it's true that there are probably close to half a million Republic ships that aren't engaged in the war with the Teroni Federation—but that's not the only real or potential threat the Republic faces. The Canphor Twins—Canphor VI and VII—have gone to war with them four times this millennium, and there's always a chance, almost a certainty in fact, that one of these days they'll try it again. When we were in the Navy, the remnants of the Sett Empire were picking up some support on the Rim, and controlled about thirty planets. Who the hell knows what's happened in the last four years? And there are doubtless other threats that we know nothing about. Most of the Republic's ships will be otherwise occupied, as long as we can keep one fact a secret."

"Only one?" said the Duke.

Cole smiled. "Only one. *We* know we're in a war with the Republic. The longer we can keep that fact from them, the greater our chance of success."

A man at the back of the room stood up. "I have a question."

"Yes, Mr. Perez?"

"It's easy to keep the fact that we're at war a secret today or tomorrow, sir, but how the hell do we keep it a secret once we start attacking their ships inside the Republic?"

"In the beginning, we'll pick them off one by one, just the way we did here on the Frontier. We won't attack any force that we can't annihilate before they can get a message off. The notion that we've reentered their territory and are engaging their ships is too outrageous for them to give any credence to, at least if we're careful."

"Dumb!" said Val.

"Oh?" said Cole. "Perhaps you'd care to enlighten us."

"We could die of old age before we kill a third of the solo ships they've got patrolling the Republic's borders. Deluros VIII is their capital world. *That's* the place we should be going!"

"That's our ultimate target," replied Cole. "How close do you think we could get as an identifiable military force? Forty thousand light-years? Thirty-five thousand?"

"So you think one lone ship can sneak through?" she persisted. "I hope you're not thinking of the *Teddy R*, because every goddamned ship and officer in the Republic is on the lookout for it. The best thing to do is put it on autopilot, fill it with exceptionally dirty pulse bombs, and aim it at Deluros."

Cole looked amused. "You must forgive her," he said to the room. "She's really very kind to her cat."

"I don't have a fucking cat!" snapped Val.

"I forgot—she ate it," he said with a smile. Val growled an obscenity, but other than that didn't respond. "As I was saying," Cole continued, "we'll pick them off whenever and wherever we can, we'll sabotage their bases, and at least half of us will be in the business not of fighting but of enlisting disillusioned members of the Republic to our cause. We have the further advantage that only four of our ships carry Navy design and insignia. That means that those are the only four ships that can be taken or even identified. If any of you run into trouble, you can cut and run, and even if your ship is identified the Navy will never know you're part of a coordinated attack force."

"By that same token, the *Teddy R* should hang back where it can't possibly be identified," said the Duke.

"In a perfect universe you'd be right," said Cole. "But if this was a perfect universe, we wouldn't be attacking the Republic."

"Okay, it's imperfect. Why does that give you leave to attack a Republic ship and be identified?"

"We call what we have a fleet," explained Cole, "but what it mostly is is a collection of small ships that were never intended for military action. Most of them have been jury-rigged and outfitted with weapons and some defenses, but the fact remains that only three of our ships can resist a Level 4 pulse cannon or a Level 5 laser cannon, and the *Teddy R* is one of them. Only one of our ships has the power to fire a Level 5 pulse cannon, and that's the *Teddy R*. There will be situations where we're the only one with the firepower and defenses to go up against certain ships or certain planetary installations." He paused. "And there's something else."

"What?"

"They don't know that the *Teddy R* isn't acting independently. If they kill or capture us, they'll assume it's over, and the rest of you will be free to operate with far less scrutiny. Which is to say, they won't be searching every ship for me."

"If they kill you, you'll be avenged," said a tall blond man.

"I certainly hope so, Mr. Sokolov," said Cole. "All right. Lieutenants Mboya and Briggs think they'll have their code finished by nineteen hundred hours station time. I'll want each of you to make your ships' computers available to them at that time, and I want at least one member of your crew, and preferably two, standing by to learn whatever they need to know about it. We'll depart the station tomorrow, after one more meeting at oh-nine hundred hours. This meeting is adjourned."

As the men, women, and aliens began returning to the casino, the Platinum Duke walked up to Cole.

"You're so calm and soft-spoken, one really has to listen to realize just how bloodthirsty you are."

A pretty brunette moved next to Cole. "We were hoping you wouldn't notice," said Sharon Blacksmith with a smile.

Cole put an arm around her and turned to the Duke. "You didn't mind financing most of this a week ago," he noted. "What made you so argumentative today?"

"A week ago eight hundred ships weren't coming after the space station that I happen to own and live on," answered the Duke.

"It was inevitable after we destroyed their force of three hundred last month."

"Inevitable is just a word," said the Duke. "Eight hundred Navy ships hell-bent on destruction is a *fact*—and you're leaving it to their mercy."

"If you really want out . . ."

"No, of course not," said the Duke. "What I really want is for us to have won already with no damage to the station."

"Well," said Cole, "I'll give you points for honesty."

"I'll give you even more for gall," said the Duke. "The Teroni Federation has thrown a couple of million ships against the Republic and hasn't made any measurable progress in twenty-nine years. And you're planning to overthrow them with a handful of ships and a crew of misfits."

"I'd rather have a fleet of five million ships manned by seasoned veterans," said Cole. "To put it in terms a casino owner will understand, you play the cards you're dealt."

"Just destroy Admiral Susan Garcia and her flagship before they blow you away," said the Duke. "Do that and I'll consider it a victory." He paused and his expression softened. "You two want some dinner?"

"Maybe later," said Cole. "I want to get back to the ship and see how they're coming on the code."

The Duke checked his timepiece. "Two hours?"

"Yeah, that'll be fine—if my Chief of Security agrees."

"We'll be there," said Sharon.

"And Duke?" said Cole.

"Yes?"

"I think you should consider coming with us. They don't want the station, but sooner or later they're going to find out who's financing us."

The Duke considered the offer, then nodded. "You have a point. I'll have some of my things transferred to the ship in the next hour."

Cole and Sharon took a tram ride half a mile out on one of the docking arms until they reached the *Theodore Roosevelt*.

"I've got to go up to the bridge," said Cole.

"I thought you hated the bridge."

"I do, but that's where Christine and Briggs are working."

"Okay," she replied. "I've got about an hour's work in Security. Pick me up there when you're ready to go back for dinner."

"Will do."

Cole took an airlift up to the bridge level and stepped out into a corridor, trying not to think of how long it had been since the ship had last been refitted. When he was still about forty feet away he stopped, walked over to a bulkhead, and tapped on it.

"Good afternoon, David," he said.

"Are we at war yet?" asked a voice from inside the bulkhead.

"All's quiet on the Western front," replied Cole.

"We're in space!" snapped the voice. "There *is* no West! And how dare you quote Erich Maria Remarque to me instead of the immortal Charles!"

"You get stranger and stranger every day," said Cole, heading off to the bridge.

"Bring me back a dry sherry," the voice called after him.

"You can't metabolize it."

"I'll be the judge of that!" said the voice.

Then they were out of earshot, and Cole entered the bridge.

"Hello, sir," said Christine Mboya, looking up from her computer. "How did it go?"

"Our side has a redhead who wants to attack all three million Republic ships at once, an egomaniacal criminal kingpin with eight hands, a platinum cyborg who's only willing to go to war as long as no one shoots back, and an alien who thinks he's David Copperfield," replied Cole with a wry grimace. "How can we lose?"

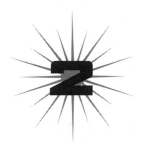

Cole sat at his usual table in a corner of the mess hall, sipping a cup of coffee and wondering why the galley created such foul-tasting cheese Danishes. The few crew members who were also there gave his table a wide berth; it was well known that he was not at his friendliest before he had his morning coffee.

One member who had no compunction about talking to him any time of the day or night was Sharon Blacksmith. She spotted him as she was walking past the mess hall, entered, walked over, and seated herself opposite him.

"Well?" she said.

He looked across at her. "Well what?"

"No red roses?"

"If I gave you a dozen red roses every time we've shared a bed together, I could defoliate an entire planet." He pushed his Danish across to her. "Settle for this instead."

She wrinkled her nose. "They're pretty awful."

He nodded his agreement. "They taste a lot better when we're fifty light-years from any inhabited planet that possesses a bakery. Maybe I'll buy a batch at Singapore Station and take them with us."

"You're really going to do it, aren't you?" she asked.

"Buy a bunch of Danishes? Probably not."

She frowned. "You know what I'm talking about, Wilson."

"I don't see that we have any choice," he replied seriously. "And if we did, I'd still choose this course of action."

"I just wish we'd had more time to build our fleet," said Sharon.

"The bigger they are . . ."

"Bullshit," she said. "Not when they're *that* big."

"Maybe not," acknowledged Cole. "I wish the odds were better. Hell, I wish we had a Republic that didn't plunder its colony planets and conscript men and women for the military against their will. I wish this was the Republic we thought we were fighting for when we all enlisted." His expression darkened. "I'd prefer a Republic that hadn't tortured my best friend to death. I'd prefer a Republic that's notion of pacifying an indigent population wasn't genocide. But it's clear we're not going to get *that* Republic until we get rid of *this* one."

She stared at him for a long moment. "You used to smile a lot more," she said at last.

"I used to have more to smile about. I can count, you know. I'm asking a force of maybe four thousand men to risk their lives against the most powerful military machine that has ever existed. Any bookmaker would say that if ten of us are still alive half a year from now, we've beaten the odds."

"Then why do it?"

"Because somebody has to," replied Cole. "Because all of us—you, me, Bull, Christine, poor Four Eyes—helped create and strengthen this monster. If we don't stand up and say 'This is not what sentient beings do to one another,' who do you think will?" He stared at her. "We've been through this a dozen times. Why bring it up now?"

"Because we're leaving Singapore Station in two hours, and there's no turning back."

A bitter smile crossed Cole's face. "If we *don't* leave, we'll be facing a fleet of eight hundred warships in less than a day." He sighed. "They're just a bunch of soldiers following orders, just the way *we* used to. If we're going to die in battle, let's do it against the people who *give* those orders."

She returned his smile, such as it was. "I thought the object was to make the other side die in battle."

He suddenly relaxed. "Well, that's certainly the way I'm going to plan it." He took another sip of his coffee. "Don't worry. I don't believe there's anything noble, or even effective, about a suicide attack. I have every intention of winning and surviving."

"Really?"

"Really."

"You're even crazier than the rest of us," said Sharon.

"There are days I think it's a prime qualification for command."

Suddenly a scream of triumph came over the ship's intercom. "Got one of the smarmy little bastards!" yelled a familiar voice.

"Val, calm down and tell me what happened," said Cole.

There was no response, and he remembered he hadn't touched the spot on the table that would open a communication channel. He placed his finger on it and repeated his statement.

"A seven-man Class H Navy ship was approaching Binder X," replied the Valkyrie as the image of her face materialized above the table. "It was probably going there for a little R and R. Two of the Octopus's ships blew it apart."

Cole frowned. "I don't suppose any of it survived?"

"A few pieces, I suppose."

"All right," said Cole. "And Val?"

"Yeah?"

"Tell the Octopus to pass the word that next time they go after a Navy ship I want them to try to destroy its antenna and then disable it."

"They're the enemy, right?" said the Valkyrie. "What do you do with the enemy? You kill him! You make the sonuvabitch wish he'd never been born! You—"

"Shut up and listen to me," said Cole irritably. "We're about to enter the Republic. Any time we can swipe the insignia from a Navy ship, that's one more of our ships that's not at risk when it's spotted. If we can get to their radio before it's destroyed, we can see if there are any new codes, we can learn how to send and respond to messages using the ship's ID, we can appropriate its weapons and give them to some of our own ships, we—"

"Why don't we just shake their hands and offer to buy all that shit?" growled Val.

"Are you going to give him my message or not?"

"Maybe."

"Maybe?" he repeated.

"Okay, probably," she said. "What if they spot our ships and shoot first?"

"If they shoot first, of course we have to defend ourselves," replied Cole. "And 'probably' isn't any more acceptable than 'maybe.'"

"All right," muttered Val.

"By the way, what are you doing on the bridge anyway?" he asked. "It's oh-seven hundred hours. That means it's still red shift. That's Jacovic's shift."

"He's still on the station, trying to recruit some new arrivals."

"Teronis?"

"Who else could he recruit?" snorted Val.

"I hope he gets some," said Cole. "It would make up a little for losing that insignia because he wasn't on the bridge."

"All right, all right," said Val, breaking the connection.

Cole pressed another spot on the table.

"Sir?" said Malcolm Briggs as his face appeared where Val's had been.

"Remind Commander Jacovic that we're departing in less than two hours, and make sure all other crew members are on board."

"Yes, sir."

"Did you get that code installed in all the ships?"

"All those at the station, sir," said Briggs. "I didn't want to take the chance of it being intercepted as a signal, so I turned a cube over to Captain Flores and told him to take it to Mr. Lafferty on Piccoli III and stay there until it was successfully installed in all his ships."

"I approve," said Cole. He paused. "His ships are spread out over a dozen planets. I don't think we'll be seeing Mr. Flores anytime soon."

"We wouldn't anyway," said Sharon. "We're all loners, at least until you tell us what you have in mind."

"Thank you, Mr. Briggs," said Cole. "That will be all."

He broke the connection.

"You're going to tell me not to correct or contradict you in front of the crew, right?" said Sharon.

He shrugged. "I don't give a damn, unless someone's shooting at us. If it makes you happy, contradict all you like."

She emitted an exasperated sigh. "What the hell kind of hero are you, anyway?"

"A live one."

She stared at him. "Come to think of it, you don't look much like a hero."

"What does a hero look like?" asked Cole.

"Bold. Tall. Strong. Handsome. Fearless."

"You've seen me with my pants off too many times. It spoils the illusion."

She laughed, leaned across the table, and kissed him. "You're hero enough for me."

Suddenly Malcolm Briggs's face appeared again. "I hate to bother you, sir," he said apologetically, "but we can't locate Commander Jacovic."

"Pass the word to Val or whoever replaces her on white shift that we don't take off without him," said Cole.

"Yes, sir."

Cole got to his feet. "I'll fetch him. We know he's recruiting, and there's only two or three Teroni hangouts on the alien levels of the station." He paused. "Tell Bull Pampas to meet me at the hatch."

"Do you think you'll need him?"

"Probably I won't," answered Cole. "But Jacovic didn't respond when we summoned him, and after Val, Bull is the best human weapon we've got."

"Then why not take Val?"

"Because she's the Officer on Deck for another hour or so. Protecting the ship is more important than protecting the Captain."

Sharon didn't agree, but decided not to argue the point, and a moment later Cole and his tall, dark-haired, heavily muscled Gunnery Chief, Eric "Bull" Pampas, boarded the tram and were soon inside the station.

Suddenly an alarm went off.

"Are you armed?" asked Cole.

"Colonel Blacksmith told me I was supposed to protect you," said Pampas as two security guards approached and confiscated his weapon. "Besides, that never happened before."

"The Duke was never worried about the Navy sending spies, saboteurs, and assassins before," said Cole. He turned to the guards. "We'll want that back on the way out."

"Fuck you," said one of the guards. "You get the Navy to come out here, and then you and all your ships leave us to face them alone. You're damned lucky I don't turn it on you."

"The Navy doesn't want *you*," said Cole. "They want *us*. Don't fire a shot and they won't either."

"And if you're wrong?" demanded the man. "If they wipe us out, are you going to avenge us? I feel all better now."

Cole could see that Pampas was tensing, preparing to try to take the laser pistol back. "Keep it," he said, taking Pampas by the arm "Come on, Bull."

"But that was my burner!" protested Pampas as he fell into step behind Cole. "They have no business keeping it!"

"Draw another one from the armory," said Cole, heading to an airlift. "I don't need you getting yourself killed on Singapore Station. We've got bigger fish to fry."

They reached the airlift, and Cole briefly read the holographic chart next to the controls. "Okay, third level," he said. "I don't spend much time on the alien levels. I couldn't remember where the Teronis congregate." They were lowered to the third level on a cushion of air. "Probably his communicator is just on the blink. But if there's any kind of situation, take your lead from me. Don't act independently unless you're attacked."

"Yes, sir."

They stepped out into a corridor. The gravity was a little lighter than Galactic Standard, the air a little thinner and dryer. The doorways were a mixed lot, some built to accommodate beings who dwarfed Men, some for aliens who barely came up to Men's waists, some exceptionally wide, others equally narrow. Cole always felt a bit disoriented on those few occasions when he had to visit this level—and this was for oxygen breathers. The lowest level was even stranger.

They walked past a few stores, some selling items as familiar as weapons, others selling things that were completely incomprehensible to the two Men. As they came to a corner, Cole looked around for a Guidebox, found one, and approached it.

"How may I help you?" asked the Guidebox as it sensed his presence.

"I'm looking for a Teroni friend. Where on this level am I most likely to find him?"

A screen materialized in the air, with three blinking lights on the schemata of the third level. "I am compelled to point out that you are a Man, and you cannot metabolize the food and drink you will encounter at these locations."

"Thank you," said Cole, heading off toward the first of them. They passed a tripodal Hesporite and four Lodinites, but no one paid them any attention, and a moment later they entered a storefront that served as a bar, a restaurant, and a casino filled with alien games.

Cole looked around, couldn't spot Jacovic, walked up to an employee, and asked if he had been there. The Teroni pointed to his ear and shook his head; clearly he didn't understand Terran. Cole reached into his pocket, pulled out a T-Pack, and bonded it to his throat.

"I am looking for a Teroni named Jacovic," he said. The T-Pack muted his Terran and broadcast an unaccented monotone Teroni. "Has he been here?"

"Ah, Jacovic!" was the reply. "He was here less than an hour ago. He said he was going to the . . ." Whatever the word was, Cole's T-Pack couldn't translate it into Terran.

"Can you direct me there?"

The alien led Cole and Pampas to the front door and pointed to another storefront about a hundred feet distant. Cole thanked him and began walking.

"You better put on your T-Pack," Cole said to Pampas. "It's obvious they don't speak Terran down here."

Pampas pulled his own translating mechanism out and bonded it to his throat. "What if we don't find him, sir?"

"Then we look harder. He was here maybe half an hour ago, and the closest planet is three light-years away. He's still on Singapore Station."

They reached the second storefront and entered through a doorway created for exceptionally tall beings.

"Val would feel right at home here," remarked Cole, and Pampas, a large man himself but a good six inches shorter than Val, nodded his agreement.

The establishment seemed a little more upscale than the first one, but Cole couldn't really be sure what Teronis considered upscale.

"Excuse me," he said, approaching what seemed to be a headwaiter, "but I am looking for Jacovic. Is he here?"

The Teroni nodded his lean, angular head. "In there," he said, pointing to a door along the back wall.

Cole and Pampas approached it. It sensed their presence and vanished until they had passed through, then took solid shape behind them.

Jacovic was standing near one wall, and half a dozen other Teronis were spread evenly throughout the room in a semicircle around him.

"Why didn't you respond when we summoned you?" said Cole by way of greeting.

"Ask *them*," said Jacovic, nodding his head in the direction of the other Teronis.

One of the Teronis produced Jacovic's communicator. "It is in safe hands," he said.

"Sir?" said Pampas, tensing.

"Stay calm," said Cole, glad that he'd taken Pampas rather than Val, who would already be among the aliens, cracking skulls and shattering bones. He turned to the alien who was holding the communicator. "You have taken something that doesn't belong to you."

"It was the surest way to get you to come here," answered the

Teroni. "We knew you wouldn't leave Singapore Station without your First Officer."

"All right, I'm here," said Cole. "Now what?"

"Now we talk."

"I'm listening," said Cole.

"My T-Pack may have said that wrong," was the reply. "Now *you* talk."

"About what?"

"Do not be obtuse, Captain Cole. Your First Officer has been trying to enlist us in what seems an ill-considered battle against your Republic."

"It's not *my* Republic, not any longer," replied Cole. "If it was, I'd be fighting *for* it, not *against* it."

"Why do you not put your forces at the disposal of the Teroni Federation?"

"Because I don't think any more highly of the Teroni Federation than I do of the Republic," answered Cole.

"And yet a Teroni is your First Officer."

"Honor and integrity are not confined to one race," said Cole. "When we faced each other as enemies, he gave me his word and kept it when it would have been very easy to break it, when there would have been no survivors to point a finger at him. That's more than most of my superiors would have done."

"You realize that the odds are millions to one against you?"

"We plan to lower them, one day at a time."

"If you actually succeeded in bringing about the end of the Republic, what would you replace it with?"

"I'm not a politician," answered Cole. "That would be for others to decide."

"Would you recommend a cease-fire against the Teroni Federation?"

"No, I would not." The Teronis tensed. "A cease-fire is temporary. I'd recommend a complete cessation of all hostilities. We've been at war for so damned long I doubt that anyone truly knows why the hell it started in the first place."

The six Teronis gathered in a tight circle. Cole could see them whispering, but he couldn't hear what they were saying. He caught Jacovic's eye, patted his empty holster, nodded toward the Teronis, and held his palms up to indicate a question.

Jacovic shook his head: *No, they are not armed.*

Well, that's a relief, thought Cole. *If things get hairy, I'll let Bull take the four biggest, Jacovic can take the one closest to him, and I'll handle the little one who's done all the talking.*

The circle widened, and the six Teronis turned to face Cole.

"We will join your cause," said the one who seemed to be the spokesman.

"I'm very grateful to hear that," replied Cole. "Why the inquisition?"

"We left the Federation's military for the same reason that Commander Jacovic did: we no longer believe that the Federation has the high moral ground, or that it is worth dying for. Jacovic assured us that you shared our values, but we have been trained all our lives to hate and distrust your race, so we felt we had to hear it from your own mouth."

"But if you have been trained to distrust everything I say, why believe me now?" asked Cole, who realized that it was a stupid and potentially dangerous question to ask, but his curiosity got the better of him.

"Oh, we knew you would tell us what Jacovic had said. But it was one answer that convinced us."

"What was that?"

"That you have no interest in being part of whatever succeeds the

Republic. There are probably hundreds of reasons for a Man to turn against his government and wish to overthrow it, just as there are hundreds of reasons for a Teroni to do the same—but ninety-nine times out of a hundred, the unspoken but true reason is egomania, and a desire for power."

"Also, we know that your Navy has been hunting you for four years," added another. He flashed the Teroni equivalent of a smile. "That helped too."

"It's a comfort to know you don't want to turn me in for the reward," said Cole.

"If you had answered wrong, we might have."

"May I have my communicator, please?" asked Jacovic, extending his hand. It was immediately returned to him.

"All right," said Cole. "I assume you all came on one ship?"

"Yes," said a Teroni.

"You're going to have to leave Singapore Station today. I'll have Lieutenant Briggs send over what you need to rig your computer so the Navy can't intercept or read your transmissions."

"Today?" said the Teroni. "We just arrived four hours ago."

"You don't want to be here tomorrow," said Cole. "There's a fleet of eight hundred Navy ships due to show up, and they don't know you've opted out of the Teroni Federation." He paused. "Whoever delivers the codes you need will also brief you on how to contact us, what we plan to do in the first phase of this campaign, what areas we'd prefer you to operate in, everything you'll need. Just tell Commander Jacovic where you're docked and we'll take care of everything else."

A few minutes later Cole, Jacovic, and Pampas were heading back out along the docking arm to the *Theodore Roosevelt*.

"So we picked up six recruits in half an hour," remarked Pampas. "Not bad."

Cole sighed deeply. Jacovic merely stared silently at the *Teddy R* growing larger and larger in the viewscreen. "Tell him," said Cole at last.

Jacovic turned to Pampas. "We recruited six men in thirty minutes. How many men you do suppose the Republic recruited on its sixty thousand worlds during that same period of time?"

"I hadn't thought of that," admitted Pampas.

"I have a feeling that we'll be a happier ship in the days to come if we ban all mathematicians from the crew," commented Cole with a rueful smile.

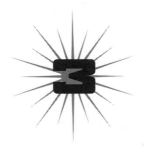

"Got one, sir!"

Cole opened his eyes and tried to concentrate.

"Sir?" continued the feminine voice.

"Is that you, Rachel?" asked Cole, swinging his feet to the floor.

"Yes, sir," said Rachel Marcos. "We've got one!"

"One *what*?"

"Take a second, sir," she said, her image hovering a few feet from the bed. "Gather your senses. Then I'll explain."

Cole blinked his eyes very rapidly. "Where the hell are we?"

"Sixteen hours out from Singapore Station, sir."

He got to his feet, walked to a sink in the corner, muttered "Cold!," waited for the water to pour out, and sloshed some on his face. Then he turned to Rachel Marcos's image. "Okay, I'm awake. What's going on?"

"We've disabled a Navy ship, sir!" she said excitedly. "And we did it before they could transmit a signal about what was happening!"

"Let me guess," said Cole. "Our redheaded friend nailed the antenna before it could send."

"Yes, sir."

Cole pursed his lips. "When she's on her game, there's none better. I'll give her that much." He paused. "What type of ship?"

"A Class K warship."

Alarm bells went off in the back of Cole's head. "And we're sixteen hours from Singapore Station? It's got to be part of the punishment party."

"Yes, sir," replied Rachel. "It was having trouble with its retarded tachyon drive, and seems to have fallen hours behind its companions. Mr. Briggs spotted it, but Val wouldn't trust anyone else to disable the transmitter and antenna, so she went down to Gunnery and did it herself, then took out its main engines."

"How did Mr. Briggs spot the ship?"

"From its SOS signal."

"Did any of the geniuses up there on the bridge figure out that if *we* could read their SOS, so could the other seven hundred and ninety-nine Navy ships?" demanded Cole.

Suddenly Val's face replaced Rachel's. "You want insignia, don't you?" demanded Val. "And their computer with all its codes? We can grab them and be back on the *Teddy R* in maybe forty minutes, and the closest Navy ship is at least three hours away."

"Leave the insignia," said Cole. "Eight hundred ships are going to know any ship displaying it is an enemy. Grab the computer and all the record cubes, and get back as fast you can. And Val?"

"Yeah?"

"No bloodshed."

"Are they the bad guys or not?" she demanded.

"Leave them be," he said, wondering how she could be so beautiful and so bloodthirsty at the same time. "We're after worse."

"You let 'em be, and they'll come back and bite us in the ass," she predicted.

"They're just following orders, the way we used to."

"The way *you* used to," she corrected him. "I was a pirate, remember?"

"Some days it's harder to forget that than others," he said dryly. "No shooting."

"There's forty-two Men on that ship, all carrying regulation sidearms," she said. "What makes you think they'll let us just walk in?"

"I'll contact them and explain that no harm will come to them if they offer no resistance. We don't even want to take them prisoner."

"How are you going to contact them?" asked Val. "I blew their antenna."

"Shit!" growled Cole. "All right, I'm leading the boarding party."

"The hell you are," said a new voice. It belonged to Sharon Blacksmith.

"Stop eavesdropping," said Cole irritably.

"I'm the Chief of Security," she replied. "Everything that transpires on this ship is my business, and you're not going anywhere. We've been through all this before: the Captain doesn't leave his ship in enemy territory."

"Enemy territory is the goddamned Republic," Cole shot back. "This is the Inner Frontier."

"Anywhere there's a Republic ship is enemy territory," Sharon insisted.

"The damned ship's disabled."

"So you enter it and get shot two seconds later. What is the rest of your fleet supposed to do? You haven't exactly given them a complete and detailed battle plan."

"If Val walks in first, she'll kill the first man who twitches, and that'll precipitate an all-out battle. I want to avoid that."

"Then send someone besides Val," said Sharon.

"Hey, wait a minute!" said Val. "I'm the one who blew away its transmitter and antenna; I'm the one who's going to claim the spoils of victory."

"It's just a goddamned computer, Val," said Cole.

"You're willing to risk your ass for it," she said. "That makes it valuable."

Cole glared at Sharon's image. "Thanks for making life so easy for me," he said bitterly.

"Just doing my job," she said. "You're the Captain and you're not leaving the ship in enemy territory."

"If I'm the Captain, then I give the orders," he said firmly. "Val, I'll meet you down in the shuttle bay. Put together a team of four, and make sure one of them knows how to open a locked hatch without blowing it apart. I want them to be able to secure it again after we leave."

"Damn it, Wilson!" said Sharon.

He waited until Val had broken the connection. "We both know that if I let her lead the boarding party, she'll kill all forty-two of them."

"They're the enemy."

"No," said Cole. "They're the enemy's weapons."

"Weapons are made to do damage, Wilson."

"Weapons can be neutralized," he replied. "Just not by someone like Val."

"So send Jacovic."

"Come on," he said. "They'll take one look at him and start shooting. The Republic's at war with the Teroni Federation, remember?"

"You have fifty-three people on this ship, and you're going to find reasons why fifty-two of them can't possibly lead the boarding party, am I right?"

"You're complicating the issue unnecessarily," complained Cole.

"And you're showboating," she said. "If you heard of any other Captain doing this, you'd call it egomania."

"If you take on the Republic with a fleet of eight hundred ships, you have to be a bit of an egomaniac," said Cole. "Now perhaps you'll let me finish waking up and concentrate on the business at hand."

"You're awake," said Sharon furiously. "If you were sleepy, you couldn't make such a dumb decision."

She broke the connection, and a couple of minutes later Cole was on his way to the shuttle bay. Along the way he passed a small, mildly humanoid alien, dressed exactly like a nineteenth-century British dandy, scurrying down a corridor.

"Good morning, David," he said. "Where are you off to in such a hurry?"

"Are you really leading the boarding party like everyone says, Steerforth?" asked David Copperfield.

"*Do* they all say it?" asked Cole, arching an eyebrow.

"Word travels fast aboard a ship."

"Not *that* fast. Someone was listening. Maybe someone from a Dickens novel?"

"But you *are* going?"

"Yes. Why?"

"Then I'm heading for my bulkhead," answered the alien. "I've laid in a supply of roast beef and Yorkshire pudding, and a bottle of port."

"None of which you can eat or drink."

"You cut me to the quick, Steerforth," said David. "I have never denied my limitations. Why do you take such delight in referring to them?"

"Stop calling me Steerforth and I'll stop pointing out who you are and aren't."

"But you *are* Steerforth!" cried the alien. "How can you pretend we aren't old school chums?"

"It's difficult, but I manage," said Cole. "Your bulkhead is calling to you. I'll let you know when we've returned safe and sound."

"You make me sound like an arrant coward," complained David.

"I don't think I ever considered the word 'arrant.'"

"It happens to be very comfortable in that bulkhead. I close my eyes and pretend I'm back in Salem House boarding school with you, preparing to go out on a date with Becky Thatcher."

"Wrong book, wrong author."

"Well, all the women in *my* book were only interested in *you*," replied David. "Little Emily, Miss Dartle . . ."

"David," said Cole, "you may be the best fence on the Inner Frontier, but you get stranger every day."

"I'll second that," said Sharon's disembodied voice.

"Well, the Platinum Duke appreciates me," said David. "He's letting me teach him a *civilized* game: whist."

"That's just what we need," said Sharon. "*Two* of them."

"I know when I'm not wanted," said David, stalking off.

"I thought *I* was the one who wasn't wanted," said Cole as he walked to the airlift that would take him to the shuttle bay.

"If you were wanted a little less, I'd be a little less annoyed when you act like an asshole," answered Sharon.

"With compliments like that, who needs insults?" said Cole as he entered the airlift.

"Just come back in one piece," said Sharon.

He emerged into the shuttle bay, where Val, Pampas, a Mollute, and a Polonoi were waiting for him.

"Which one?" asked Val, gesturing toward the four shuttlecraft.

"The *Kermit*," answered Cole, walking over to it.

"You always choose that one."

"So?"

"It's the most expendable," answered Val.

"What makes it any more expendable than the others?" asked Cole.

"It's the oldest. "

"So am I," he said, entering the shuttle. He went directly to the back, donned his body armor, and waited for the others—except for the warrior-caste Polonoi, who had almost-impregnable natural armor on the front of his body (and almost none on the back)—to do the same. "All right," he said when they were assembled at their stations. "Once we're inside the ship, no one shoots except on my command."

"Until they kill you," said Val as the shuttle left the *Teddy R* and began approaching the Navy ship, which hung in space about a quarter of a million miles away.

"Try not to be so optimistic," said Cole. "We don't want to hurt them, and there's no sense taking their insignia or any other ID. All we want is their computer, and there's every likelihood they'll destroy it when they see us approaching rather than turn it over to us. Nothing on that ship is worth anyone dying for."

Val muttered something under her breath, but knew enough not to argue with him in front of others now that the mission had begun. The rest were silent, all eyes turned to the viewscreen, where a hugely magnified image of the Navy ship appeared as a tiny dot.

Cole activated his communicator. "Jacovic?"

The Teroni's image appeared a few feet away. "Yes, sir?"

"It occurs to me that we're depending on the goodwill of a ship that we've helped disable," said Cole. "We're a sitting duck as we approach. Fire a couple of warning shots, not close enough that they'll think we were trying to hit them, but close enough to let them know that you're prepared to take them out if they fire on us."

"Yes, sir."

A moment later a beam of solid light from a laser cannon and a ball of energy from a thumper—a pulse cannon—shot out in the general director of the Navy ship, missing it by clear but close margins.

"That should do it," said Cole. "We'll approach with our shields up. If they fire even a single shot, we're turning tail and running back to the ship, and you'll aim your next couple of shots a little better— but I don't think it's going to happen. They know we can destroy them at will. The fact that we haven't ought to convince them that we have no intention of doing so."

"You hope," said Val.

"I hope," he replied.

They approached without being fired upon, bonded hatch-to-hatch, and the Mollute quickly opened the lock on the Naval ship's hatch. Cole was about to enter when Val pushed him to the back and walked in first, followed by Pampas and the Polonoi.

All forty-two crew members stood facing them, weapons drawn, but no one fired a shot. When Val was sure they weren't going to fire first, she stepped aside and let Cole walk to the front of the boarding party.

"We mean you no harm," he said. "We have disabled your transmitter and antenna, but once we have what we came for, we'll broadcast an SOS to the remainder of your fleet, and we won't leave the area until we know it has been received. We seek no prisoners. We want one item from your ship. It is not any of your weaponry. If you make no attempt to hinder us, no one on either side will be hurt, and we'll be off your ship and sending that SOS inside of ten minutes."

The two sides stared at each other silently for a long minute. Finally the captain of the ship holstered his weapon, and the rest of his crew followed suit. Then Cole turned to Pampas. "Okay, Bull, go pull it and take it back to the shuttle."

Pampas walked over to the main control panel, studied it, shook his head, and began looking around the deck. Finally he saw what he wanted and began making his way to it. An ensign, almost as powerfully built, moved to block his way.

"None of that," said the captain of the ship, and the ensign stepped aside.

Pampas pulled out some tools, signaled for the Polonoi to help him, and in four more minutes they had the computer disconnected and detached.

"Okay," said Cole, as Pampas lifted it in his massive arms, "take it back to the shuttle and we'll be on our way."

Pampas walked past him to the hatch, but Cole paid no attention to him. He was watching a crewman who was staring intently at him, his body tense, his fingers flexing nervously.

"It's him!" the crewman finally shouted.

The ship's captain turned to him questioningly.

"It's Wilson Cole!" he yelled.

"Don't do anything stupid, son," said Cole.

"You son of a bitch, we've been after you for four years!" said the crewman. He reached for his weapon. Val put a beam of solid light between his eyes before his fingers touched it.

Suddenly more weapons appeared. Val began cursing and firing, as did the Polonoi and the Mollute. Pampas dropped the computer and went for his weapon. Energy pulses and solid light bounced off Cole's body armor as he pulled his own burner and began firing.

It was a slaughter. One side had body armor, one didn't. In a matter of thirty seconds the crew of the Navy ship lay dead or dying on the deck. The Mollute was also dead, brought down by a shot to his unprotected head. Cole turned to see if Pampas, who had been standing behind him, was all right, and saw him kneeling next to the computer, which had been melted by a stray laser blast.

"Wonderful!" muttered Cole angrily. "Just wonderful!"

"Do you want to move any of the wounded to the *Teddy R*, sir?" asked the Polonoi.

Cole surveyed the carnage, and finally shook his head. "There are nine or ten still twitching. Our infirmary can't handle that many, and they're in a bad way."

"Shall we send the SOS, then?"

"No," said Cole. "If they save a single survivor, they'll know the *Teddy R* did this and they'll have the whole fucking Navy after us—and we're only three hours ahead of them. Let's get back to the shuttle."

"What about our dead comrade, sir?" asked the Polonoi, indicating the Mollute.

"Leave him," said Cole. "He's past caring, and we need to obliterate all trace of him."

They rode the shuttle in silence back to the *Teddy R.* Cole went directly to his office and poured himself a stiff drink, then contacted Jacovic, who was still on the bridge.

"Sir?" said the Teroni.

"Kill the Navy ship," said Cole. "Obliterate all trace of it. Sooner or later they'll figure out what happened to it, and maybe even who was responsible—but later is better."

"Yes, sir," said the Teroni.

A few minutes later Sharon entered his office.

"I heard what happened," she said.

He stared at her and made no answer.

"I'm glad you survived."

"Forty-three men didn't," he replied. "All for a piece of melted metal."

"The fortunes of war," said Sharon.

"We're supposed to be better than them," answered Cole grimly. "This was not the most auspicious beginning."

"Three more hours, sir," said the image of Domak, a warrior-caste Polonoi.

"Until what?" asked Cole, who was sitting alone in his office, watching a musical entertainment on a holoscreen.

"Until we're inside the Republic," answered Domak.

"There shouldn't be any welcoming committee, not if Mr. Briggs has picked the right approach route." He paused. "Let me know when we're actually in Republic territory."

"Yes, sir."

"Any word from Singapore Station?" said Cole.

"Yes, sir," said Domak. "The Navy ships surrounded it, and when there was no opposition, they simply docked and made use of the facilities."

"Make sure the Platinum Duke knows that, would you, please?"

"Yes, sir." Domak's image vanished.

Cole decided it was time to inspect the ship's battle readiness. Actually, the ship was always ready these days, but inactivity bored him, so he began making the rounds. First was the shuttle bay, containing the shuttlecraft that were named after four of Theodore Roosevelt's six children. (They were on their second *Archie* and *Quentin* and their third *Alice*, but somehow the original *Kermit* had survived.)

Next came the Gunnery Section, which was usually run by Bull Pampas, but he was sleeping, and the shift was being manned by Bujandi, a Pepon. The infirmary had no permanent patients—Cole considered overnight to be permanent on a warship—and had a full complement of supplies.

He then went down to the guts of the ship, where he queried Mustapha Odom, the Chief Engineer, about the vessel's readiness, then nodded sagely as he realized he didn't understand half of the technical answers Odom was supplying.

He stopped by the undersized Officers' Lounge, where he found six of his officers playing various card and board games.

And finally, when he couldn't avoid it any longer, he went up to the bridge. Over the years he'd come to loathe it. The formality bothered him, and the tendency of normal men and women to speak in sentence fragments the moment they set foot on the bridge bothered him even more. There was a sense among the crew that all important decisions had to be reached on the bridge, whereas in truth he was fully as capable of commanding the ship from his office, or his cabin, or his table in the mess hall. There was nothing that was said or seen on the bridge that couldn't be transmitted to any part of the ship, but still it retained its special aura. Of all his officers, only the dead Forrice had felt no obligation to remain on the bridge when he was the Officer on Deck. As the Molarian used to say with a wink of one of his four eyes, "There's nothing in the Code of Conduct that says *which* deck."

Cole stepped out of the airlift, turned right, and began approaching his destination.

"Captain on the bridge!" Christine Mboya called out, and she, the alien Domak, and Ensign Idena Mueller all stood and saluted.

Cole considered not returning their salutes, but he knew they'd remain at attention until he did, so he gave them a halfhearted salute. He further resisted the temptation to point out that Christine had left the verb out of her sentence.

"All this formality really isn't necessary," he complained for the hundredth time.

"It's regulation, sir," said Christine.

"It's a regulation created by the military machine that we're going to war with," he replied.

"It's also a sign of respect."

"It's also a way of letting the enemy know who to shoot first," he said wryly.

"I will remember that the next time we leave the ship together, sir," said Christine.

"Tell me something, Lieutenant Mboya," said Cole.

"Sir?"

"Did you ever lose an argument with a parent, a teacher, anybody?"

"Not that I can recall, sir," said Christine.

"Why am I not surprised?" He looked around the bridge. "Neat as a pin. I assume everything's in order?"

"Yes, sir."

"Then I won't keep you any longer." A quick smile. "We must visit again sometime."

A computer flashed off to his left.

"Just a moment, sir," said Domak. "We have a coded message coming in."

"From?" said Cole.

"It's from Mr. Lafferty, sir."

"On Piccoli III?"

"I don't think so, sir. It doesn't seem to be coming from that sector."

Cole frowned. "Anything to imply it's private?"

"No, sir."

"Okay, play it right here."

Lafferty's tan, wrinkled face appeared in the center of the bridge.

"Got a surprise for you, Mr. Cole," said the old man with a sly grin. "You're gonna like it."

"Well?" replied Cole after a moment.

"It's not a live transmission, sir," interjected Domak just before Lafferty's image began speaking again.

"I don't trust subspace transmissions," continued Lafferty. "I've been intercepting and reading the Navy's for years, so why shouldn't they be able to read mine? Anyway, we have to meet. You'll figure out where. I'll wait three days for you to show up. If you don't, I'll try to contact you once more, then assume you're dead and carry on myself."

Lafferty's face vanished.

"That's all?" asked Cole.

"That's the whole of it," said Domak.

"And based on that, I'm supposed to figure out where in this whole galaxy to meet him? Hell, the only time I've ever seen him face-to-face was on Piccoli, and the only other time I've ever been within light-years of him was when we were both defending Singapore Station last month."

"Maybe he means Piccoli III," suggested Idena Mueller.

Cole shook his head. "His transmission didn't come from there. And he said I'd figure it out; Piccoli doesn't take any figuring."

"He certainly can't want to meet at Singapore Station," said Christine. "We don't dare go back there this soon."

"Then what the hell location am I supposed to figure out?" said Cole, frowning.

"Had he mentioned some other world during your visit with him?"

"No," replied Cole. "We were together less than an hour. Mostly we were trying to arrange for me to get safely back to the Inner Frontier with the Navy hot on my tail."

"Then I'm afraid I can't help you, sir," she said. "Probably none of us can."

"I know," said Cole. "I'll just have to work it out myself."

He walked to the airlift and went back down to his office, where he sat, staring at a wall, for the next ten minutes.

"Sometimes it helps if you talk things out," said Sharon, her image flickering into existence.

"Don't you ever sleep?"

"You'd be the best judge of that," she replied. "I suppose it depends on how clumsy you were the night before."

"Fine," he said. "Get a good night's sleep tonight. I'll pester Rachel or some other svelte crew member half your age."

"No, I couldn't do that to Rachel," said Sharon. "She's young and impressionable. She's never seen a forty-five-year-old man trying to prove he's twenty-two. She could be giggling for years." She paused as a smile crossed Cole's face. "Besides, she's sleeping with Mr. Bellamy."

"She is?" he said. "How do you know?"

It was her turn to smile. "I'm the Chief of Security. I know everything that happens on this ship."

"All right—so what do you want?"

"I thought I'd help you," she replied. "Two heads are better than one."

"You were listening?"

"It's my job."

"Okay," he said. "Any suggestions?"

"No," answered Sharon. "But then, I've never met Lafferty. By the way, has he got a first name?"

"He never shared it with me, but I suppose he must," answered Cole. "It's probably on the registration of the ship he gave me."

"Could the hint be on the ship?"

"I sure as hell hope not. We left it and appropriated a little three-man Navy ship."

"We?" she repeated. "You and Lafferty?"

"No, me and that little alien friend of his. What the hell was his name? Oh, yes—Dozhin. I think he's still on Singapore Station."

"Do you want to contact him?"

Cole shook his head. "No. The Navy's there now. I don't want them to be able to trace the signal. Besides, I don't know what he could tell me. He's almost as big a coward as our friend David, but without David's virtues."

"David has virtues?"

"He has contacts. That qualifies in his business—and ours." He frowned. "The answer has to be with Dozhin. Lafferty knows he came out to the Frontier with me. Maybe he—" Cole froze for a moment. "Oh, shit! I've got it." He touched the spot on his desk that contacted Christine.

"Yes, sir?" she said.

"Tell Pilot to take us to Cicero VII as fast as he can."

"Do you know where it is?"

"I've no idea. Not too many parsecs from Piccoli III, I should think."

"Yes, sir."

Her image vanished, but Sharon's remained, her face an open question mark.

"Dozhin's home planet," said Cole. "He told me he left it when the Navy pacified it."

"Won't they still be there?"

He shook his head. "Lafferty wouldn't invite me there if they were."

"Let's hope you're right," she said. "And our pilot's name is Wxakgini."

"I can't pronounce it," said Cole. "He knows that."

"You should try, as a sign of respect."

"Every time I screw it up he winces. Just Pilot is better."

"That's why he never calls you 'sir.'"

"I can live with it."

"It's hard to imagine you were once the pride of the regular Navy," she said with a smile.

"I think pride is a bit of an overstatement," he said wryly. "They took two captaincies away from me."

"And gave them back eventually."

"No choice," said Cole. "They lost a lot of captains in the war."

"You know, you can be really annoying when you're being modest," she said.

"Okay, I'll brag to the crew about what you told me during an exceptionally interesting moment last night."

"Fine."

"You don't mind?"

"Not if you don't mind sleeping alone for the next six hundred years," she said, and her image vanished.

"Pilot?"

Wxakgini's image appeared, his head connected as always to the navigational computer by a series of tiny tubes, his body similarly connected to nutrient solutions.

"Yes?"

"What's our ETA on Cicero VII?"

"We'll be traversing the Glover Wormhole. Seventeen minutes to reach it, seventy-three minutes in transit, and approximately two hours at the other end."

"Once we're out of the wormhole, have whoever's the Officer on Deck make sure there are no Navy ships patrolling the Cicero system before you begin our approach."

"I will do so," said Wxakgini.

Cole broke the connection, felt restless, and went to the mess hall for some coffee and a sandwich. Val was just finishing a meal when he got there.

"I hear your friend Lafferty's got a surprise for us," she said when as he sat down two tables away.

"So he says."

"I also heard from Lieutenant Sokolov," she continued. "He's killed three ships since this started."

"Little ones, I hope."

"Have you got something against killing big ones?"

"In a ship the size of Sokolov's I do," said Cole. "He's too small to kill anything above a Class J without blowing its nuclear pile and killing everyone on board."

"That's the point of going to war," said Val, "to kill the other guys."

"You go to war to get the resolution you want to a particular problem. The more people you kill, the less likely the other side is to give in until you've all but annihilated them."

"So?"

He sighed deeply and stared at the Valkyrie, marveling as always at the combination of beauty and brutality. "You are the finest warrior I've ever seen, maybe the finest there's ever been. If I had a hundred like you I could conquer the galaxy." He paused. "I just wish somewhere along the way they'd given you a course in peacemaking or maybe ethics."

"I learned at a harder school," she replied.

"I know."

"The bars and whorehouses are filled with women who learned how to make accommodations," said Val. "I'm not one of them."

"I value you for what you are," Cole assured her. "I was just musing about what you might have been."

"I might have been a five-foot-tall hunchback with a prosthetic leg and steel teeth," she said.

"Point taken."

"So what do you think's waiting for us on Cicero?" asked Val

Cole shrugged. "We'll know soon enough."

Suddenly she smiled. "If it bites, I'll protect you."

"Fine," said Cole. "And if it kisses, I'll protect *it*. I've seen you wear out the androids in that brothel back on Singapore Station."

"I go there because they're the only ones I *can't* wear out," she replied with a laugh.

Cole and Val both experienced a sudden sense of disorientation.

"I guess we've entered the wormhole," he said.

"I guess," she replied, getting up from the table. "I'm going to grab two hours of sleep, just in case there's some fighting to do when we get there."

"We'll wake you if we need you."

Then she was gone, and Cole ordered his coffee and sandwich. They arrived, he took a bite of the mock hamburger, and made a face, wondering why after all these millennia soya products still tasted more like soybeans than all the things they were *supposed* to taste like.

He spent another half hour finishing his sandwich, sipping his coffee, and getting the details of Sokolov's three conquests after the pilot filed a report with Christine. He was about to go to his cabin when the Platinum Duke wandered in, sat down at his table, and ordered some coffee, artificial eggs, mock steak, and something that wasn't quite toast.

"Good evening," said Cole.

"It's my morning," answered the Duke.

"Don't burn your lips on the coffee," said Cole as the Duke's meal arrived. "It's very hot."

"I don't have any lips," said the Duke, lifting the cup to his mouth. A moment later he cursed and put it down. "I do have a tongue, though."

"You heard that your beloved Singapore Station is unscathed and probably turning a hell of a profit."

"You were right," said the Duke. "I still don't like running and hiding."

"*You're* running and hiding," replied Cole. "*We're* running and attacking."

"I think I liked you better when you were a customer," said the Duke.

"I liked you better when you supplied me with elegant meals from your private kitchen."

The Duke chuckled. "We had a good thing going. David and I would line up lucrative contracts, and you and the *Teddy R* would fulfill them." He paused. "How the hell did we get from there to here in so short a time?"

"We had help," said Cole grimly.

"Yes," agreed the Duke, remembering the attack on Singapore Station and the events that had precipitated it.

They sat in silence for a few moments. Then Cole felt a familiar wave of dizziness, and realized that they had emerged from the wormhole and would now be approaching the Cicero system. If Briggs or Christine were looking for signs of the Navy, it could be an hour before the *Teddy R* left the vicinity of the wormhole. Jacovic would take half that time and be almost as thorough—and Val, if she was on duty, would glance at the viewscreen, declare the area free of Navy ships, and hope she was wrong as she proceeded to Cicero.

The Duke finished his meal and left. Cole was on his third cup of coffee when the all-clear signal came through and the *Teddy R* lurched forward.

"Sir, would you like to come to the bridge and take command?" asked Christine.

He stared at her image. Unspoken was the fact that she had been promoted to Second Officer for her loyalty and her other skills, but that she was totally unversed in spacial warfare.

"You're in charge during white shift," replied Cole. "Take us to Cicero VII."

"I have no landing coordinates to give to Wxakgini."

"Lafferty knows that."

"I don't follow you, sir."

"He didn't invite us out here as a practical joke. When you get close enough, I'm sure you'll be told where to land. If you aren't, that'll be time enough to discuss our options."

"Yes, sir," said Christine. "Thank you, sir."

He resisted the urge to tell her to call him "Wilson" or "Cole" or "Hey You," only because he knew it wouldn't do the least bit of good, and ordered a piece of pie to go with his coffee.

David Copperfield spotted him and entered the mess hall.

"Hi, David," said Cole as the little alien approached his table.

"Good morning, Steerforth. I heard the all-clear."

"You know anything about the Cicero system?"

"I know a smuggler named Krieder or Krieter used it as a storage dump for a year after the Navy killed off the local population. There are ten planets in the system, six small ones close in and three gas giants far out. I believe the only oxygen planet is the seventh one. Not very hospitable to us humans."

Cole decided not to comment on David's last sentence. "Any word about the Navy setting up a small station anywhere in the system?"

David shook his head. "Nothing of value, once they locked Kreider away and confiscated his goods."

"Why would they pacify an out-of-the-way planet like Cicero VII?" continued Cole.

David shrugged. "Why do they do anything? They're the Navy."

"I used to be part of that Navy," said Cole. "There had to be a reason. Maybe not a good one, but a reason."

"You can't prove it by me," said the dapper alien.

"Fuel costs money. Ammunition costs money. Taking a ship away from the war with the Teroni Federation costs money and men. You don't do that on a whim, not in peacetime, and certainly not in the middle of a war."

"It's the middle of a war to you and me, Steerforth," said David. "But half the people fighting it can't remember a time when there *wasn't* a war."

"Even so . . ."

"We'll land and you'll see for yourself," said the alien.

"Sharon, are you peeking in again?" said Cole, raising his voice.

"But of course," she replied as her image flickered to life.

"I don't believe the Navy wiped out Dozhin's race for no reason."

"I'd prefer not to believe it, but we'll never know."

"Maybe we will," said Cole. "Get our best computer ace— Christine's on duty, so is Briggs, so it'll be Domak or Jack-in-the-Box—and work with him or her. They'll be able to dig out almost any fact, hack into any computer in nearby systems, but they won't know what they're looking for. I want you to oversee and direct them, and see if you can find out just what the hell the Navy wanted with Cicero VII."

"All right," she said. "But if they did wipe out the race to get their hands on something, it's gone by now."

"Let's find out anyway," he said.

"Okay, I'm on it," said Sharon as her image vanished.

"Why go to the effort, Steerforth?" asked David. "As Colonel Blacksmith says, whatever it was is almost certainly gone by now."

"Didn't they teach you anything in that boarding school, David?"

"Hah!" cried the alien happily. "You admit we were classmates!"

"It was a rhetorical question," said Cole. "Let's find out if whatever they wanted was a renewable resource, like drugs or organic medicines. And even if it's not renewable, wouldn't you like to learn what the Republic wanted so badly that they wiped out an entire planetary population to get their hands on it? Not only that, but they didn't want your pal Kreider to find it."

"How do you arrive at that conclusion, Steerforth?"

"There's a war on. The Navy doesn't waste its time arresting smugglers. They leave that to planetary or system police—unless the smuggler is either trading in something they desperately want, or is likely to stumble upon the Navy's cache."

"It's their cache," said David suddenly.

"You're sure?"

"Krieder dealt in fine jewelry and expensive art," answered the little alien. "You're right: the Navy wouldn't waste their time with that." He smiled. "I do believe between us we've figured out that there's something valuable there."

Cole returned the smile. "The benefits of a public school education."

David chuckled and ordered a cup of coffee. The table asked him if he wanted any cream or sweeteners, and he explained that he-men took their coffee black.

"David . . ." began Cole as the coffee arrived.

"It's been a good day so far. I'll break my diet."

"You're not on a diet, and if you want to live to the end of the day you can't drink any coffee. You know that, David."

"Maybe I'll sip it, maybe I won't," replied David. "Don't ruin the celebratory mood."

"Could be worse, I suppose," said Cole.

"I beg your pardon?"

"You could have read Mowgli or Tarzan. At least you don't kill your food in mortal combat, and you remember to wear clothes to the table."

"Why do you persist in making fun of me, Steerforth?" said David.

"I thought I was complimenting you."

The coffee arrived. David stared at Cole, then his coffee, then Cole again. "It's too hot," he said. "I'll let it cool."

"Good idea," said Cole. He decided to take pity on the little alien. "I've got some work to do in my office," he said, getting to his feet. "You'll want to stay here and finish your coffee."

"Yes," said David. "I'd just spill most of it if I tried carrying it. I'll join you when I'm done."

Cole left, and figured David would dump the coffee out by the time he reached his office. He sat at his desk and contacted the bridge. "Any sign of the Navy?" he asked.

"So far so good, sir," said Briggs, who was still manning the scanners.

"That's a comfort," said Cole. "While I'm thinking of it, any sign of Lafferty?"

"No, sir."

"Well, he'll be in touch when he's ready."

Cole broke the connection, called up a book he'd been reading on his holoscreen, and picked up where he had left off. A few minutes later David Copperfield entered the office.

"How was your coffee?" asked Cole.

"Well, it wasn't Brazilian, but I suppose it was all right, considering our circumstances."

"You have a drop on your chin."

David continued the fantasy by wiping the nonexistent drop away. "No sign of the Navy yet?"

"No," said Cole. "I don't think we'll have to put your bulkhead's defenses to the test today."

Suddenly Sharon's voice rang out: "*Bingo!*"

"Bingo?" repeated Cole, making a face.

"You prefer 'Excelsior'?" she asked as her image popped into existence.

"Just tell me what you've got."

"Cicero VII was rich in fissionable materials," said Sharon.

"*Was?*" repeated Cole.

"All mined out in a four-year period," she replied. "The planet has been abandoned for the past five years. Dozhin and his friends and relations can go back now—if they want to."

"Thanks," said Cole. "See if you can dig up anything else."

"We're on it, Domak and me," said Sharon as her image vanished.

David stared curiously at Cole. "You are smiling from ear to ear."

"Humans can't smile from ear to ear," said Cole. "But if we could, I would."

"Why?"

"You heard the same thing I did," said Cole. "Use that Salem House education, David."

"Stop teasing me and just tell me what you think you know!"

"The Navy could have negotiated for mining rights," began Cole. "They could have just bought the whole damned planet. But instead they killed off the entire population. Why?"

"Clearly they were short of fissionable materials," said David. He frowned. "But that's obvious."

"*Think*, David," said Cole. "They needed the materials so much that they chose to wipe out an entire race rather than take the time to negotiate a lease. It can only mean one thing: the war was going badly, probably still is, and they couldn't take even an extra month to get their hands on that stuff."

"It makes sense," admitted the alien.

"It also means we aren't going to run into any opposition in this sector."

"Why do you think so, Steerforth?"

"The planet's mined out. It was the only thing they wanted or needed, and they're long gone. There's no sign of them, and Mr. Briggs is as thorough as Christine. If they'd left a single ship behind, he'd have spotted it. It's obvious that they've moved their ships to where they're needed against the Teronis." He raised his voice. "Sharon?"

There was no response.

"Damn it," he said. "The one time I wish she was listening, she's doing something else. Okay, David, I'll let you do it."

"Do what?"

"Tell the bridge they can stop searching for the Navy. It's not there, and it's time we kept our rendezvous with Mr. Lafferty."

"They won't listen to me," said the alien.

"Sure they will," said Cole. "Tell them I'll confirm it if need be, but I can almost guarantee they won't bother asking."

"What makes you think so?"

"Because you're out of your bulkhead. That means you have inside information that it's safe."

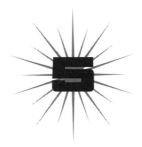

"Approaching planet, sir," said Christine's voice.

"Approaching *the* planet, goddammit!" muttered Cole to himself. Aloud he said, "Where does he want us?"

"Coordinates have been fed into our computer. It seems we meet inside an extinct volcano."

"Okay. Patch me through to the planet on every available frequency."

"Done."

"Lafferty, this is Wilson Cole. We've got your coordinates, but the *Teddy R* can't land. It was built in space and will die in space, hopefully not in the immediate future. I'll bring a party down in two shuttlecraft."

"Not necessary," said Lafferty's voice. "I was going to take you, but I suppose it's just as easy to lead you. You sure no one's followed you?"

"Pretty sure."

"That'll have to do."

"Not to worry," said Cole. "No one's bothered us since we left Singapore Station, and this system is some of the least desirable real estate in the Republic."

"Tell me that in an hour," said Lafferty.

Jacovic's image suddenly appeared. "That was piped all over the ship, sir. What do you think he's got?"

"Beats me," said Cole with a shrug. "Maybe he's found some uranium or plutonium that the Republic missed."

"I found better," said Lafferty's voice. "First I had to make sure no one was tailing you; that's why I directed you to Cicero VII. Now you can follow me."

A ship emerged from within the volcano and began making its way toward an asteroid belt between Cicero VIII and IX.

"Follow him, Pilot," said Cole.

"You're going to need a shuttle or two when we get there," said Lafferty.

"Son of a bitch likes guessing games, doesn't he?" said Cole.

"I request permission to accompany you in a shuttle," said Jacovic.

"Granted," replied Cole.

"Thank you, sir," said Jacovic as his image vanished.

Cole left his office and began making his way to the shuttle bay. When he reached the airlift he met Bull Pampas and Braxite, his one remaining Molarian officer.

"Should we draw our weapons from the armory, sir—or should we use those from the shuttles?" asked Braxite.

"We're visiting allies, not enemies," answered Cole.

"If there's an attack, we could be virtually helpless," continued the Molarian.

"There won't be," said Cole. "The Republic hasn't had a presence here in years. Besides, Jacovic's coming with me, and Christine's shift is almost over. That means Val will be in command. Do you really think she's going to let anyone attack us?"

"How deep into the duty roster do we go, sir?" asked Pampas.

"Five per shuttle," answered Cole. "I assume you and Braxite were at the top of the list?"

"Yes, sir."

"Interesting," said Cole. "You were at the top the last time too, Bull."

"Val puts me at the top every time," replied Pampas uneasily. "She says I'm the only crew member who can last a full minute in the ring with her."

"She's probably right. Okay, I'll be in one shuttle and Jacovic will be in the other. He stays in orbit until I give him an all-clear signal. You're in charge of the crews; split 'em up any way you choose."

Pampas saluted. "Yes, sir."

"One more thing, Bull. I assume we're going to be among friends down there—but nobody salutes anybody whenever we're out of the ship."

"I know, sir."

"I'm sure you do, but since the guy who gets saluted instantly has a bull's-eye pinned on his back, I hope you don't mind my repeating it."

"Yes, sir. I mean, no, sir." Pampas looked flustered. "I mean . . ."

"It's okay, Bull. Just relax and get on down to the shuttles."

"Aren't you going there?"

"I was, but I thought of one last thing I have to do. I'll be down shortly."

He stopped at the airlift and contacted the bridge.

"Christine, is Val there yet?"

"Right here," said the Valkyrie's voice, and a moment later her image replaced Christine's.

"This figures to be absolutely routine," said Cole. "I don't know what the hell Lafferty feels we had to come all the way out here to see, but we've checked it out and the whole system looks to be deserted except for Lafferty's ship. We'll be taking off in the shuttles as soon as we get to the asteroid belt, and we'll land wherever he wants us to. I don't know how long we'll be on the ground, but I can't imagine it'll be more than twenty minutes, maybe half an hour. Should be a piece of cake."

"Fine," said Val. "Now tell me why you contacted me."

"It *looks* to be routine, but I could be wrong. I'm going to feed a seven-digit code into the computer. That'll serve as our password. When we come back, if we can't supply it, blow the shuttles to hell and gone."

"Wait a minute, Wilson!" said Sharon's voice.

"What is it?"

"What if you're incapacitated? Does anyone else know this code? You can't program it into the shuttle, because that way the shuttle will respond no matter who's aboard it."

"Good point," acknowledged Cole. "I'll give it to Jacovic and Braxite as well." He paused. "I'm going down to the shuttle bay. I'll feed you the code once I'm onboard the *Kermit*."

Cole entered the airlift and floated down to the shuttle bay on an almost-solid cushion of air. *I can remember when visiting a friend in an isolated, deserted star system wasn't a military operation fraught with security concerns*, he thought, and wondered if it would ever be that way again.

"Everybody aboard?" he asked as he entered the *Kermit*.

"Yes, sir," said Braxite. "Commander Jacovic showed up about a minute ahead of you. He's in the *Archie*."

"Fine," said Cole. "Let's go."

As the *Kermit* took off, Cole sent the code back to the ship's computer, then relaxed as they began following Lafferty's ship.

"What do you suppose we're going to see, sir?" asked Braxite.

"Beats me," said Cole. "If I knew what it was, I'd probably have told Lafferty that it wasn't worth a trip out here." He stared at asteroids in the viewscreen. "I keep wondering what the hell you can find or hide in an asteroid belt."

"We'll find out soon enough, sir," said Braxite. "He's slowing down."

A small two-man shuttle emerged from the belly of Lafferty's ship. "We're just about there," said his voice. "Follow me."

"We've *been* following you," said Cole irritably.

"See that golden one off to starboard?" said Lafferty. "That's our destination."

"It's a big one," remarked Cole. "Are we landing there?"

"Yes."

"Okay. Jacovic, have your crew get into their space suits." He turned to his own crew. "You do the same."

"*Very* slowly now," said Lafferty, "or you might overshoot it."

"Overshoot *what*?" said Cole.

"You'll see."

Lafferty's shuttle began circling the large golden asteroid, with the *Kermit* and the *Archie* following him. Finally he slowed down even more, and then landed.

"Preparing to land, sir," said Idena Mueller, who was at the controls. "I still don't see what's there."

"We'll find out soon enough," said Cole, testing his suit's oxygen. "Put me through to the *Archie*, coded and scrambled."

"It's done, sir."

"Jacovic, this is Cole. I want you to start lagging behind."

"Do you want us to go into orbit, sir?" asked Jacovic.

"No, I don't think so. I've walked into my share of traps, and this just doesn't feel like one. Just stay about two minutes behind us. Once we land, I'll signal you to bring your shuttle down. If I don't within, say, thirty seconds, take off like a bat out of hell and get back to the *Teddy R* any way you can."

"Considering that we've pretty much checked the place out, we're being awfully cautious," remarked Braxite.

"That's how you stay alive for four years when you're the most wanted man on the most wanted ship in the galaxy," replied Cole with no sign of annoyance.

"I'm sorry, sir," said Braxite, flustered. "I didn't mean . . . that is—"

"It's all right," said Cole. "I feel like we're moving through molasses too . . . but the operative word is 'moving,' not 'molasses.'"

"Prepare for landing," announced Idena as Lafferty's shuttle vanished from sight.

"Where the hell did he go?" asked Cole.

"Look!" said Idena, pointing to the viewscreen. Lafferty had landed in what seemed to be a huge quarry, left over from some forgotten time when Men or some other race were mining the asteroids. He vanished from sight when he was still eighty feet above the ground, and could only be seen from directly overhead. Idena set the *Kermit* down forty yards away from him.

Cole checked the viewscreen and saw Lafferty leading a number of his men out to the ship. "Get me the *Archie*," he said.

"Done, sir."

"Jacovic, bring it down."

"We're on our way," replied the Teroni.

The shuttle crew had waited for Cole to indicate what he wanted done next. He signaled Idena to open the hatch, and he stood in it until the ramp extended and lowered to the ground.

"Good to see you again," said Lafferty, stepping forward and extending his hand.

"And you," said Cole. "Don't get too far from the shuttles. I've got another on the way down."

They watched the *Archie* make its careful descent, finally landing less than thirty yards from the *Kermit*.

Jacovic and his crew emerged, and Cole made some brief introductions. "All right," he said at last. "Suppose you show me why the hell you dragged us all the way out here."

"Happy to," replied Lafferty. "Do I have a big excrement-eating smile on my face?"

"Couldn't be bigger," said Cole.

"Well, there's a reason. Come this way."

Lafferty crossed the bottom of the quarry, which was perhaps half a mile in diameter. After they'd gone a hundred yards he came to a stop, and Cole could see in the dim light that there was something *very* large and formless obscuring his vision.

"Stop or you'll walk into it."

Cole stopped and stared. *Something* was carefully camouflaged, but he couldn't make out what it was.

"Kill the screen," ordered Lafferty, and suddenly the holographic camouflage vanished and Cole found himself looking at a Class L Navy starship without a mark on it.

"What do you think?" said Lafferty, still grinning.

"I'm impressed," said Cole. "That's what the *Teddy R* evolved into over a century. Six Level 5 thumpers, three Level 5 and three Level 4 burners . . . It can absorb anything Level 4 or lower in any quantity, and it can take—I can't remember the new specs—two or three Level 5 hits a second with minimal damage."

"You know your stuff," said Lafferty.

"I was a part of the Navy until four years ago," replied Cole. "Holds a crew of seventy-two."

"Not anymore," said Lafferty. "Fifty-six these days. They've automated that many more functions."

"Where the hell did you get it?" asked Cole. "You sure as hell didn't shoot it down. It's clean as a whistle."

"Kobernykov II."

"Never heard of it."

"And you never will again," said Lafferty with a trace of pride. "It's about eighty light-years from here. The Republic just opened it as a shipbuilding world." A grin. "We just closed it."

"I saw what you had at Singapore Station," said Cole. "A Class L ship like this should have been able to fight fifty of your ships to a standoff."

"Probably it would have," agreed Lafferty. "*If* it had an engine." Cole just stared at him. "We found it in the one structure we didn't destroy. It was just sitting there like a newborn baby. But no one had spanked its bottom yet. We knew the Navy hadn't been in the Cicero system for several years, so we towed it here until we could figure out what to do with it." He looked proudly at his trophy. "We couldn't put it down on a planet without destroying it, but there's almost no gravity out here."

"Has it got all its weaponry?"

"Yes."

"Operational?" asked Cole.

"Yes. We tested them out just inside Cicero IX to make sure. I assume the screens and shields work too, but they draw their power from the engine."

Cole studied the ship for a long minute.

"I suppose the next step is to hunt up an engine, forge some insignia, get right next to some other Navy ships, and blow them away before they know what hit 'em," said Lafferty.

Cole shook his head. "No, we have a better use for it."

"Better than destroying a few thousand ships?"

"Much better," said Cole. Suddenly he turned to Lafferty. "As of this moment, you are no longer a combatant."

"What am I?" said Lafferty.

"A mechanic. The sole duty of you and any men you need is to get an engine installed in this ship. It doesn't have to be the one that was designed for it, as long as it's powerful enough to run the ship. And you'll need insignia."

"That's what I said," replied Lafferty. "We get an engine and some phony ID, and we start blowing ships away."

"No," said Cole.

"But you just said—"

"You get the engine and the insignia, but then you wait right here for my orders."

"What are you talking about?" demanded Lafferty. "I could kill fifty ships a day with this. We could keep killing them for months before anyone figured out what was happening."

"And once they did," said Cole, "they'd destroy you, and they'd still have three million ships."

"And what do you think *you're* going to do with this ship?" said Lafferty heatedly.

Cole looked at the ship again.

"Win the war," he answered.

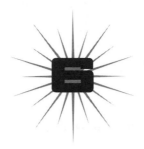

The *Teddy R* had left the Cicero system far behind, passing one deserted planetary system after another.

"What the hell has gone on here?" asked Briggs as his sensors came up with another lifeless world, its buildings destroyed, its thoroughfares cratered.

"War has gone on here, Mr. Briggs," said Cole, who had found himself driven to the bridge through boredom. "The Teroni didn't leave any bases, because there was nothing here worth fighting for once the Navy pulled out—and the Navy didn't come back and rebuild because there was nothing valuable or interesting enough to keep the Teroni here. The only losers are the people who used to live here."

"Maybe they'll resettle someday," said Rachel Marcos.

Cole shook his head. "There's no infrastructure anymore, and if they build it, there's always a chance the Teronis will come back and destroy it again. We're out in the boonies; clearly the Navy doesn't consider this sector important enough to leave a residual force behind."

"It just doesn't make any sense," she said.

He looked at her youthful, unlined face and thought: *How can you be so innocent and uncynical after four years aboard this ship?* He suddenly realized that he envied her.

He shook his head as if to clear it of uncomfortable thoughts, then wandered over to where Wxakgini sat high above the floor, his brain connected to the navigational computer, his body connected to the nutrients that kept him alive. The Bdxeni were unique in the galaxy, the only race that never slept, and hence the ideal starship pilots. Cole had never met one with a name he could pronounce.

"How are we doing, Pilot?" he said.

"I don't understand the question," replied Wxakgini, once again omitting "sir" as a protest against Cole never calling him by his name.

"Just making conversation."

"I am pursuing an erratic course with no destination in mind, as per your orders."

Cole stared at the Bdxeni for a moment, wondered how anyone ever held a conversation with him, and then decided that he had a limited perspective on "conversation," that Wxakgini was conversing silently with the computer every minute of the day.

Suddenly the Platinum Duke's image appeared in front of Cole.

"I did it!" he cried happily.

"Did what?" asked Cole.

"Beat the little bastard at whist!"

"You actually played whist?"

"I had to," said the Duke. "He damned near cleaned me out at blackjack."

"That's what you get for gambling with a member of the British middle class," said Cole.

"Sir?" said Rachel, and the Duke's image vanished.

"Yeah?"

"We have a message coming in from Mr. Moyer."

"Coded and scrambled, I trust?"

"Yes, sir. He has just made another kill. That is his fifth."

"Good for him."

"You don't seem very elated," she noted.

"He's killed five ships, and that's impressive," admitted Cole. His expression darkened. "We still have three and a half million ships to neutralize. That's less impressive."

She studied her computer for a moment. "He wants to speak to you, sir."

"This will translate him into Terran, and my reply will go out scrambled to his ship, right?"

"Yes, sir."

"Okay, put him through."

"It will just be audio. It would take too long to transmit a live holo at this distance."

"Fine."

"Sir," said Moyer's voice, "I need some guidance. I have a prisoner here, a survivor from the last ship I destroyed. I couldn't just let him starve or run out of air in a safety pod. What should I do with him?"

"Put him down on an oxygen world," replied Cole. "It can't be a Republic world; they'd never let you take off again. If you can find some colony world, maybe a farming planet, drop him off there."

There was a pause while the message reached Moyer and his reply came back.

"Our charts may be out of date, sir. What we have as a colony world may have been assimilated into the Republic since we left. I think it might be safe to drop him on an uninhabited oxygen world, and contact a Republic world a week later with his coordinates. He's in good physical shape, no wounds at all; he can make it for a week, and I can be pretty far away by then."

"Makes sense," said Cole. "All right, handle it that way."

He signaled Rachel to break the connection.

"You still look unhappy, sir," she noted.

"We can't have all our ships cruise aimlessly, picking off small Navy ships whenever we can sneak up on them," said Cole. "We're not fighting some little warlord who commands twenty ships back on the Inner Frontier. This is the Republic. They don't even notice that we're here."

"Commander Jacovic says you have some master plan that has something to do with the ship Mr. Lafferty is equipping."

"Mr. Lafferty could be months or even years stealing or assembling an engine that can run that thing," said Cole. "Or he could get captured trying. If he accomplishes it, fine; but we can't just sit around waiting for him to do so." He suddenly looked around. "By the way, where's the Officer on Deck?"

"I'm coming," said Val, stepping off the airlift with a beer in her hand. "Briggs, did you finish that sweep?"

"Yes," he replied. "It's just a meteor storm."

"Good." She turned to Cole. "You can't be too careful. I used meteor storms for cover more than once in my pirate days."

"Damned dangerous," commented Briggs.

"Damned effective," replied Val with a smile.

"You could have lost your ship," said Briggs. "If something had hit you, there was nothing you could do."

"Sometimes you have to take bold action," said Val with an unconcerned shrug.

"You're right," said Cole suddenly. "Sometimes you do."

Val, Briggs, and Rachel turned to him.

"What the hell are you talking about, Cole?" asked Val.

"As far as the Republic's concerned, we're less than a gnat," said Cole. "They don't respond, because they don't even know we're here. We could pick off ten ships a day, and at the end of the week they'd have built more ships than we eliminated. We have to start being bolder; we have to make them aware of our presence."

"Won't that just mean they'll come after us with overwhelming force?" asked Rachel, frowning.

"They won't know where to come," said Cole. "Besides, they're fighting a war of attrition against the Teroni Federation. They're not coming anywhere in force."

"A fleet of eight hundred ships may not seem like a force to *them*," noted Briggs, "but *we* couldn't survive against it."

"Our job isn't to survive it," said Cole. "Our job is to mobilize and misdirect it."

"I don't understand," said Rachel.

"Neither do I," said Val with a smile. "But I think I like it."

Cole turned to Val. "Who would you say are our two best pilots?"

"Me and someone else," she replied.

"I'm being serious."

"So am I."

"Damn it, Val!"

"All right. After me, the two best you have are Sokolov and Moyer."

"I agree."

There was a momentary silence.

"Have we won the war yet?" asked Val sardonically.

"Mr. Briggs, is there a way for me to send a holo, coded, scrambled, unreadable by anyone but one of the ships whose computers you and Christine rigged before we left?"

"Of course."

"I'm not done yet. Can we then transfer that signal to a captured ship?"

"Yes."

"I'm still not done. Now, the captured ship won't have a computer that you worked on, so I assume the signal should probably be put in a cube and hand-delivered to the captured ship's system?"

"That'll work," said Briggs, "but I don't see—"

"One final question," said Cole. "Can that signal then be transmitted, unscrambled and uncoded, to a destination of our choice?"

"Well, yes, if whoever transfers it to the captured ship's computer programs the ship's computer to do that."

"Is it difficult?"

Briggs shook his head. "All the difficult work has been done, encoding the initial signal so that it's undecipherable."

"Now, once those captured ships have been rigged to send the signal, we can also program them *when* to send it, right?"

"No problem at all."

"Thank you, Mr. Briggs." He turned to Rachel. "I want to send a coded, scrambled message to Vladimir Sokolov and Dan Moyer. I don't care if they can see me or not."

"Ready," she said, concentrating on the computer's controls.

"Gentlemen, this is Wilson Cole. I commend you on your recent kills. Now I have what will almost certainly be a more difficult task for you. I want each of you to capture or disable a small Republic ship—Class H would be perfect, certainly nothing bigger than Class J. Set the prisoners down on an uninhabited oxygen world, and I stress uninhabited. I don't want them on any world where they can make contact with anyone who might be sympathetic to the Republic. Leave them with all their food and all their medical supplies. You can also leave their weapons; just toss 'em out the hatch as you're closing it."

He paused, cleared his throat, and continued. "In a few minutes we will be transmitting a second message, a prerecorded holographic one. Mr. Briggs will tell you exactly how to handle it and what I want you to do with it. Once you have done as ordered, I want you to clear the hell out of the sector, whatever sector you're in. If there is anything you don't understand about your instructions or about the message you will soon be receiving, contact either Mr. Briggs or Lieutenant Mboya."

He looked over at Rachel and nodded his head, and she sent the messages off.

"Okay, this next will be the message I discussed with Mr. Briggs. And it has to be holographic, not just audio."

"All right," said Rachel. "Ready whenever you are."

"Now," said Cole.

"Go."

"This is Wilson Cole, speaking to you from the bridge of the *Theodore Roosevelt*. If you have any doubt of my identity, run a voice-print." He paused to give them the opportunity to do just that. "Four years ago you imprisoned me for an action that saved five million human lives. That is a disagreement between you and me, and I was content to live out my life on the Inner Frontier, well beyond your jurisdiction. But your pursuit of me has enlarged our disagreement to include literally billions of men, women, and aliens. You have committed genocide, you have practiced torture, and you have proven yourself totally unworthy of the trust the citizens of the Republic have placed in you. You have one Standard day in which to resign your position. If you do not, then be assured that you will be forcibly removed from it. This is not an idle threat, and I am not grandstanding: if you have not resigned within one Standard day, we shall be at hazard. And this time I won't be running *from* you, but *toward* you."

He nodded to Rachel, who coded and scrambled the message, then turned back to Briggs.

"This will be transmitted to Sokolov and Moyer," he said. "Once they've each captured or disabled a ship, I want these messages sent uncoded to the recipients I name, but I don't want them sent separately. I want them sent within a minute of each other, from totally different sectors."

"That shouldn't be a problem."

"Good. And even though Sokolov and Moyer aren't in military ships, I want them to get the hell out of the area, at least fifty light-years, before those messages are sent. If they can't find the proper wormholes, have them contact Pilot; he's been around forever and he knows every damned wormhole in the galaxy—or at least it feels like he does."

"I'll tell them, sir," said Briggs. "You haven't told me where you want the message sent."

"I want Moyer's sent to the *Xerxes*—Admiral Susan Garcia's flagship."

"It'll probably be picked up by thirty other ships first. It could take a long time to go through channels and reach her."

"Once they check my voiceprint, it'll take about twenty seconds," replied Cole confidently.

"And the other message, the one we're giving to Vladimir Sokolov?"

Cole smiled. "You haven't guessed? Have it sent to Deluros VIII, to the personal attention of Egan Wilkie, the Secretary of the Republic."

"So you're sending them a threatening holo," said Val. "So what? They'll laugh their heads off."

"No, they won't," said Cole. "They'll home in on the two ships, which I hope will be a couple of thousand light-years apart, and blow them to hell and gone—but at the same time they'll realize that we're a force of more than one. And then they'll start checking on how many of their ships have turned up missing. Probably some were brought down by the Teronis, and a few malfunctioned, but we'll take credit for—and be blamed for—every last one. Any power plant blows, any shipbuilding world is sabotaged—some will be our doing but most won't—they'll credit it all to us. They'll spread themselves thin, thinner than they should be while they're fighting the Teronis, and while we keep feinting and ducking, they'll keep responding—and sooner or later we'll find the weakness in their armor."

"It's a hell of a way to fight a war," snorted Val.

"I know it's going to disappoint the hell out of you," said Cole, "but I have no interest in fighting a war." She stared at him curiously. "I'm only interested in winning the war, and if I can do it without firing a single shot, I'll be just as happy."

"We're growing a strange crop of heroes this year," said Val.

"Heroes fight bravely and die young," said Cole. "I'm just a guy who's playing the cards that were dealt to him."

"Besides," said Sharon's disembodied voice, "maybe Garcia and Wilkie will take the hint and resign."

"Yeah," said Val. "Right after the stars stop in their courses and I run off with David Copperfield."

"If I were a bookmaker," said Cole, "I'd call it six-to-five pick 'em."

Cole's messages had an immediate and deleterious effect. Not on the
Teddy R, which was a third of a galaxy away from Deluros VIII, but on
almost anything that moved and didn't bear the insignia of the
Republic.

A convoy of eleven ships, carrying ore from the mining worlds of
the Frontier to the shipbuilding world of Spica II, didn't identify itself
quickly enough and was obliterated.

Two men—one high on whiskey, one high on drugs—got into a
fight on Bishawn IV. Weapons were drawn, a single pulse blast was
fired, it went wild and hit a bystander, more guns and shots were fired,
the bartender sent out a distress signal that people were shooting at
each other, the Navy picked it up, and a moment later the tavern and
all seventy-one of its customers and employees were vaporized.

Every ship, whether business or pleasure, was inspected, released,
then inspected again in the next system, and the system after that.
Anyone who didn't give the Navy the answers they wanted, or who
didn't give them fast enough, or clearly enough, or often enough, was
incarcerated without appeal.

Loyal alien worlds, longtime members of the Republic, were suddenly viewed with suspicion. Terrified ambassadors—Cole's messages
had passed through channels and had leaked within an hour—insisted
on Navy escorts. Private ships became convinced that other private
ships were in the employ of the notorious Wilson Cole, and began
firing on each other.

"I should have thought of this a long time ago," remarked Cole as the most recent reports came in.

He was sitting in the mess hall, where he had been joined by Sharon, David Copperfield, and the Platinum Duke.

"You know, we may win this conflict without firing a shot," said David.

"That's the best way to win a war," replied Cole.

"I hear that the Seventh Fleet is being recalled to defend Deluros," said the Duke. He chuckled. "Against *us*!"

"It all seems to be going smoothly now," said Sharon, "but pretty soon they're going to notice that we're not attacking them, on Deluros VIII or anywhere else."

"Sure we are," said Cole with a smile. "And they can prove it. After all, haven't they already destroyed two hundred of our ships, and pretty much decimated five planets that we've used as bases?"

Sharon shook her head in wonderment. "Who'd'a thunk it?" she said in bemused tones.

"My friend Steerforth," answered David promptly. "No one but an Englishman would be this subtle and this brilliant."

"David, give it a rest," said Cole. "I've never even been to Earth."

"Stop contradicting me!" demanded David irritably. "Of course you're British! If you weren't, you couldn't have thought of this."

"Why don't you just agree with him?" suggested the Duke. "That is, if you want to discuss another subject anytime in the next few weeks."

Jacovic's image flickered into existence. "It's official, sir. They've pulled back the Seventh Fleet, and there are rumors that they'll soon be recalling the Fourth to bolster their planetary defenses as well."

Cole frowned. "That doesn't make any sense," he said. "If they call back the Fourth, they're ceding the Matheson Sector to the Teronis."

"Evidently they're more afraid of you, sir," suggested Jacovic.

"They can't be that incompetent," said Cole. "We're not that lucky." He paused and considered the situation. "They've been pouring men, ships, money, *everything* into that sector for fifteen years. Now they're just going to walk away because of a threat from one ship?"

"They don't know how many ships we have, Wilson," said Sharon "The only thing they *do* know is that they sent three hundred ships out to Singapore Station last month, and none of them returned." She paused. "They don't know that it was touch-and-go all the way, and that we lost close to two thousand ships."

Jacovic's image faded and vanished.

"It just goes to show you," said the Duke. "Never underestimate the power of fear."

"I know Admiral Garcia," replied Cole. "And if there's anything in the galaxy she's afraid of, I'm not aware of it, and neither are you."

"Then why do you suppose they're reacting like this?"

"I don't know Egan Wilkie," said Cole. "I suspect this is being done on his orders, not hers."

"You know," said Sharon, "this just might convince him to sign a truce with the Teroni Federation. If he decides he can't fight both the Teronis and the threat from within, he might choose to fight the latter."

"It's not going to happen," said Cole firmly.

"Why not?"

"First, this can't last. They've got to figure out pretty soon that we haven't fired a shot yet. And second, the Teronis are no fools. If he's too eager and offers them too many concessions, they'll know he's doing it out of weakness. They've been at this for more than a quarter of a century; what's one more year if your enemy is in deep trouble?"

"Then what was the point of all this?" asked David Copperfield. "I mean, if they'll know in a week or a month or even three months, what real damage have we done them? All we've done is tell them that the *Theodore Roosevelt* is inside the Republic."

"They don't even know that," replied Cole. "All they know for sure is that we weren't at Singapore Station when their fleet of eight hundred ships arrived."

"Then I repeat: why have you gone to the trouble of doing all this?"

"I sent one message to two locations," replied Cole easily. "It wasn't any trouble at all."

"Damn it, Steerforth! You're toying with me!"

"Use your brain, David," said Cole.

The little alien frowned. "I'm thinking," he said. "Nothing's coming."

"Domak?" said Cole, raising his voice.

"Yes, sir?" said Domak's image, appearing over the table.

"Have you got the latest damage reports?"

"There's been no damage to the ship, sir."

"I mean inflicted by the Republic in the McAllister Sector."

"Yes, sir. I have it right here."

"Stick it on a holoscreen and transmit it down here, please."

A holographic screen with a three-dimensional map of the McAllister Sector and a long readout below the map suddenly replaced Domak's image. Cole scanned the readout intently for a few seconds, found what he was looking for, and leaned back.

"Thank you, Domak," he said.

"Will there be anything else, sir?"

"Yeah. Tell Jacovic we're going to New Lenin, and have Pilot lay in a course to get us there. Tell him we don't want to arrive in less than three days. We wouldn't want to run into any Navy stragglers."

"I'll get right on it, sir," said Domak, ending the connection.

"What was that all about?" asked David.

"New Lenin is the banking and trading capital of the McAllister Sector," said Cole. "Or at least it was until two days ago."

"What happened?"

"The Navy decided we had a secret base there," answered Cole. "End result: there are an estimated sixty-three thousand dead, most of the major buildings in the capital city of Gromyko have been destroyed, and as far as I can tell the *Teddy R* remains unscathed."

"That's tragic, of course," said David, without much emotion. "But what does it have to do with what we were just discussing?"

"David," said Cole, "if we're going to defeat the Republic, we're not going to do it with eight hundred ships and four thousand men."

"I'm still not following you."

"New Lenin has a population of three million," answered Cole. "Their planet has just been attacked for no valid reason by the Republic." He paused and looked into the little alien's eyes. "Now, if you were going to recruit a few thousand motivated men and their ships to our cause, where would you look for them?"

"I see!" said David, his eyes widening.

"That's where we're heading now. And every time the Republic overreacts against another world, we'll be there signing them up."

"That might even make mean old Mr. Creakle proud of you, Steerforth!"

"Who the hell is Mr. Creakle?"

"Our headmaster," said David reproachfully. "How could you forget?"

"I must have lost my head," answered Cole as Val entered the mess hall. "Or maybe I confused him with Barkis."

"Ah!" said David happily. "'Barkis is willin'.'"

"Good," said Val. "Let's recruit the son of a bitch."

During the flight to New Lenin, Cole had Christine locate alien colonies and enclaves along the way. He sent Braxite out in the *Archie* to recruit Molarians from the alien enclave on Kipling V. Domak was given the *Alice* and told to recruit Polonoi from the colony on Bednari III.

"We have two shuttles left," noted Sharon. "Who do we send out next?"

"We have one shuttle left." They were in Cole's office, and she looked at him questioningly. "The *Teddy R* can't land, so we'll need the *Kermit* to take us down to New Lenin's surface." He paused. "I'll probably turn the *Quentin* over to Jack-in-the-Box."

"His name's Jaxtaboxl."

"He doesn't mind," noted Cole. "No reason why anyone else should. Anyway, there's a fair-sized Mollutei population on Win-schlaager VI. I think we'll let him try his luck there."

"What about David?"

"He's the only member of his race any of us have ever seen, he insists that he comes from nineteenth-century London, and besides, if they're all like him, do you really want a bunch of them fighting on our side?"

She laughed. "You have a point." Then: "Who are you sending down to New Lenin?"

He simply stared at her silently.

"No!" she said adamantly. "The Captain doesn't leave his ship in enemy territory, damn it!"

"It hasn't been enemy territory for a few days," said Cole. "*We* didn't decimate it."

"They're a part of the Republic. You're the Republic's most wanted criminal."

"We're going there because we're betting that they don't consider themselves part of the Republic either," said Cole. "I want them to see me, hear me, question me, and convince themselves that contrary to what the Navy's been telling them for the last few years, I'm not the Antichrist."

"How about convincing *me* and following regulations?" demanded Sharon.

"Whose regulations?" he shot back. "The same Navy we're fighting against? We haven't been part of it for four years now."

"Damn it, Wilson!"

"I'll come back intact and unharmed, guaranteed."

"What is your guarantee worth?" she asked bitterly.

"Not *mine*," he corrected her. "Val's." She stared at him uncomprehendingly. "I'm taking her along as my bodyguard. Feel better now?"

"Okay, she'll protect you from them," said Sharon. "Who'll protect *them* from *her*?"

"She'll be all right," said Cole. "I've used her in this capacity before."

"Will you at least signal ahead and make sure they won't shoot you before you open your mouth?"

"Of course."

"You promise?" she said suspiciously.

"My Chief of Security's opinion to the contrary, I'm not suicidal."

"Maybe not, but you seem to think you can only be killed by a silver bullet. You've been one hell of a lot luckier than you deserve to be."

"That helps too," acknowledged Cole.

"Sir?" said Christine urgently as her image popped into existence.

"What's up?"

"A lone Class H Navy ship is approaching under a white flag."

"How many men aboard it?"

"None, sir."

"A bomb?"

"No, sir. I didn't make myself clear. Mr. Briggs has scanned it. It has a crew of two, both Lodinites, not Men. There are no explosives on board."

"Have they sent a signal?"

"Not yet," said Christine. "Wait a minute. Yes, here it comes. They want to talk to you."

"Ship-to-ship or face-to-face?" asked Cole.

"They don't care."

"Then make it ship-to-ship and patch it through to my office."

Instantly the images of two furry Lodinites appeared above Cole's desk.

"Which of you is Captain Cole?"

Cole was tempted to say "The ugly one," but realized that standards of beauty varied from race to race, and if they immediately began conversing with Sharon he might get a momentary chuckle out of it but it wouldn't keep him very warm when he went to bed alone for the next few nights, so instead he said, "What can I do for you?"

"We come under a flag of peace," said one of the Lodinites.

"I know," said Cole. "That's why we allowed you to come this close."

"We are members of the Navy."

"I know that too."

"There are more than a million Lodinites in the Navy. We fought at Man's side in the Sett War, and the Battle of the Brazi Cluster, and we have been fighting with Man against the Teroni Federation for twenty-nine years."

"Then what brings you to the Republic's most wanted criminal under a flag of truce?" asked Cole, hoping he knew the answer already.

"It was just serendipitous that we spotted the *Theodore Roosevelt*. We were on our way to the Inner Frontier."

"Why?"

"The Republic has put Lodin XI under martial law!" growled the one who had remained silent. "We are their most loyal ally, and they have the temerity to do that to us, just because some of our leaders spoke out against their overreaction to your threat against Secretary Wilkie."

"We want to join you!" chimed in the other one.

"I think that can be arranged," said Cole. "With a couple of stipulations."

"What are they? What pledge must we take?"

"No pledge, no oaths. You're here; that's proof enough that you don't want to be *there*. I want one of you to come aboard the *Teddy R*—"

"The what?" interrupted the first Lodinite.

"The *Theodore Roosevelt*," replied Cole. "One of you comes here, and one of our crewmen will transfer to your ship."

"May I ask why?"

"He'll know our codes and program them into your computer, and he'll be able to extract things from your ship's computer you didn't even know were there. And the one of you who's transferred here will learn our methods and our rules. It won't be permanent; the two of you can be together again in a few days—but probably not on that ship."

"Why not this ship?"

"It's a Navy ship. I'm going to want one of my best pilots to have it. If he can pick off the occasional Class H or Class J Navy ship, and let the survivors identify him, the Navy will start wondering how many of their ships we control. They might start seeing ghosts and shooting each other, just the way they're currently shooting up planets that we've never touched down on. Anyway, that's my plan, and that's my offer. You can accept it or you can retreat out of range of our weaponry before we call an end to the truce."

"Will we eventually join the crew of the *Theodore Roosevelt?*"

"Yes, if you wish."

"Then we accept it."

"Good. We'll send a shuttle out with our man very shortly, and bring one of you back here."

He broke the connection, then contacted Christine.

"Yes, sir?" she said.

"Can we do without Briggs for a few days?"

"I suppose so, sir," she said. "But if so, then let's reschedule Lieutenant Domak so we're not both on duty at the same time."

He nodded his head. "Spread the expertise out. Makes sense. Put me on the ship's audio."

"Done."

"Mr. Briggs," said Cole as his voice echoed throughout the *Teddy R,* "pack a few days' worth of clothes and edibles, and get down to the shuttle bay."

He waited a moment, then directed Idena Mueller to pilot the *Kermit* to the Lodinites' ship, trade Briggs for one of the Lodinites, and then return to the *Teddy R.*

"Can you give me a few minutes, sir?" she asked, her voice fuzzy with sleep. "You just woke me."

"Sorry," said Cole. "Yeah, take as much time as you need. The Republic's been around a couple of thousand years. I don't suppose another ten minutes makes much difference."

The trade was effected half an hour later, and Cole had Luthor

Chadwick, Sharon's second-in-command in Security, locate Val for him. She was working out with Bull Pampas in the makeshift gym near the infirmary. He waited another half hour until they had finished, showered, and gotten back into their uniforms, then contacted Val and asked her to come to his office.

"I need a beer," she said. "Lifting weights is thirsty work. Why don't you meet me in the mess hall, or in that undersized closet that passes for the Officers' Lounge?"

"The mess hall is fine," said Cole. "Five minutes?"

"I'll be on my third beer by then."

He just shook his head in puzzlement. "I will never figure out how you can drink like a fish and stay so damned good-looking."

"Good genes," she replied with a smile. "And my workouts would kill you—or anyone else on the ship besides Bull."

He showed up in four minutes, and found she was just finishing her second beer.

"I hear some Navy ship just surrendered to us," she said by way of greeting.

"Not quite," Cole replied. "It was a little Class H job, and they've joined us."

"Can you trust them?"

"Can *they* trust *us*?" he replied. "I've got Briggs over there working on their computer right now."

"Okay, enough polite small talk," said the Valkyrie. "Who do you want me to lean on?"

"Hopefully no one," he said. "I'm going to take the shuttle down to New Lenin. I want you to ride shotgun and protect my back."

"You got it," she said.

"Don't look so damned eager. We're trying to recruit these people, not go to war with them."

"Do *they* know it?"

"They will, before we land."

"Men like you take all the fun out of war and carnage, you know that?"

"I'll try to live with the shame," replied Cole.

Val ordered another beer from the galley. "You want one? My treat."

"What do you mean, your treat? Nobody pays to eat on the ship."

"No one's paid me since the battle back at Singapore Station, so it's a wash. Now, do you want one or not?"

"Not," said Cole. "And go easy on that stuff after today. No one likes a drunken pirate queen."

She stared at him for a moment. "That's a pretty daring challenge."

"Forget I said it," said Cole. "Just be ready."

He got up and left the mess hall. He wasn't sleepy, and he felt a little claustrophobic in his office after they'd been in space for a week or more. He considered the exercise room, but he hadn't lifted weights or run on a treadmill in almost twenty years. He went down to Gunnery, ostensibly to inspect it, actually just to pass the time and talk a bit with Bull Pampas, but Pampas was off duty and he had nothing to say to the Mollute he found there. Mustapha Odom was always good for a chat, but when Cole went down to Engineering he found that Odom was on his sleep shift.

Some life! he thought. *I traverse the galaxy, I visit star clusters you can't even see from my home world, I have the universe at my fingertips—and I spend most of my adulthood feeling like a goddamned sardine in a can.*

He looked in at the Officers' Lounge and found David Copperfield and the Platinum Duke playing cards.

"Hi, Steerforth," said David, looking up.

"I didn't realize you two were officers," said Cole wryly.

"We're gentlemen," replied David. "That's just as good."

"Still playing whist?"

"It's a proper game for gentlemen."

"And it's the only one I can win at," said the Duke. "If I can ever figure out the odds, I'm going to add a table when we get back to Singapore Station."

Cole merely stared at him.

"I know, I know," continued the Duke at last. "But if I didn't believe there was a chance, then what the hell am I doing on this ship?"

"There's a chance," said Cole gently.

He left them playing their game, and eventually wound up on the bridge. Christine was the Officer on Deck, speaking rapidly to the main computer in a language Cole was sure only the two of them understood. Idena Mueller and Bujandi, a native of far Peponi, were also on the bridge, tending to their various stations.

He walked over to Idena. "No problem with the transfer?"

"I thought we already reported to you that it was successfully accomplished, sir," she replied. "I believe Colonel Blacksmith is debriefing the Lodinite in Security right now."

"Fine," said Cole. He turned to Christine. "Everything going smoothly for Mr. Briggs?"

"He reports that he's familiar with the computer, and should be done coding it and downloading its public and private contents within twenty Standard hours."

"Tell him he'll be staying until we've thoroughly indoctrinated the Lodinite whose place he's taking."

"Meloctin, sir."

"Meloctin to you, too," he said, frowning in puzzlement.

"That's the Lodinite's name, sir—Meloctin."

"Fine."

He wanted to strike up a conversation, but all three crewmembers were busy performing necessary tasks. Suddenly he became irritated with himself. *What's* wrong *with being bored in a war zone?* he asked himself. All right, no one was shooting at anyone and there were no enemy ships within a parsec, but even so the entire Republic was a war zone for anyone aboard the *Teddy R*, and especially its Captain.

He considered visiting Sharon in Security, but he knew she was busy with the Lodinite. He was just about to go to his office and call up another musical entertainment—he'd seen them all a dozen times—when Christine suddenly turned to him.

"Sir?"

"Yes?"

"A coded message from the Octopus is coming in."

"Open it up and let's see it."

An instant later the image of the Octopus hovered in front of the main viewscreen. He was still shirtless, and the six hands that stuck out of his rib cage seemed to be clenching and unclenching independently of him. Cole wondered if they kept doing it when he slept.

"Hi, Wilson," he said in his gruff voice. "We're on the trail of a hot one."

"You want to explain?" said Cole.

"There's a Navy convoy—maybe a dozen ships but only two Class Ls—heading back to Deluros from the Quinellus Cluster. And guess what they're carrying?"

"Why don't you just tell me?"

"About twenty tons of gold! They just plundered some of the Frontier mining worlds. There are a dozen races that have no confidence in the credit, and insist on being paid in gold."

"You're not seriously telling me that you plan to rob a Navy convoy?" said Cole disbelievingly.

"I wish I could," said the Octopus, "but I haven't got enough fire-power."

"Then what the hell are you talking about?" asked Cole "You're contacting me to tell me you're *not* going to rob it?"

"I'm going to blow it to smithereens!" said the Octopus. "We know which ship's got the gold and which are the decoys. Maybe I can't steal it for myself, but I can destroy it, and that'll have the same effect on the Republic. They won't be meeting their alien payroll this month!"

"How many ships have you got?"

"Seven."

"Against a dozen ships, including two Class Ls?" said Cole dubiously.

"They've got to pass through a dust cloud two parsecs beyond the Beaufort system," said the Octopus. "Well, through it or near it. We'll be waiting inside it. And they'll immediately move into a formation to stop us from *stealing* the gold. They'll never guess that we're out to destroy it."

"I think you're biting off more than you can chew."

"You just don't want someone else to be the Republic's most wanted felon," replied the Octopus with a laugh.

"I can't stop you," said Cole. "So good luck, Godspeed, and give 'em hell."

"That I will do," promised the Octopus, ending the transmission.

"What do you think, sir?" asked Christine.

Cole shrugged. "He was the most powerful criminal kingpin on the Inner Frontier before he teamed up with us. He knows his stuff. Maybe he can pull it off. . . ."

"But?" she said.

"But if I was a betting man, I'd bet against it. He can defend his ship against one Class L attack . . . but two of them acting in concert?

I don't know." He paused. "Still, if he can destroy that gold and word gets out—and we'll make sure it does—that'll do more damage to the Republic than knocking off a thousand ships."

"I don't know," said Idena. "They'll be late on the payroll, but they're hardly impoverished."

"It's got nothing to do with the value of the gold," explained Cole. "It's a public demonstration that they can't defend something that's very valuable to them—and if they can't defend *that*, how can you expect them to defend your planet against the Teronis or the *Teddy R*?"

"I hadn't thought of it that way," she admitted.

He smiled. "More wars are won with headlines than with bombs."

"I suppose when you get right down to it, the concept of propaganda has been around a lot longer than the reality of bombs," said Idena.

"Which doesn't mean I hope the Octopus attacks with words rather than thumpers and burners," said Cole.

He stayed on the bridge for a few more minutes, then went to his cabin. He called up an entertainment, decided he wasn't interested in it, and spent the next two hours watching sporting events that the ship captured from powerful pan-galactic transmitters. Finally he fell asleep, fully clothed, while watching the holo of a murderball game between Rockgarden and Far London.

When he woke up he found Sharon, also fully clothed, sleeping beside him. His stirring woke her, and she sat up, rubbing her eyes.

"Good morning," he said.

"There are no mornings in deep space," said Sharon.

"Right," said Cole. "Good afternoon." He paused. "Did we do anything—I mean, you and me?"

"You snored. I slept the innocent sleep of a fairy princess, dainty and delicate as a dragonfly's wing."

"Please," he said. "Not before breakfast."

"All right," she said, getting to her feet. "I was hoping you'd grow a beard overnight so no one on New Lenin would recognize you, but it hasn't happened, so we might as well have what could very well be our last breakfast together."

"Try not to display so much faith in me," said Cole dryly. "It might make me overconfident."

They left the cabin and headed toward the mess hall. Upon arriving, Cole contacted Jacovic, who was the Officer on Deck.

"What's our ETA for New Lenin?" he asked.

"We'll be in orbit in about an hour, sir."

"They don't know yet that we're the Good Guys," said Cole, "so I want all our defenses activated *before* we enter orbit."

"Yes, sir," said Jacovic. Then: "Sir?"

"Yes?"

"I request permission to accompany you."

"Request denied," replied Cole. "I appreciate the offer, but this is the wrong venue. The Republic attacked them, so there's a chance I can convince them that we're on their side. But they've been at war with the Teroni Federation for a quarter of a century. I can't present them with a wanted mutineer *and* a Teroni and expect them to sit still long enough to listen to what I have to say."

There was a momentary silence. "I agree, sir," said Jacovic. "I hadn't thought it through."

"All right," said Cole. "I assume the Valkyrie is up and around?"

"Yes, sir. I believe she's in the exercise room."

"Figures. Well, she knows when she has to be ready."

He and Sharon ordered their breakfast. The Platinum Duke showed up before they had finished.

"You're really going to do it?" he said by way of greeting. "You're really walking into the lion's den?"

"The Republic destroyed the den, and all the lions are out shivering in the cold," answered Cole. "I'm just going to offer them a blanket."

"Spare me your metaphors," said the Duke. "If we were back on Singapore Station, I could get fifteen-to-one against you living out the day. Can't you just talk to them from up here?"

"I could."

"Then why don't you?"

"I'm not looking to pick up twenty or thirty ships, or a couple of hundred recruits," answered Cole. "There are close to three million people on this planet who have good reason to hate the Republic. But they also have good reason—or so they think—to distrust the Republic's enemies. If I do it right, I could practically conscript the whole damned planet. I want them to see me, talk to me, to get a feel for what I'm saying, for what I am. I don't know if I could do that via a transmission. Would *you* follow someone who was afraid to land on your world?"

"Shouldn't you have warned them before now that you were coming?"

"Why give them three days to argue about whether to let me land or not?"

"So with half of Gromyko blown away, who do you contact? What government is left?"

"I have no interest in governments," replied Cole.

"Then who?"

"I have some ideas. I'll play it by ear."

"Here's hoping that no one puts a laser beam in that ear," said the Duke.

"Nobody's going to touch him," said Val, who was standing at the entrance of the mess hall.

"I'm counting on you to make sure of that," said Sharon.

"As long as I'm being talked about as if I'm not here," said Cole, getting up from the table, "I think it's time for me to go announce our presence to New Lenin."

"I'll drink to that," said Val.

"Not today, you won't," said Cole.

Val looked like she was about to argue, then shrugged. "You're the boss," she said.

"I'm glad someone remembers that," said Cole as he left to send his message.

Cole stood on the bridge, and nodded to Domak.

"Okay," he said. "Widest possible bandwidth; I want everyone on the damned planet who wants to see and hear me to be able to."

"Are you sure you wouldn't rather do this from your office?" said Jacovic. "It might appear less threatening. After all, they were just attacked by warships exactly like this one."

Cole couldn't repress a grin. "Not exactly like this one," he replied. "They were probably ninety years younger and a century more advanced. But to answer your point, I *hope* they'll listen to reason and greet me with open arms—but I want them to know that we're not a sitting duck up here, and that if they take any action against us on the assumption that we are still the enemy, we have the wherewithal to defend ourselves." He turned to Domak. "This will override every broadcast and show up on every computer and holo-screen, right?"

"In theory," said Domak. "Lieutenant Mboya could probably make absolutely certain of it."

"Let her sleep," said Cole. "She's putting in twelve-hour shifts with Briggs gone. Let's assume you're as good as I think you are and get this show on the road."

"Now," said Domak.

Cole stared at where he imagined a camera was.

"Greetings, citizens of New Lenin. My name is Wilson Cole, my ship is the *Theodore Roosevelt*, and until a few days ago you probably thought I was your enemy. Since that time, you have experienced first-hand the morality, thoughtfulness, loyalty, and compassion of the Republic, which I personally encountered almost four years ago. They have destroyed most of Gromyko and killed tens of thousands of loyal New Lenin citizens because they have overreacted to a threat that was made against only two people, neither of whom was within fifteen thousand light-years of New Lenin."

He paused to give them a moment to digest what he had said, then continued. "I would like to come down to the surface of New Lenin and speak to some of you personally. I have no objection if you have holo cameras and other mechanisms that will transmit what is said all over the planet. I want a guarantee of safe passage for myself and one assistant to take a shuttlecraft down to any location of your choice. The *Theodore Roosevelt* is in orbit around New Lenin. If my offer is refused, there will be no repercussions; we will simply leave. If I am offered safe passage and you should renege upon that offer, there *will* be conse-quences, but I hope, and I am sure you hope, that it does not come to that. I will give you one hour to consider my offer and reply to it. A failure to answer will be considered a negative response, and we'll take our leave of the system immediately thereafter."

He waited a few seconds for his conditions to sink in, and then concluded. "I am coming with a proposition. If it is rejected, we will leave immediately and in peace. I await your decision."

He nodded to Domak, who cut the transmission.

"Keep every channel we've got open," he said. "They'll take about forty minutes to argue it out, and then they'll invite me down."

"You sound awfully sure," said Sharon.

"They'll realize that if we wanted to fire on them, we'd have done it before announcing our presence and giving them a chance to activate whatever defenses they still have."

"Four Eyes was right," she said. "You think too much to be a hero. Heroes walk in, weapons blazing."

"Look where it got him," said Cole bitterly. "There are an awful lot of heroes buried all across the galaxy." He looked around. "I assume Val's waiting in the shuttle bay?"

"I think she's down in Gunnery, seeing how many cannons she can lift," said Sharon with a smile.

"See?" responded Cole, returning her smile. "We have a hero after all. Rough, tough, fearless, redheaded, maybe two or three inches under seven feet—what more could you want?"

"You announced her as your assistant," noted Sharon. "When she walks in fully armed, they might have a little difficulty with your definition."

"They'll have more important things to worry about."

Suddenly an alarm sounded.

"Incoming?" asked the Mollute who was at one of the stations.

"No," said Sharon, frowning. "That's an internal Security alert." She raised her voice. "Luthor, do you read me? What's going on?"

"No problem," said Chadwick as his image popped into being. "Just a little problem with our newest crew member."

"The Lodinite?" asked Cole.

"Right," replied Chadwick. "Meloctin, I think his name is. He got confused, thought he was one level down, and walked into the infirmary by mistake. The situation is resolved, and he's back in his quarters."

His image vanished.

"It's hard to imagine someone getting lost aboard this old hulk," offered Domak.

"That's because you've been aboard her for, what, seven years?" said Cole. "He's been on it less than a day. It *is* a big ship. It's outdated, and battle-scarred, and tired, but it's as complex as most Class Ls."

They killed time for another half hour, and then the message Cole had been waiting for came in.

"Captain Cole, this is Augustus Lake," said a tall, thin man with a shock of unruly white hair. "I'm the Acting Mayor of Gromyko. More to the point, I'm the only member of the city or planetary government left alive. We are willing to hear what you have to say. I'll feed the landing coordinates into your computer—you'll be setting down atop one of the few undamaged buildings. When you emerge, you'll find yourself facing an array of armed men and women. We will not fire without provocation, but you have to understand that we have lost our trust in people who proclaim they mean us no harm."

"That's understandable and acceptable," replied Cole. "My assistant will also be armed, but if there is no immediate threat to my person, she will not use her weapons."

"Give us thirty minutes to set everything up," continued Lake. "We'll take you to a secure room, what's left of what might be called our leading citizens will be there to hear what you have to say, and we'll have holo cameras standing by to transmit what you say to the rest of our citizenry."

"Fine. Just give my computer the coordinates, and we'll be there in half an hour."

"I apologize for our appearance," said Lake. "We've barely begun digging out of the rubble."

"I understand, and I sympathize."

The transmission ended, and Cole turned to Sharon.

"Feel a little better?" he asked.

"Augustus Lake seems like a decent man," she replied.

"I told you there was nothing to worry about.

"You didn't let me finish," she said. "He seems like a decent man, but you're going to be confronted by dozens, perhaps hundreds, of armed men and women, many of whom lost loved ones just a few days ago."

"They know we didn't do it."

"They also know we were the reason it was done," said Sharon. "You don't know that a couple of them won't be so blinded by their grief that they decide to kill the cause of it the reason the Navy went berserk."

"It *didn't* go berserk," said Cole. "It coldly and calmly attempted to destroy a planet that's been a part of the Republic since it was first colonized. That's what this is all about."

She sighed deeply. "I know. I just want you to stay alert."

"I've got Val. She's alert enough for both of us."

And a few minutes later Cole and Val took off in the *Kermit*, spiraling gently down to the appointed rooftop in the shattered city of Gromyko.

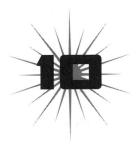

Gromyko smelled of death. Most of the bodies hadn't been removed yet, and the odor wafted up to the roof where the *Kermit* had set down.

Cole turned to Val before opening the hatch. "No sudden moves. These guys figure to be more on edge than most."

"Got it," she replied with no show of concern.

"I mean it, Val. If your hip itches within four or five inches of your burner or your screecher, let it itch. You reach to scratch it, I can almost guarantee someone's going to take that as an excuse to shoot."

She frowned. "Then why the hell am I here anyway?"

"Not to face thirty or forty armed men," said Cole. "But once we get in the studio or whatever it's called, I want you to keep your eyes open."

"You don't really think the Republic's got a spy here?" she said dubiously.

"No, not after what happened," replied Cole. "But don't forget—there's still a twenty-million-credit price on my head. You don't have to favor either side to want to collect it."

She nodded. "Okay, it makes sense."

"I'm so glad you approve." He opened the hatch. "Let's go."

They emerged onto the roof, where they found themselves facing some fifty armed men and women dressed in street clothes—which was logical: no one would wear a Republic uniform on this planet, and they wouldn't have had time to organize and equip an independent force.

Augustus Lake stepped forward. "The notorious Captain Cole," he said by way of greeting. "Will your assistant relinquish her weapons?"

"No," said Cole before Val could refuse in even harsher terms. "She won't use them without cause, but I wouldn't want to be the guy who tries to take them away from her."

Lake looked up at Val, who towered a foot above him, and shrugged. "As you wish. We will have to trust one another." He headed off to an airlift. "Follow me, please."

Cole fell into step behind him. Val looked like she wanted someone to take a shot at him, but no one moved, and she joined them in the airlift as it descended a dozen levels.

"How bad was it?" asked Cole.

"Worse than I hope you can imagine," answered Lake. "Here we are."

They stepped off the airlift and entered a large room. There were perhaps thirty chairs, and each of them was filled. There were three holographic cameras, each of which turned to him and tracked him as he walked to the front of the room.

Cole waited until Lake seated himself. Val stood about ten feet to his left, her arms folded, scrutinizing each member of the audience in turn.

"I want to thank you for allowing me to address you," began Cole. "I know the propaganda you've been subjected to since the Navy and I parted ways. I'd like to begin by telling you the truth of what transpired. Every member of my crew who was with me at the time will vouch for it, and so, if she's being honest, will Admiral Susan Garcia.

"The *Theodore Roosevelt*, under the command of Captain Podok, a warrior-caste Polonoi, was charged with patrolling the Cassius Cluster, with myself as First Officer. Our orders were to protect large fuel depots on two worlds, Benidos and New Argentina, and not let that fuel fall into the hands of the enemy.

"One day the Fifth Teroni Fleet showed up in force, some two hundred ships strong, and headed for Benidos. There was no way our single ship could stand against them. Captain Podok interpreted our orders to mean that the fuel was to be kept from the Teronis at all costs."

Cole paused, the muscles in his jaw twitching as he remembered that fateful day. "She gave the order to destroy Benidos rather than allow the fuel to fall into Teroni hands. In the process, she killed three million Republic citizens.

"She then directed the *Theodore Roosevelt* to do the same thing to New Argentina, which was home to five million human colonists. I couldn't let her slaughter them, so I relieved her of command and made an accommodation with the Commander of the Fifth Teroni Fleet: if he would take the fuel and do no harm to the citizenry, we would not try to hinder him, nor would we do to New Argentina what Podok had done to Benidos. I might add that that same Teroni Commander eventually came to the conclusion that his Federation is no more worth his loyalty than the Republic is worth mine or yours, and he is currently the First Officer aboard the *Theodore Roosevelt*.

"I surrendered myself to the military authorities and was perfectly willing to defend myself at a court-martial. But while I was awaiting trial, Captain Podok went to the press and claimed that I had taken control of the ship solely because she was a Polonoi. It happens that most of the inhabitants of Benidos, though members of the Republic, were not Men. No one knew what she planned to do to Benidos until it was done, but the press broadcast the story that I only took the ship away from her when she threatened members of my own race on New Argentina.

"Word reached my attorney that because of pressure from the media, the result of the trial was predetermined, that I and two so-called accomplices were to be found guilty to avoid a public relations disaster, and officers who objected to the verdict were quietly being replaced by those who didn't. My crew broke me out of the brig, and we have spent the past three years on the Inner Frontier."

He surveyed his audience, trying to determine if they believed him. No one had any questions, so he continued.

"I had intended to remain on the Inner Frontier for the rest of my life, but the abuses of the Republic don't end at the Republic's border. They have plundered colony planets, conscripted men and women, and otherwise exercised a power and authority that was never given to them, and they've been doing it for as long as they have existed. The tipping point came last year. They captured my First Officer and tortured him to death in an attempt to learn the *Theodore Roosevelt*'s whereabouts from him. Then, to punish the planet where they had found him, they came back in force and obliterated it and every living thing on it.

"I declared that the Inner Frontier was now off-limits to the Navy. I formed some unlikely alliances, and the thing came to a head a little more than a month ago, when the Republic sent a force of three hundred ships after us. We emerged victorious, but then they recently sent a larger force, and I realized that we could meet each force in battle until we were finally defeated, or we could go after the source of our problems, which was not the Navy, but the people who created the Republic's policy and gave orders to the Navy—and as you know, they're all on Deluros VIII."

"How many ships have you got?" asked a woman.

"About eight hundred."

"It's suicide," said a man. "Eight hundred ships against the Republic!"

A middle-aged man stood up. Val eyed him like a predator eyes its prey as he walked up to the stage and stood next to Cole. "Last week I had a wife and three children. Today I don't." He extended his hand to Cole. "Captain Cole, you've got eight hundred and one ships."

And suddenly half of the audience was on their feet, pledging their support.

"I assume this is what you came here for?" said Lake.

"Eventually we're going to need ships, equipment, money—everything that any navy needs," Cole confirmed. "But right now we need to organize, which means we need recruits and recruiters." He waited until all the pledges and promises died down and then addressed the room again. "Man needs a government, and in a frequently hostile universe we need a Navy as well. I don't want to upset the social order. I don't want to disband the Navy. I don't want anarchy. I simply want the Republic to do what it was empowered to do, and if that means getting rid of Secretary Wilkie and Admiral Garcia, then that's what I plan to do. The Republic is like a poorly trained pet or a misbehaving child. If you ignore its faults and don't correct them, eventually it assumes they are not faults but virtues, and suddenly you've got a monster on your hands. Men have been looking the other way for too long; we're faced with a monster, and we're going to have to do something about it. And we can. There are sixty thousand worlds in the Republic. They haven't all been abused in quite the same devastating way as New Lenin, but an awful lot of them bear major grudges, not against the concept of a Republic but against the abuses of *this* Republic. When the time comes, I'll ask you to join us in the battle, but right now you can be of much greater value to me if you'll go to other Republic worlds and recruit a goodly number of their citizens to our side."

"I'll join," said one man, "if you'll turn Egan Wilkie over to us when you finally get him."

Cole shook his head. "I can't promise that. There are hundreds, probably thousands, of worlds with an equal claim to him."

"So you just want cannon fodder, not justice," said the man angrily.

"If you believe that, don't join me," said Cole.

"You can't win without us, and a hell of a lot more like us!" persisted the man.

"Perhaps not," said Cole. "But I'm not going to make any promises or commitments that I can't keep."

They spoke for another twenty minutes, and when Cole and Val finally returned to the ship, he was convinced that he had won most of them over, and that they, in turn, would win thousands of citizens of New Lenin, and even more from other worlds, to his cause.

He was feeling exceptionally pleased with himself by the time the *Kermit* touched down in the shuttle bay and he set foot on the *Teddy R.*

Then Jacovic told him what had transpired while he was gone, and his euphoria vanished.

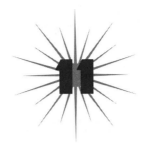

"When did it happen?" asked Cole as he reached the bridge.

"Hard to say," replied Jacovic. "Somewhere between two and ten hours ago."

"I *told* him he couldn't hold off two Class L ships," said Cole. "What about his other ships?"

"We don't know. They may be destroyed; they may have been captured."

"But he's definitely a prisoner?" continued Cole.

"Yes."

"Any idea where he's being held?"

"No," said Jacovic.

"Fucking grandstander!" muttered Cole. "He knew better! He cost maybe a hundred men their lives."

"If he'd succeeded, he'd have disrupted their economy for a few weeks," said Jacovic in defense of the Octopus.

"A *tiny* portion of it," growled Cole. "So he would have destroyed twenty tons of gold—big deal! There are sixty thousand goddamned worlds in the Republic. That's less that a pound of gold per world!" He paused. "I don't suppose Christine or Briggs put in some distress signal that only we can read?" Jacovic merely stared at him. "No, I didn't think so." He raised his voice. "Sharon, I assume you're eavesdropping again?"

"I am," she replied. "And I'm sorry about the Octopus."

"I'm a hell of a lot sorrier for his crew," said Cole. "The Republic is already making Men a little rarer than they were. He had no call to waste them like that." He tried unsuccessfully to force the tension from his body. "I'm going to grab a sandwich. Why don't you meet me there?"

"I've got some busywork to finish," she said. "I'll be there in ten minutes."

"Fine." She broke the connection and he turned back to Jacovic and Domak. "Any other good news?" he said sarcastically.

"We heard from Lafferty . . ." began Domak.

"And?"

"He still doesn't have an engine, but he says he thinks he has a lead to one."

"Well, compared to the Octopus, I suppose that's good news," said Cole. He walked over to Wxakgini. "Pilot, there's always a chance that the Navy will come back to admire their handiwork. Get us out of here."

"Where to?" asked Wxakgini.

"How far are we from the Pollux system?"

"Thirty-six light-years."

"How long to get there?"

"Using the Cormean Wormhole, nine hours," answered Wxakgini. "However, the wormhole has been unstable lately, so it could take considerably longer to traverse."

"Use it," said Cole, turning away from him and approaching Jacovic. "Pollux IV is the only inhabited world in the system, it's got a population of less than ten thousand, almost all of them farmers. No way the Navy is going to show up there, and we could use some fresh supplies for the galley. I can't be the only person who's sick to death of soya products."

Jacovic nodded his head. "I'll contact them after we emerge from the wormhole."

"Fine," said Cole. "See you later."

He walked to the airlift and took it down to the mess hall. He'd just finished ordering his sandwich when Sharon showed up.

"Val tells me you were a smashing success," she said.

"Really?" he said. "I thought she only considered a mission a success when she got to kill some guys on the other side."

"Are you going to let what happened to the Octopus color everything you say for the rest of the day?" she said. "There are five empty tables here. I could sit at one of them."

"I'm sorry," he said. "I just hate waste, and he wasted seven ships and who knows how many lives." He reached across the table, took her hand, and squeezed it gently. "Okay, the subject is closed."

But it wasn't.

It was an hour after they emerged from the Cormean Wormhole when Christine's voice and image woke him from a nap he'd been taking in front of a mystery holo.

"Yeah?" he said, collecting his senses. "What is it?"

"We just had a communication from Mr. Sokolov, sir."

"And?"

"He has a prisoner."

"He's in a two-man ship," said Cole. "What the hell is he doing with a prisoner?"

"He went out of his way to capture this one, sir," she said.

"Do you enjoy stringing this out?" said Cole irritably. "Just tell me what's going on."

"I wanted to make sure you were totally awake."

"I am now."

"Thanks to the coded upgrades Mr. Briggs and I installed in Mr. Sokolov's computer, he was able to pick up a signal from another small ship, concerning the disposition of the Octopus."

"Well?" demanded Cole, suddenly alert.

"I gather they've got him and about eighty survivors. They intend to transfer him—well, probably all of them—in the next two days. They plan to hold a show trial that will be broadcast throughout the Republic, and when they find them guilty of treason, which of course they will, there will be a public execution."

"Where's the trial to be held?"

"I don't know."

"Doesn't matter anyway," said Cole. "Wherever it is, it'll be all but impregnable. Where's the Octopus now?"

"I don't know."

"Does Sokolov?"

"No."

"How far away is he?"

"Wxakgini says if Mr. Sokolov uses the Bellermaine Wormhole, he can be here in two hours."

"Tell Sokolov to get his ass in gear!" said Cole. "We just may be able to pull some Octopus fat out of the fire after all."

"Yes, sir."

She contacted him again less than three minutes later.

"Problems?" asked Cole.

"No, sir. Mr. Sokolov is on his way."

"Then what is it?"

"I was wondering: should I contact any of our allies? I mean, if we're going to try to rescue the Octopus . . ."

"Not yet," said Cole. "First we have to find out where he's being held. There's no sense telling any of our ships to rendezvous here if we're a thousand light-years from where we need to be."

"I hadn't thought of that," she replied. "I'm sorry, sir."

"Not a problem," said Cole.

"Val would have thought of it instantly," continued Christine.

"Probably," agreed Cole. "But Val couldn't have rigged Sokolov's computer to pick up that conversation."

She finally smiled. "I hadn't considered that. Thank you, sir."

Cole got to his feet, left his cabin, and went to Security.

"Hello, sir," said Luthor Chadwick, standing and saluting as he entered. "I assume you wish to speak to Colonel Blacksmith?" He began walking toward the door.

"Stay here," said Cole. "I want to talk to both of you."

Chadwick looked surprised, but remained standing at his desk.

"Sharon," Cole said, facing her private office, "come out here."

She emerged a moment later. "I hear we're about to get a prisoner."

"That's what we have to talk about," said Cole.

"All right," she said. "Talk."

"The Octopus is still alive," began Cole. "So are most of his men. We don't know where they are, but it figures to be near the dust cloud where he made his attack. The problem is that there are at least thirty habitable planets in the general area. They're moving him and the others in two days, maybe sooner, and we have to assume they're moving him closer to the center of the Republic where it'll be impossible to rescue him. I don't think we can pull it off while they're in transit; it's too hard to get to the ship without one side or the other destroying it." He paused and stared at each in turn. "That means we've got to get that information from our prisoner *fast*, in time to attempt a rescue before they're moved."

"How much time would you say we had, sir?" asked Chadwick.

"The prisoner will be here in maybe two hours. Figure you'll have six hours to break him."

"That fast?"

"We could need ten, fifteen hours to get to where they're holding the Octopus. Or one hour. We won't know until you get that information. And of course we'll have to come up with some kind of plan, which we can't do until we know where they're incarcerated. We can't just blast our way in; we'd probably kill the prisoners as well as the jailers."

"Six hours," said Chadwick dully.

"Tops. Three would be better."

"Well, we can try some bliathol," said Sharon thoughtfully.

"What's bliathol?" asked Cole.

"One of the newer truth drugs," she replied.

"Have you ever used it before?"

"When's the last time we grilled a prisoner?" she said.

"Not since I've been on the *Teddy R*," he admitted. "What if it doesn't work?"

"I'm not sure," she replied. "We don't have a sensory deprivation tank."

"Too bad we don't have any telepaths in the crew," said Chadwick.

"There are only two known telepathic species in the galaxy, and neither has any use for the Republic," said Cole.

"Why don't you leave us to discuss it?" said Sharon.

"All right," said Cole. "I'll check back with you later."

"We'll be here," she replied.

He went back up to the bridge.

"Christine, patch me through to Mr. Sokolov, coded and scrambled."

Vladimir Sokolov's face appeared above Christine's computer.

"Good work, Vladimir," said Cole.

"Thank you, sir."

"I've been getting this secondhand. What, exactly, did you hear that led you to capture your prisoner?"

"The voice at the other end of the transmission—I couldn't trace its location—was saying that they'd just captured close to eighty prisoners," said Sokolov. "When he described the leader, I knew it was the Octopus. Anyway, he told my prisoner that they'd transfer the Octopus and the others to a much safer location in the next two Standard days. They were expecting a Class N dreadnought, but just in case it didn't show or was late, they wanted all the firepower they could muster, including my prisoner's ship. When I heard that I homed in on his signal and disabled his ship before he knew I was there. I killed his antenna, his transmitter, and his Level 2 thumper, and then started blowing bits and pieces of his ship away until he surrendered."

"Surrendering bespeaks a certain interest in reaching an accommodation with his captors," said Cole hopefully.

"He's given me his name, his rank, his serial number, his home planet, everything I could possibly want," said Sokolov. "Except the location where they're holding the Octopus."

"Sharon and Luthor will try their best to help him remember," said Cole. "See you soon."

He cut the connection.

"What will we do if he doesn't talk?" asked Christine.

"That's not an option," answered Cole grimly. "If he doesn't talk, eighty good men and women will die."

Sokolov arrived ninety minutes later and brought his captive aboard the *Teddy R*. The Navy pilot was in his late twenties, clean-cut, in his seventh year in the service. His name was Alberto Torres, and he seemed none the worse for undergoing the unnerving experience of having his ship shot apart while he was still in it.

He was brought before Cole by Ensigns Brill and Dunyach, two members of Sharon's Security team.

"Welcome to the *Theodore Roosevelt*, Mr. Torres," said Cole. "I notice that you failed to salute me."

"You are a mutineer and a felon," replied Torres. "I will salute only members of a legitimate military."

"You know why you're here, of course?"

"I know," said Torres.

"I will ask you once before I turn you over to the tender mercies of my Chief of Security: will you tell me where your eighty prisoners are currently incarcerated?"

"I will not."

"Okay," said Cole to the security men. "Take him away."

They turned and marched Torres to the airlift, and then to Security.

"He seems like a nice young man," remarked Christine. "I hope we don't have to be too harsh with him."

"Let's see what Sharon's miracle drug can do."

He found out an hour later when her image popped into view above his table in the mess hall.

"It's not working," she told him.

"It's a dud?"

"I doubt it," she said. "I think he's probably been conditioned against it."

"How about some old-fashioned hypnotism?" asked Cole.

"I'm no hypnotist. Besides, if he can resist bliathol, he can almost certainly resist hypnotism too."

"Well, see what else you've got in your drug cabinet. We're losing time."

She sighed deeply. "Right."

She broke the connection.

Val entered a moment later, got herself a beer, and sat down opposite him.

"Has he talked yet?" she asked.

"No."

"You're going to have to get rough with him," she said. "I assume your lady friend's tried drugs and they're not working."

"So far."

"Let me know if you need a little help with him."

"We'd like him to survive long enough to tell us what we need to know," replied Cole dryly.

She laughed. "I told you the first time you met him that the Octopus was an asshole. If you save him, he'll just do something dumb again."

"He may be an asshole," said Cole, "but he's *our* asshole. More to the point, he's got eighty men facing death because they followed his orders. We have to try to get them out."

"Things were a lot simpler when I was a pirate," she said. "I had just one rule: Everyone's expendable."

Cole saw Sokolov walking past and called him in.

"Sir?" said Sokolov.

"Sit down, Vladimir," said Cole. "I want to talk to you about Torres."

"No bleeding-heart mumbo jumbo for me," said Val, getting up and taking her beer with her. "I'm outta here."

She left the mess hall, and Cole gestured Sokolov to take her seat.

"Tell me about him, Vladimir."

"There's nothing much to tell. He never saw me coming, and I had his ship disabled before he could fire a shot."

"I don't mean about his piloting abilities," said Cole. "What's he like?"

Sokolov shrugged. "He seems nice enough. If we were still in the Navy, I think he could become a friend."

"Did he say anything, talk about anything, while you were bringing him here?"

"Nothing important, sir. The first thing I did was question him about where they're keeping the Octopus, so he knows why we want him. After that, he pretty much clammed up."

"Pretty much?" repeated Cole.

"He thought I was Navy at the beginning, and wanted to know why I was attacking him. I believe he actually thought it was a test of his loyalty, or his ability to keep the location a secret, until I explained that I was from the *Teddy R* and you were my Captain. From that point on he refused to discuss anything concerning the military except his name, rank, and serial number."

"So he was silent for almost two hours?"

"No, sir," said Sokolov. "We talked about sports."

"Just sports?"

Sokolov smiled. "And girls."

"Did you probe for any weak spots, anything that might get him to talk?"

"That's out of my bailiwick, sir," answered Sokolov. "I'm no psychologist. Any probing I do is in deep space, with my ship."

"Okay," said Cole. "Thanks, Vladimir."

Cole got up and wandered back to his office. After half an hour he contacted Sharon again.

"Any luck?"

"No," she replied. "Drugs aren't going to work on him, Wilson. If we give him any more, we could blow every neural circuit in his brain." She sighed. "He was *well* conditioned."

"How's he doing?"

"He's okay. Probably got some fuzzy vision, but that'll pass in time."

"We can't wait much longer," said Cole. "The message Sokolov overheard was that they're moving the prisoners in two days or less, not two days or more. I don't think we've got more than three more hours, four at the outside, to break him."

"Well, we're not going to do it with drugs, that I can guarantee you."

"Then we'll have to do something more forceful."

"How much more forceful?"

"Whatever it takes," said Cole. "You can't start with half measures and work up to truly harsh interrogation techniques. First, we haven't got the time—and second, we know his mind is resistant to drugs, but we don't know how much punishment his body can take. We can't have him passing out before he's told us what we need to know."

"I'll discuss it with Luthor and the rest of my staff and see what we can come up with."

"Just don't take too long," said Cole. "I'll be on the bridge. Christine is checking his serial number. Maybe she's dug up something useful on him by now."

Fifteen minutes later Sharon's image appeared on the bridge.

"Wilson," she said, "you'd better come down here."

"He talked already?"

"No."

"You didn't kill him?" he demanded harshly.

"No."

"Then what is it?"

"Security has a staff of five, counting myself," she said.

"And?"

"Two of them refuse to participate," continued Sharon. "They claim that there's no difference between harsh interrogation and torture, and they won't be a part of it."

"The difference is that if we don't apply it, eighty men are going to die," said Cole.

"You don't have to convince *me*," she said. "Tell *them*."

"They're down there with you?"

"Yes."

"I'm on my way," said Cole.

"They're right," said Ensign Walsh, who was manning one of the stations. "If we do it, we're no better than the Republic we're fighting."

"The Republic we're fighting is going to kill eighty men if we don't do it."

"That's the fortunes of war," said Walsh.

"We captured Alberto Torres, and now we're going to find out what we need to know," replied Cole. "That's the fortunes of war, too."

"There's a difference," insisted Walsh. "The Octopus's men were captured on the battlefield, so to speak."

"One-third of the galaxy is a battlefield," said Cole. "Torres was captured on it too."

"They were captured committing an act of aggression. He wasn't."

"I haven't got time to argue the fine points with you, Mr. Walsh," said Cole. "Too many lives depend upon the results of this interrogation."

"It's not interrogation—it's torture."

"Granting for the moment that it is, consider this: Torres is going to live through it, because if we kill him he can't tell us what we need to know. Then ask yourself which is worse: harshly questioning one man who is going to survive, or letting eighty other men go to a certain death."

Cole left the bridge while Walsh was formulating an answer, and entered Security two minutes later. Sharon was waiting for him.

"Where are they?" he said.

"In the next room."

He walked into the room and found himself confronting Brill and Dunyach, the two ensigns who had taken Torres down to Security.

"I understand you two refuse to follow your superior officer's orders," he said.

"It's torture any way you cut it, sir, and I'm not going to participate," said Brill.

"You know what's at stake?" said Cole.

"We're at war. They took their chances. They lost."

"Can't you say the same thing about our prisoner?"

"Put him in the brig," said Dunyach. "Or execute him, if that's what you want. But don't ask me to help torture him."

"'Torture' is an easy word to throw around," said Cole. "We're going to question him with some degree of harshness, that's all."

"You're playing word games, sir," said Brill. "You're asking us to cause him so much physical pain that he breaks and tells us what we want to know."

"That's right."

"That's torture," said Brill.

"Is it?" asked Cole. "What if one solid punch to the belly gets him to talk?"

"It won't."

"But if it does—is that torture?"

"No," said Brill reluctantly.

"How about four punches to the belly?"

"I see where you're going with this, sir," said Brill. "I don't know where it crosses the line from harsh interrogation to torture, but I don't plan to be a participant when it does."

"Has Colonel Blacksmith asked you to do anything you explicitly find repugnant?" said Cole. "Has she suggested you gouge one of his eyes out, or drive bamboo splints under his fingernails?"

"No, sir," said Dunyach. "But I won't hold him down while someone else does that to him."

"Would you hold him underwater until he drowned?"

"No!"

"Would you hold him underwater until it simulated drowning— maybe sixty seconds, maybe seventy?"

Dunyach seemed to be weighing the question. Finally he just stared into Cole's eyes. "I'm all through talking, sir. Do to me what you do to the prisoner, but I'm not going to participate."

"Even though it means eighty men will surely die?"

"Yes, sir."

"And if you knew some of those eighty men would undergo harsh interrogation, as they surely will before they're executed, would that make a difference to you?"

Again Dunyach seemed to be struggling with himself. Finally Brill spoke up.

"We're not going to do it, sir, and that's final."

"All right," said Cole. "You're confined to quarters, and we'll put you off on the next populated oxygen world we come to."

"For not torturing a prisoner?" demanded Brill.

"No," said Cole. "For disobeying a direct order, and for being willing to let eighty allies die rather than causing some serious discomfort to one enemy. Now get out of here."

They left without another word, and Cole went back to Sharon's office.

"Whatever you were going to do, can you do it with three people instead of five?"

"I don't know," she said. "I suppose we can ask Val for help if we need it."

"No," said Cole.

"No?" she asked curiously.

"I'm the ultimate authority who approved it. If you need help with whatever technique you apply, you come to *me* for it—no one else."

"Are you sure, Wilson?"

"I can't throw those men off the ship for refusing to do something I wouldn't do myself—and I can't let eighty men die when we have a chance to save them."

"All right," said Sharon grimly. "Time's running short. Let's get to work."

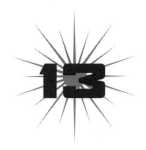

It wasn't pretty and it wasn't painless, but it was relatively quick, and in less than half an hour they had the information they needed. Cole left Security and returned to the bridge with it.

"Did he talk?" asked Val when he arrived.

"He talked," answered Cole.

"I thought he would," she said. "He looked too damned wholesome." Then: "Is he still alive?"

"Yes."

"Is he ever going to be able to function normally again?"

"Yes," said Cole.

"He talked too soon," she replied decisively.

"We can't all be like you, Val," said Cole. "I feel sorry for the poor bastard. He was minding his own business out in the middle of nowhere. He didn't ask for that information, or to have the transmission overheard. He's just a victim of circumstance."

"We're all victims of circumstance," she replied. "The competent ones make use of it or overcome it."

Cole wanted to tell her that she couldn't stand up under the kind of interrogation Torres had suffered, except that he had a feeling she was the one person on the ship who could. Instead he walked over to Wxakgini.

"Pilot, take us hell for leather over to the Malagori system."

"Hell for leather?" repeated Wxakgini.

"Old-fashioned slang. It means fast as you can."

"It's not a matter of how fast *I* can go, but rather how fast the ship—"

"Just do it!" snapped Cole. "I've had a lousy day, and I don't need any arguments about semantics!"

Wxakgini turned back to the navigational computer without another word.

"Malagori?" said Rachel, frowning. "What's there? I thought it was unpopulated."

"They colonized Malagori V a few years back," said Cole. "It's called Thistlepatch now."

"Why?" mused Domak.

"I suppose we'll find out when we get there," answered Cole. "Anyway, I gather it's mostly a shipping world. They've got a few dozen huge warehouses where supplies from the outer colonies, plus those they steal from the Inner Frontier, are temporarily stored and then sent off to those worlds that have ordered them."

"Do they *have* a prison for eighty people there?" asked Rachel.

"I doubt it. That's why they're transferring them so soon. They're probably just locked in another warehouse."

"What kind of defenses do they have?" asked Val.

"The usual planetary defenses," said Cole. "Nothing that can bother the *Teddy R.*"

"This should be a piece of cake," she said.

He shook his head. "Don't understand me so fast. They have no *planetary* defenses that can harm us—but we have to assume they'll have military ships patrolling the system. They won't know for sure that the Octopus didn't get off a coded distress signal before they captured him."

"Will we be asking some of our allies for help?" said Domak.

"I don't know what good it'll do," answered Cole. "We have only two other ships capable of going up against the kind of massive fire-power that could hinder the *Teddy R*. One of them has no engine, and the other was just captured by the Navy." He paused. "We may need something other than a direct approach." He turned to Rachel. "Sokolov's still on board, right?"

"Yes, sir."

"And his ship's still attached?"

"It's bonded to the *Teddy R*, sir."

"All right," said Cole. "Have Pilot pick a rendezvous location for us, Moyer, Perez, and Flores—oh, and Jonah, the Octopus's son, if he wasn't captured with the others. Then contact them and have them meet us there in ten hours."

"Yes, sir."

"Let me know if there's any problem."

Cole walked to the airlift, and Val called after him. "Where are you going?"

"To the Officers' Lounge, to pour myself a stiff drink and try to get the taste of the past hour out of my mouth."

Cole walked to the airlift and descended two levels. He thought of asking Sharon to join him, but she hadn't looked like she wanted any company, even his, when he'd left Security twenty minutes earlier.

David Copperfield and the Platinum Duke were playing an alien card game when he entered.

"You're teaching him another game?" Cole asked of David.

"He's teaching *me*," answered the little alien. "It's the only way he'll agree to play whist with me."

"Well, we all have to make sacrifices," said Cole, plopping down on a leather chair.

"Did our prisoner give us the information we needed?" asked the Duke.

"Eventually," said Cole.

"How long did he hold out?"

"Eighteen, maybe twenty minutes," replied Cole. He grimaced. "It must have felt like an eternity to him."

"I won't ask what you did to him," said the Duke, "but I do have a question."

"Yes?"

"Would you have done the same thing if you'd been after strategic information that you didn't know would save eighty lives?"

"I don't know that *this* will," said Cole. "It just gives us a chance at it. I have no idea what the Navy left behind to guard the prisoners."

"You didn't answer my question."

"I don't know the answer," said Cole truthfully. "I hope I never have to find out."

"Well, that's honest, anyway."

"*I* can answer it," interjected David Copperfield. "My friend Steerforth would never resort to torture under any circumstances."

"I don't believe you were listening," said the Duke. "He already did."

"Is the prisoner alive?" persisted David. "Will he recover fully?"

"Yes to both questions," said Cole.

"Then it was just interrogation, not torture."

"There's a very fuzzy line, David," said Cole. "I don't know if we crossed over it or not. I just know if we hadn't done what we did, we'd have condemned eighty men to their deaths. This way there's at least a chance we can save them."

"War is hell," said David.

"To quote General Sherman," said Cole.

"No, it was Admiral Vosburgh, right before she destroyed Pinchon V."

"You're both wrong," said David. "It was the immortal Charles."

"David," said Cole, "not every brilliant line belongs to Dickens."

The little alien pulled a deck of cards out of his pocket and held it out to Cole.

"Cut the cards," he said.

Cole cut to a seven.

"My turn," said David. He cut to a jack, flashed a triumphant smile, and put the cards back in his pocket.

"What was that all about?" asked Cole.

"I won."

"Okay, you won. So what?"

"So Dickens said it."

"What do you suppose he'd have been like if he'd read the *Communist Manifesto* first?" the Platinum Duke asked Cole.

"I suppose it could be worse," said Cole. "He could have read *Fanny Hill*, and none of the female crew would be safe."

"Or that Canphorite poet Tanblixt—the one who uses all that cosmic imagery."

"Will you please stop speaking about me as if I'm not here?" demanded David.

"But you're *not* here," replied the Duke.

"I beg your pardon?"

"You've been replaced by someone who loves Charles Dickens so much that he thinks he's David Copperfield."

"Steerforth, throw that man in the brig!" demanded David.

"Calm down, both of you," said Cole.

"He insulted me!" said David.

"David, I like you," said the Platinum Duke. "But the fact remains that you're certifiable."

"*Shut up!*" yelled Cole. The other two simply stared at him. "I just did something that I took a solemn oath never to do," he said. "I don't need any more hassles today."

Before they could either apologize or argue, Cole was on his feet and out the door. He walked through the aging corridors and past the dented bulkheads until he reached Security. Sharon was alone, and he walked up to her.

"How do you feel?" he said.

"Rotten."

He took her hand and pulled her to her feet. "Come on," he said.

"Where are we going?"

"My cabin," he said. "We can feel rotten together."

"I was hoping you'd ask," she said.

They emerged from the Baxter Wormhole three light-years from the outermost planet of the Malagori system.

Within an hour Moyer and the others had rendezvoused with them.

Cole, who seemed to find himself on the bridge more and more often, much as he disliked it, turned to Jacovic. "There's no way we can see what they've got defending Malagori V from here, and if we get close enough to see them, we're close enough for them to see us. I don't know who's better equipped to program a probe, Christine or Mr. Odom, but have one of them do it. We want it to get close enough to see what's there and transmit the information back to us, and then I want it to plunge into Malagori."

"Malagori?" repeated the Teroni. "You mean the star, not the planet?"

"Right. Probably they'll blow it apart first, but if not, let's not give them a chance to capture it and see what it's learned and where it's sent that information."

"I think that Mr. Odom would be best," said Jacovic.

"Okay, but just to be on the safe side have him work in concert with Christine so the signal can't be read by anyone but us," said Cole. "Damn! I wish Mr. Briggs was with us. I have a feeling I'm going to work Christine around the clock, and I need her to be sharp."

"I might be able to help in that regard," said Sharon's voice.

"Oh?" said Cole.

"Meloctin—the Lodinite who just joined the crew—is a computer and communications expert. He's passed muster on every psyche test I could give him, always remembering that he *is* a Lodinite and their psychologies are different from ours. I think Christine could show him the codes and everything else he'd need to know in maybe an hour, and then he could spell her when she gets too tired to stay alert."

"If you vouch for him, that's good enough for me," said Cole.

"I vouch for him *conditionally*."

"That'll do. Once Christine's through with the probe, have her show him whatever it is he has to learn."

It took a little longer than Cole had anticipated to program the probe, but after forty minutes it was launched. It hit light speed in another minute, and after a few more minutes it began sending back images.

"Damn!" muttered Cole, looking at the holographic image. "That's a Class M ship."

"Nothing else, though," noted Vladimir Sokolov, who had joined Cole on the bridge until he had to return to his own ship. "Just the one."

"That one has more firepower than the *Teddy R* and thirty of our Class H and Class J ships combined," said Cole. "We can't square off against it. And that's one of the newer ones. I don't know if we have anything that can pierce its defenses."

The image vanished.

"What happened?" asked Cole. "Did they shoot it down?"

"No, sir," said Mustapha Odom's voice. "It made its transmission and is now plunging into the star at many multiples of light speed."

"All right," said Cole. "Thank you, Mr. Odom."

"Sir?" said Domak.

"Yes."

"I've pinpointed some neutrino activity on the surface of Malagori V," said the Polonoi. "I think it has to be the complex where they're keeping the Octopus and the others."

"Unless they've built some settlements that we don't know anything about," said Sokolov.

"I don't think so," said Cole. "If there's a new settlement, then Domak should be picking up two sets of neutrino activity." He turned to the Polonoi. "Keep checking, but if you don't find any more, we're going to have to assume you've found the prisoners."

"Any instructions, sir?" asked Jacovic.

Cole shook his head. "Let's give Domak half an hour to make absolutely sure there's no other activity on the surface."

"Won't the Navy ship be aware that we're nearby, sir?" asked Sokolov. "I mean, they couldn't have missed the probe."

"They know it," said Cole.

Sokolov frowned. "Then—"

"Relax, Vladimir," Cole interrupted him. "They're not coming after us."

"Why not, sir?" asked Domak.

"Because all they saw is the probe. They don't know how many ships we've got. They're just one—a huge, powerful one, to be sure, but just one—and they're not going to leave the planet to go hunting for us when they don't know where or how many we are."

Christine Mboya appeared on the bridge.

"Nice job on the probe," said Cole by way of greeting.

"It was mostly Mr. Odom's doing, sir," she replied. "I knew the codes, but he knew how to program the probe."

"Okay, I take it back," said Cole. She seemed flustered. "I was kidding, Lieutenant."

"Oh, sir," she said without smiling.

"Ask Meloctin—that's the new Lodinite—to come up to the bridge, and when he gets here I want you and Domak to show him everything he needs to know to work your station once you're relieved."

"Yes, sir," she replied.

"Sir?" said Sokolov.

"Yes?"

"To get back to what you were discussing with Lieutenant Domak, if they won't leave orbit, how the devil are we going to get past them to rescue the prisoners?"

"*We* aren't," said Cole. "Val is."

"First bright thing you've said all month," said Val as her image appeared over Christine's workstation.

"Thanks for that vote of confidence," replied Cole dryly.

"So how are we going to do this?" continued Val.

"I'm working on it."

"Well, you'd better work fast," she replied. "No sense getting there after the prisoners are gone."

"I thought you didn't care about the Octopus."

"I don't. But I care about killing the guys who are holding him."

"You missed your calling in life," said Cole.

"Yeah?"

"You should have been a pacifist."

"Well, that's a change," said Val. "Briggs and Sokolov keep telling me I should have been a figure model, and the Duke is always trying to hire me as his pit boss."

"Just go get your beauty sleep," said Cole. "I'll let you know when we need you."

"I'm not sleepy."

"If we don't go into action for another eight or ten hours, I want *someone* to be awake and alert, damn it!"

"Keep your shirt on," said Val, her image beginning to fade. "I'll be ready."

The image vanished completely, and Cole turned to Sokolov. "She will, you know."

"I know, sir." Sokolov paused awkwardly. "Perhaps, sir, you're now ready to tell me how we're going to rescue the Octopus and his men?"

"Well, we're not going to meet the Navy ship head-on, that's for sure," said Cole.

"Then how—?"

"I'm working on it."

Cole walked over to Wxakgini, who sat high above the floor in his permanent station, half hammock and half cocoon, his eyes closed, his brain tied in to the navigational computer's brain, using its eyes instead of his own.

"Pilot, I need to talk to you."

"I am right here," was Wxakgini's response.

"Are there any wormholes within the Malagori system," asked Cole, "and more specifically, between the fifth and sixth planets?"

"One."

"Where does it lead?"

"It will let you out by the Benadotti system about twenty-nine light-years from here."

"That should do it," said Cole. He turned to Domak. "How many moons around Malagori VIII and IX?"

"Malagori VIII has eleven moons, and Malagori IX has six," answered the Polonoi.

"Okay. Jacovic, what have we got in the way of small craft?"

"There are the four shuttles, sir," said the Teroni, "plus Mr. Sokolov's ship."

"And in space?"

"Mr. Moyer, Mr. Perez, Mr. Flores—and Mr. Briggs in the Lodinite ship. He seems to have made the jump, too.

"Which would you say is the least hospitable of the seventeen moons on Malagori VIII and IX?" asked Cole.

"I would say the fourth moon of Malagori VIII, sir," replied Jacovic. "Methane atmosphere, uneven surface covered by jagged crystal, almost ninety-five degrees below zero Centigrade, frequent massive windstorms of hurricane strength . . ."

"That'll do, Jacovic," said Cole. "I accept your analysis." He began walking across the bridge toward the airlift. "I'll be in the mess hall."

He descended to the proper level, entered the mess hall, and walked to his usual table. He was not surprised to find Sharon there waiting for him.

"May I take your order?" asked the table.

"Coffee and cheesecake."

"Thank you."

"Cheesecake?" said Sharon. "I thought you were on a diet."

"If we die in the next fifteen or twenty hours, no one will care," answered Cole. "And if not, I'm celebrating our victory a little early."

"I take it you have a plan."

"I do."

"I hope it doesn't involve confronting that Navy ship."

"I hope so too," he said with a smile.

She relaxed noticeably. *"That's* a relief."

"I knew you'd appreciate it," said Cole. "How's the young man?"

"Alberto Torres?" she asked. "I checked on him an hour ago. He's sleeping soundly, and doesn't seem too much the worse for wear."

"Good," said Cole. "We'll know in a few hours if it was worth it."

"Of course it was worth it," replied Sharon. "We couldn't even *attempt* to rescue them if we didn't know where they were."

"True enough."

"So what's your plan?"

"Stick around, and you'll hear it when everyone else does. I need to talk to Pilot one more time."

"Then why aren't you doing it?"

"Because talking to him usually annoys the shit out of me, and I thought it'd be nice to digest my cheesecake *before* I talked to him."

"Farseeing and resourceful," she said with a smile. "No wonder you're the Captain."

The coffee and cheesecake arrived and he began eating.

"What do you think of it?" she asked curiously.

"The coffee's okay. The cheesecake tastes a little like paste, but not as good." He sighed. "I really miss eating on Singapore Station."

"Live with it," she said. "We're not going back for a long, long time."

"I know," he said, getting to his feet. "Well, the sooner we get rid of the bad guys and overthrow the strongest government that has ever existed, the sooner I can have veal parmesan at Duke's Place."

"You're not going to eat the rest of your cheesecake?" she asked as he headed to the doorway.

"It's all yours."

She took a small piece on a fork and brought it to her mouth. "You were wrong," she said.

"About what?"

"It doesn't taste like paste."

"It does to me."

She shook her head. "Paste has much better flavor, to say nothing of smoother texture."

"You're right," he said with a smile, and left.

He was back on the bridge a moment later, and speaking to Wxakgini again.

"Is there a wormhole in or near the system that'll get a ship way the hell out of here?"

"I told you."

"I mean another one."

"I shall have to check," said Wxakgini.

"I'm not going anywhere."

"Then why do you need a wormhole?"

"A figure of speech," said Cole. "It means I'll wait while you check."

"Terran," muttered Wxakgini irritably. A moment later he looked down at Cole. "There is the MacGruder Wormhole, currently one hundred and thirty degrees around the sun in approximately the same orbit as Malagori IX, that will deposit you some four hundred light-years away, near the fourth planet of the Delamere system."

"That should do it," said Cole. "Thanks."

But Wxakgini had merged with the navigational computer once more, and paid him no further attention.

Christine Mboya and Domak were schooling Meloctin when Cole approached her.

"I hate to intrude," he said, "but I'm going to need you for a few minutes, Christine." He turned to the Lodinite. "I'm sorry, but this is vital."

"I quite understand, Captain Cole," said Meloctin.

"What it is, sir?" asked Christine.

"I want you to talk to Pilot and get the exact coordinates of the wormhole he just told me about—it's out past Malagori IX—as well as the coordinates of the Delamere system at the other end of it, and I want you to program them into Mr. Moyer's ship, Mr. Sokolov's, Mr. Perez's, Mr. Flores's, the Lodinite ship Mr. Briggs is on, and our four shuttles. Finally, I want you to program the exact location of the neutrino activity on Malagori V into each. Can you get that done in fifteen minutes?"

"Yes, sir."

"Good. Do it."

Cole next contacted the Valkyrie.

"Val, are you awake?"

"Of course I'm awake."

"We're sending four shuttles to carry the passengers. It'll be a little crowded, but you'll have to manage until we can transfer them to the *Teddy R*. I want you to pick a twelve-member combat team and spread them over the four shuttles. Have them ready to go in twenty minutes—and don't take off until I address all of you. Got it?"

"About time," was her only answer.

Twelve minutes later Christine looked up from her computer. "All done, sir," she announced.

"Good," said Cole. "Let me know when Val and her crews are down in the shuttle bay."

He became aware of an increased tension on the bridge, as it became clear he'd settled on his strategy and the rescue attempt was about to begin.

"I'll be back shortly," he said, and walked to the airlift. A moment later he opened the door of the Officers' Lounge, where he knew he'd find David Copperfield and the Platinum Duke engaged in another card game.

"David," he said, "I don't want to distress you, but I think you might want to spend a little quality time in your bulkhead."

The little alien didn't say a word, but simply placed his cards on the table, got up, and scurried right out of the room.

"And you might want to start laying bets on whether we survive or not," added Cole to the Duke.

"If we live through this," replied the Duke, "I'm going to spend the rest of my ill-gotten gains and buy you a sense of humor."

"If we're still alive tomorrow, I promise to laugh at one of your jokes," said Cole.

"I'll hold you to that."

"Just not the one about the minister and the dancing girl, please."

Cole left and returned to the bridge.

"They're all on their way to the bay, sir," said Christine.

"Correction," said Val's voice. "We're all here."

"Fine. Christine, connect me to the bay, and to Moyer, Perez, Flores, and Briggs. Oh, and to Vladimir Sokolov's ship."

"Don't bother about that," said Val. "Sokolov's with me."

"All set, sir," said Christine.

"Okay," said Cole. "Val, the four shuttlecraft leave the ship on my signal and go immediately to the fourth moon of Malagori VIII. I don't want you to go into orbit, but to land on the far side. I want the four small ships to do the same. I know we're masking our transmissions, but I want all eight craft to maintain a total communications blackout."

"What then, sir?" asked Dan Moyer. "Our understanding is that the prisoners are on the fourth planet."

"They are, but with the Class M Navy ship patrolling the planet we can't possibly get through. Your eight craft will remain on the moon until the *Teddy R* can draw the ship away. Pilot tells me there's a wormhole between the fifth and sixth planets that will let us out near Benadotti some nine light-years away. Once we lure the Navy ship into it, *then* I want you to leave your moon and do whatever has to be done to free the Octopus and his men. Christine has programmed their location into your crafts."

"Okay," said Val. "We free them. Now what? The Navy ship's

either going to catch you or it isn't, but it's not going to stay away too long."

"In fact, you're going to make sure of that," said Cole. "Once you're there and the prisoners are freed, I want you to set off every alarm they've got—local, subspace, whatever—before you leave." He paused to make sure there were no questions. "We've programmed the coordinates of the MacGruder Wormhole into each of your ships. It'll let you out almost four hundred light-years away from here. Once there head to the third planet of the Delamere system and wait for us—and if we're not there within, say, six hours, assume we're not coming, turn over command of your mission to the Octopus, and good luck to you. Now get going."

He cut the connection, then watched on the main viewscreen as they took off and made their way to the fourth moon of Malagori VIII.

"ETA?" he asked.

"About twelve minutes, sir," said Jacovic.

"We'll give them twenty," said Cole. "Who's in Gunnery? No, strike that; it doesn't matter. We'll aim and fire from here."

"I doubt that we can do them any damage, sir," offered Jacovic.

"We just want to annoy them," replied Cole. "Any chance we can knock out their transmitter?"

"I doubt it, sir," said the Teroni. "Both the transmitter and antenna are very well protected in the Class M."

"All right," said Cole. "It's probably faster than we are, but I don't think it's so much faster that we can't reach the Benadotti hole first. Besides, we know where we're going and they don't."

"Once they realize we might be leading them away, won't they just turn around and go back?" asked Christine.

"Pilot says it's almost impossible to make a one-eighty in a wormhole," said Cole. "He's never been wrong before. This would be a very unfortunate time for him to make his first mistake."

"Once we emerge, we're still in a very awkward situation, sir," she said. "They'll be able to narrow the distance until we're within range."

Cole turned to the Teroni. "Tell her, Commander."

"That is why Val is setting off all the alarms," said Jacovic. "Given a choice between racing back to defend Malagori V against an attack and protecting the prisoners or chasing the *Theodore Roosevelt*, they will choose the former."

"If everything goes according to plan," added Cole.

They waited in silence until twenty minutes had passed. Then Cole instructed Wxakgini to approach Malagori V.

"No subtlety, no subterfuge. Just approach it directly, and make sure we're always a lot closer to the Benadotti Wormhole than they are."

"Will you require evasive maneuvering if they start firing on us?" asked Wxakgini.

"Only if it doesn't conflict with my first order, which is to keep closer to the wormhole. Beyond that, take your orders from Commander Jacovic. He's been through this kind of thing often enough."

"Thank you for your confidence," said Jacovic softly. "But in fact I have never been in an analogous situation."

"We'll let that be our little secret," said Cole as the *Teddy R* began approaching Malagori V.

"Are we getting near that damned hole?" asked Cole as they passed the sixth planet of the Malagori system.

"It's about equidistant between Malagori V and VI."

"They have to have spotted us by now," said Domak.

"Of course they have," said Cole. "That's a Class M ship. Trust me, if we can see them, they can see us."

"They why don't they *do* something?" persisted Domak.

"Because they don't know how many of us there are, or what directions we might be coming from."

"Then why will they chase us?"

"I suppose we'll just have to irritate the shit out of them," said Cole with a smile.

"That means he has a plan," said Sharon's voice. "Of course, if he dies of a heart attack right now, none of us will ever know what it was."

"Sir?" said Christine.

"Yes?"

"They're asking for us to identify ourselves."

"No answer."

"Why aren't they shooting?" asked the Duke, who had just arrived on the bridge.

"Because we're a Navy ship. Not one they can instantly identify, though they will before much longer."

"They're asking again, sir."

"Can you make an answer break up, or simulate static, or anything like that?" asked Cole.

"A ship as sophisticated as a Class M will see right through it, sir," answered Christine.

"All right. Tell them we're on a secret mission, we have top priority, and what the hell are they doing here?"

She just stared at him for a moment.

"Just do it," said Cole. "If it makes them think for half a minute, we'll be thirty seconds closer to the Benadotti hole."

She did as instructed. There was no response for almost a minute, and then they demanded identification again.

"Jacovic, where do we stand?" asked Cole.

"We're considerably closer to the wormhole now than they are," responded the Teroni. "I would say that we can reach it in approximately one minute, and the Navy ship is almost two and a half minutes away."

"Let me know when we're thirty seconds from it."

"Sir, they're warning us off," said Christine. "They want us to leave the system."

"Tell them we have every right to be here in the Shoemacher system," said Cole.

This time she asked no questions, but did as he said.

"That ought to buy us a few seconds," said Cole.

As they waited for a response, Jacovic caught Cole's eye and nodded his head. "Thirty seconds, sir."

"Good," said Cole. "Christine, the next time they send a message, let's have it on visual and audio and respond in kind."

"Incoming," she said a moment later.

A square-jawed square-shouldered middle-aged man wearing a captain's insignia suddenly flickered into sight.

"I am Trevor Gladstone, Captain of the *Midnight Star*," he said. "This system is off-limits to everyone. You have consistently refused to answer us, and when you *have* answered they have been obvious lies. I will ask you one last time: who are you, and what is your business here?"

"Captain Gladstone, this is Wilson Cole, Captain of the *Theodore Roosevelt*, and my business here is to free the prisoners you are holding on Malagori V. Will you peacefully release them in my custody?"

Gladstone's eyes narrowed as he studied Cole's image. "By God, you *are* Wilson Cole! I demand that you surrender your ship to me, sir!"

"That's funny," said Cole. "I was going to make the same demand of you." He glanced quickly at Jacovic, who held up ten fingers. *Ten seconds.*

The *Midnight Star* broke out of orbit and began approaching the *Teddy R.*

"Commander Jacovic, open fire," said Cole, and Jacovic sent four Level 5 pulse torpedoes at the Navy ship.

"Jacovic?" repeated Gladstone. "The Teroni Fleet Commander? What the hell is going on?"

Cole smiled at Jacovic. "Your reputation precedes you."

"Incoming laser and pulse fire, sir," announced Domak.

"Mr. Odom?" said Cole. "How are we holding up."

"We're good for a few more blasts," said Odom's voice, "but we can't withstand a sustained attack, not against a Class M's firepower."

"Maybe we'd better fall back and regroup," said Cole for Gladstone's benefit. He gestured to Christine to shut down the communication.

"Pilot, get us into that wormhole, top speed, and get us out the other end as fast as you can!"

The *Teddy R* jumped forward, and was inside the Benadotti Wormhole in a matter of nine seconds. The *Midnight Star* took up the pursuit, and entered the wormhole less than two minutes later.

"I need instructions for when we reach the other end," said Wxakgini.

"Just keep going as fast as you can," said Cole. "If there's any garbage out there—meteor swarm, dust cloud, anything like that—head for it."

The ship swayed gently.

"It feels like we're slowing down," said the Duke.

"There's no fast or slow in a wormhole," replied Cole.

"But I heard you order him to speed through it."

"Force of habit," said Cole. "Wormholes are a wonderful shortcut, but once you're inside them you go at the speed *they* want you to go. Hell, the longer we're both inside it, the more time Val's got to effect a rescue."

They emerged eight minutes later, twenty-nine light-years from Malagori, and reached maximum speed instantly.

The Navy ship burst out of the hole two minutes later and took up the pursuit, firing its awesome weaponry as it went. The *Teddy R* shuddered twice as its shields suffered direct hits, but nothing got through its defenses and it continued speeding through the galaxy—and then, suddenly, the *Midnight Star* came to a sudden halt, circled around, and headed back toward the wormhole.

"It's done!" said Cole.

"Are you sure?" asked the Platinum Duke.

Cole nodded an affirmative. "They didn't stop chasing us when they came out of the hole because Val hadn't effected the rescue yet. But once she did, she set off all the alarms. That's why they turned around and went back. But when they get there, they aren't going to find any prisoners. Our ships should make the MacGruder hole, which is on the far side of the star, before the *Midnight Star* can even reach Malagori V, which is on this side." He smiled. "Good time of year to effect a rescue."

He walked over to Wxakgini. "Is there another way to get to the Delamere system without either taking the MacGruder Wormhole or traveling through normal space?"

"There is always another way, just less direct."

"Can we make it in five hours?"

"I must think and compute," said Wxakgini, closing his eyes.

"You, or the navigational computer?" asked Cole.

"There is no difference," said Wxakgini, and Cole concluded that he was probably right. The pilot was silent for almost a full minute, and then opened his eyes again. "We can traverse an as-yet-unnamed wormhole to the Beethoven system, and from there seek out the Yamaguchi Wormhole. It will let you out within reach of the Delamere system, and you can travel through normal space for the remainder of the voyage. ETA will be six hours and forty-three minutes."

"How long before we're out of the Yamaguchi Wormhole?" asked Cole.

"Five hours and thirty-seven minutes."

"Okay, do it." He turned and saw that everyone on the bridge had been listening. "We can contact Val and the others in five and a half hours, when we get out of the wormhole. I told them to wait six hours before writing us off."

"So we pulled it off!" said the Duke.

"In theory," said Cole.

"What are you talking about? Val got the prisoners, and we got out with our asses intact."

"We don't know for a fact that their guards didn't kill every last prisoner when they saw the ships and shuttles coming in for a landing," replied Cole. "We don't know if we lost any of our people. Let's wait seven more hours before we celebrate."

They made their rendezvous on schedule, and transferred the Octopus and his men to the *Teddy R* shortly thereafter.

"This ship wasn't built to hold a crew of a hundred and thirty," said Cole as the Octopus joined him for a drink in his office. "We're going to have to find someplace for you and your men."

"I've been giving it some thought," said the eight-handed mutant. "We're not that far from the Bellermaine system. There's a small military outpost there. Why not use the *Teddy R* to take it out? Leave a few ships undamaged and my men and I will appropriate them."

"They won't do you a bit of good," said Cole.

"Why not? They'll be Navy ships."

"And the Navy will know two minutes after you leave what each one's registration number is, what its name is, and what codes have been programmed into its computer. You'll be the most easily identified ships in the Republic." Cole stared at him and shook his head. "Sometimes it's difficult to believe you were really the biggest pirate on the Inner Frontier."

"I was *not* a pirate," said the Octopus adamantly. "I was an *entrepreneur*. Your good-looking redheaded friend—*she* was the pirate." Suddenly he grinned. "I can't tell you how many times she plundered my chosen prey before *I* could."

"Let's get back to the subject at hand," said Cole. "We've got to get your men off the ship in the next couple of days, before tempers start fraying. We're cramped for living space as it is. And I'm not about to attack a Navy base just to make you happy."

"It's a small one," insisted the Octopus. "It's ripe for the taking."

"Why tell the Navy where we are?" Cole shot back. "We just made fools of them not eight hours ago. Let's capitalize on that first."

"I'm here instead of on Malagori V. How much more capitalizing do you need?"

"Let's find out," said Cole. He contacted Jacovic.

"Yes, sir?" said the Teroni as his image appeared.

"How many probes do we have left?"

"I'll have to check." A pause as he called up the information on a screen Cole could not see. "Five, sir."

"I guess we can spare one," said Cole. "Thanks." Then: "Let me speak to Meloctin."

The Lodinite's face immediately appeared. "Yes, Captain?"

"If I want to record a message, can you capture it, insert it in a probe, and program it to be sent at a certain time?"

"There should be no problem at all," answered Meloctin.

"I'll want it broadcast to as many worlds as can receive the signal, but I also want it transmitted via subspace radio directly to one person."

"I don't foresee any difficulty, sir."

Cole smiled. "I'm glad to have you aboard, Meloctin—and I'll bet Christine Mboya, Malcolm Briggs, and Domak are going to be even gladder. I'll be up to record the message shortly."

He broke the connection.

"What's that all about?" asked the Octopus.

"Want to be a video star?"

"What are you talking about?"

"Finish whatever it is you're drinking and come with me," said Cole.

A moment later the two of them were on the bridge, and Cole approached Meloctin. "Are we ready?"

"Yes, sir," said the Lodinite.

"Where do you want me to stand?"

"Anywhere you want."

"Right where I am is fine." He turned to the Octopus. "Stay where you are until I signal you to join me." He looked around. "Jacovic, stay well away from me while we're recording. If they see you, they're going to convince themselves this is some trick perpetrated by the Teroni Federation."

Jacovic nodded and backed away.

"Say when," Cole told Meloctin.

"Any time," replied the Lodinite.

"Now." Cole looked straight ahead. "Hello again, Secretary Wilkie. This is Wilson Cole aboard the *Theodore Roosevelt*, still free and still approaching Deluros. You took eighty of my friends prisoner two days ago, and held them incommunicado on the planet of Malagori V. This, of course, was unacceptable, so we freed them without losing a single man to your Navy. Since you are rarely within hailing distance of the truth, I expect you to deny this vigorously. But before you do, I'd like to introduce you to a friend of mine." He gestured for the Octopus to join him. "This man is the notorious Octopus, one of the most feared entrepreneurs"—the Octopus laughed out loud—"on the Inner Frontier. Yesterday he was in your custody on Malagori V. Today he is standing next to me on the bridge of the *Theodore Roosevelt*. You are unquestionably going to claim that is it an actor, which is ludicrous unless you assume that we carry eight-handed actors among our crew . . . or perhaps you will think that he is nothing but a special effect. So I am going to ask him to say a few words to you, so that anyone who wants to run a voiceprint can do so."

Cole turned to the Octopus, who stared where Cole had been staring.

"Hello, you ugly little worm," said the Octopus. "You had better hope Wilson Cole reaches you first, because if I do, I plan to tear you into so many pieces that they can never find all of them. Speaking as an unelected criminal kingpin to an elected one, your days of plundering the galaxy are done. You can step aside, and I personally hope you don't, or you can cling to your office for a few more days, after which I will personally toss you aside before doing quite a few other exceptionally nasty things to you."

Cole waited until he was certain the Octopus was done, and then spoke again. "Your days of abusing the citizens of the Republic and the Inner Frontier are coming to an end. You are the primary villain, and your days in power are numbered, but we won't be satisfied to replace you with another tyrant. This time we're going to have a government that does what it is supposed to do, whatever that takes."

He nodded to Meloctin, who deactivated the recording device.

"Got it all?" said Cole.

"Yes. Would you like to edit it before I insert it in the probe?"

Cole shook his head. "No, we said what we had to say."

"Where would you like the probe sent?"

"Pilot?" said Cole, approaching Wxakgini.

"Yes?"

"What's the longest wormhole in the vicinity?"

"Define vicinity."

"Half a day."

There was a momentary silence while Wxakgini consulted with his mechanical counterpart. "That will be the Miranda Wormhole."

"If I shoot a probe into it, where will it come out?"

"Twenty-three thousand light-years away."

"How soon?"

"Approximately fourteen hours."

"Damn, that's fast, even for a wormhole!" exclaimed Cole. Then: "When it comes out, how close to Deluros will it be?"

Wxakgini closed his eyes and bonded with the computer again. "Thirty-two hundred light-years."

"Thanks." Cole returned to Meloctin. "Get all the coordinates you'll need from Pilot," he said. "Where the wormhole starts and ends, how to direct the transmission to Deluros once the probe is out the other end. Then rig it to broadcast and send twenty minutes after it emerges."

"That's cutting it very close," noted the Lodinite.

"We can't chance waiting any longer. A probe pops out of a wormhole just three thousand light-years from the Deluros system, you can bet they'll destroy it the second they know it's there."

"All right, sir," said Meloctin. "I should have it ready to go in half an hour."

"One more thing," said Cole.

"Sir?"

"Rig it to self-destruct immediately after it transmits our message. If you think you might need help, ask Mr. Odom."

"I've worked with probes before, sir," said Meloctin.

"All right," said Cole. "It's all yours." He turned to the Octopus. "Come on," he said. "We have to talk."

The Octopus followed him to the airlift, and a moment later they were in Cole's office.

"Now what?" said the Octopus, seating himself opposite Cole's desk.

"Now we put our heads together and try to solve your problem."

"*My* problem?"

"You're a navy without any ships."

"And you won't attack a Navy base?"

"Not a chance," said Cole. "They have no idea where we are. They won't find the probe before it self-destructs, but they'll trace the signal and assume we're three thousand light-years away. If we attack out here, if we're even seen by a Navy ship, then all that misdirection was for nothing."

"Yeah, well, picking off a Class H ship every couple of days is not going to win this war," said the Octopus.

"I'm working on it."

"*Are* you, Wilson?" he asked sincerely.

"Of course I am," said Cole irritably. "Believe me, there are better and safer ways to feed my ego than going to war with the Republic. I meant what I said: I intend to take the Republic down, or at least take down Wilkie and Garcia and see to it that some fundamental changes are made."

"Then why are we hiding to hell and gone?" demanded the Octopus. "If we don't send that message on the probe, Wilkie doesn't even know we exist."

"He knows," said Cole.

"Yeah? How?"

"Because a very foolish man got himself and his men captured, and we stole them back from right under the Navy's nose," said Cole. "He knows, all right."

"Okay, I shouldn't have tried it," admitted the Octopus. "But we weren't accomplishing a damned thing out here. Hell, we're still not!"

"That's just out-and-out wrong," said Cole. "With under a thousand ships, we've got the Republic shooting anything that moves, decimating entire worlds, overreacting to everything we do. I wish we had a couple of million ships, but we don't, so we'll have to fight this war with our brains and not our overwhelming force."

"Just tell me that you really have a plan."

"I really have a plan," replied Cole. "Plus about ten contingency plans, since nothing is guaranteed against an enemy of this magnitude and with its resources."

"But you have a plan?" repeated the Octopus.

"I have a plan."

"Fucking well better!" growled the Octopus.

"Now, if you're through with your little fit of pique, let's see what we can do about getting your people the hell off the ship before we can't stand the sight of you and vice versa."

"If you're that damned anxious to get rid of us, set us down on the next oxygen world."

"I'm anxious to get you outfitted and back into the fight," answered Cole.

"Okay," said the Octopus, "if you won't attack a Navy base, how about a spaceliner? We take everyone prisoner—pilot, crew, and passengers—set them all down on a planet, and my men and I take the ship deep into the Republic, maybe all the way to Deluros, without being challenged."

"Not unless you're prepared to kill every passenger and crew member aboard the ship," replied Cole. "You have to figure ninety percent of them will have communicators that can reach the nearest police or Navy ships—and once you're identified, you're even worse off in a spaceliner than a stolen Navy ship, which at least can defend itself."

"We'll strip 'em naked—a delicious thought in itself, at least regarding those passengers of the female persuasion—and then set 'em down on an uninhabited world."

"With no weapons, no communications, no medicine—just a bunch of naked people on a totally unpopulated world? And actions like that will make them prefer you to the Republic? Don't forget—all this presupposes that neither the ship nor the passengers can get off an SOS identifying you before you take control of it."

The Octopus stared at him for a long minute. "I think I hate you most when you're right," he said. "I don't like you very much at this moment."

"I'll take that as a high compliment, or as close to a compliment as you're capable of," said Cole easily. "Got any other suggestions?"

"We both know you'll just shoot 'em all down," said the Octopus sullenly. "You've known all along what you want me to do, haven't you?"

"I've had a pretty good idea," replied Cole. "But I thought I'd see if you had any better suggestions."

"Don't make me play guessing games," said the Octopus. "Just tell me what we're going to do about my situation."

Cole stared at him for a moment. "I think we'll start by procuring a cargo ship for you. The right one will be big enough to hold your men, and you can move freely through the Republic in it—or most of the Republic, anyway. And unlike a passenger ship, we'll only be taking two or three men prisoner, and possibly none at all; a lot of these ships are fully automated."

"But we'll still be in an unarmed ship," said the Octopus.

"Initially," Cole agreed. "Before long you'll be in a dozen unarmed cargo ships." Cole paused. "The advantage is that you can *land*. Choose a planet that has a major Republic presence, maybe the capital world of one of the galactic sectors, and harass and disrupt it on the ground. They'll be looking for an attack from space, by the *Teddy R* or some Teroni ship. You'll actually have an easier time of it with a ground attack."

"It's a thought," said the Octopus.

"I can't help but notice that most of your men are thieves and cut-throats," continued Cole. "That's a definite advantage in a guerrilla war, which is what we're fighting. If you need weapons, or more cargo ships, or money, they'll know how to get it on whatever planet you find yourselves."

"I hate to admit it, but it's got possibilities."

"Also, once you get more ships, you can coordinate your attacks. Say you have two Republic worlds in neighboring systems. Start harassing one until help arrives from the other, and then have the other half of your team hit the other."

"Okay, I'm convinced," said the Octopus.

"Just one thing," said Cole.

"Yeah?"

"I don't want you to engage in any pitched battles. The whole point is to keep them off balance, keep them guessing about our strength and our whereabouts until we're ready to do something major."

"*Are* we doing something major?" asked the Octopus.

"When the time comes."

"And we're not going to die of old age before then?"

"*I'm* not," said Cole. "You could be a lot older than you look."

The Octopus laughed. "All right," he said at last. "No pitched battles."

"Okay," said Cole. "By tomorrow we'll have your ship."

The Octopus got to his feet. "I'm going back to your mess hall," he said. "You wouldn't believe the slop they fed us back on Malagori."

"Of course I would," replied Cole. The Octopus stared questioningly at him. "I was a serving officer for eighteen years. I *know* what passes for food in the Navy."

The Octopus laughed and left the office. As soon as the door snapped shut Sharon's image appeared in front of Cole.

"You were eavesdropping, of course?" said Cole.

"Of course."

"And?"

"I don't know, Wilson," she said. "He's like Val but without her skills. How long do you think he can keep his word before he does something really dumb?"

"He functioned for years on the Frontier," replied Cole. "I think he's just having a little trouble adjusting to a new situation. Where he comes from, no one could match forces with him."

"How fast a learner is he?"

Cole shrugged. "We'll find out. If they capture him again, he's on his own. We can't keep rescuing him. We've got more important things to do."

"*Do* you have a master plan?"

"I wouldn't call it that," said Cole. "There are too many variables."

"But you know what you *want* to do."

"I want to win the war."

"You know, sometimes you can be very annoying to talk to. I think the Octopus had a point."

"Probably he did."

"Damn it, Wilson! Why won't you tell me?"

"For the same reason I won't tell Jacovic or Val or any of the others," said Cole. "If you're captured, I don't want them to be able to extract it from you the way we extracted information from Alberto Torres."

She stared at him. "I love you," she said at last, "but you can be a cold son of a bitch."

"It goes with command," said Cole. "I liked myself much better when other people got to make these decisions." He got to his feet. "I think it's time to go to work again. We're not going to run out of air or food, but in a couple of days it's going to *feel* like we will. Let's get the Octopus his ship, and move his crew the hell off ours."

He left the office and was going to direct the operation from the mess hall, which was his preferred command station, but he remembered that the Octopus was there so he went to the bridge instead. Val was now on duty, Jacovic was either eating or sleeping, and Meloctin seemed completely comfortable at Christine's computer.

"Val," he said, "start hunting for a cargo ship, something big enough to hold eighty men if we dump the contents."

"It shouldn't be that hard," she said. "Delamere IV is an agricultural world. There should be a steady supply of cargo ships."

"Just pinpoint it," said Cole. "No shooting. We need it intact."

"Gotcha."

Meloctin had adjusted to the lack of salutes, but he seemed a little shocked by "Gotcha" rather than "Yes, sir." Cole smiled and decided that the Lodinite would get used to Val before long.

Nothing happened for almost an hour, and then Val spotted a cargo ship.

"Incoming," she announced. "It's out by Delamere VII now." She turned to Cole. "Couldn't be better. He'll be deadheading until he can load mutated corn and wheat into his ship, so we won't have to dump a bunch of stuff that can be traced."

"Good point," said Cole. "All right, let's intercept him near one of those Delamere VI moons."

The *Teddy R* jumped ahead, and was waiting for the cargo ship as it neared the sixth planet of the system. Cole ordered it to stop, it refused, and he fired a laser beam across its bow. *That* stopped it.

It turned out that the pilot, a woman named Gentry, was the only entity on the ship. She'd made a short jump from the neighboring Kilgore system, and would be replaced by a fresh pilot once the ship was loaded.

As the Octopus and his men transferred to the cargo ship, Gentry was brought to the bridge, where Cole was waiting for her.

"You're going to be our guest for a few days," he told her. "I'm not going to put you off on some uninhabited world where you'd live and die alone and undiscovered, and I can't drop you on a Republic world where you can report what happened, so you're going to stay aboard the *Theodore Roosevelt* until my friends have had time to change your ship's appearance and registration and to leave the vicinity. If you accept our terms and behave yourself, you won't be confined to the brig, but will be given a cabin and treated with every courtesy."

"The *Theodore Roosevelt*?" she said, her eyes widening. "Are you really Wilson Cole?"

"Yes."

"I expected something with horns and a tail," said Gentry. She paused for a moment, considering her options. "I accept your terms."

"Rachel," said Cole on the ship's intercom. "Please come to the bridge, and escort our guest to an empty cabin."

"They're all a mess, sir," replied Rachel. "The Octopus's men are many things, but neat isn't one of them."

"That's all right," said Cole. "Our guest is going to have a lot of time on her hands. I'm sure she won't mind cleaning her cabin."

Rachel arrived a moment later and led Gentry off the bridge to an airlift.

"We're on our way," said the Octopus, and Cole saw from his image that he was on the cargo ship.

"Not just yet," said Cole. "Mr. Briggs will be boarding your ship in a minute or two to put our codes into your computer."

"Sure, why not?" said the Octopus with a shrug. "Hell, what's another hour?"

At it turned out, it took Briggs only forty minutes, and then the Octopus took off for a new system where he planned to disguise the ship, create a new registration, and acquire a few new cargo ships.

"What now?" asked Val when the Octopus had left.

"Now the distractions are over, and we get back to fighting the war," said Cole.

Val stared at him. "Why do I assume when you say that, you're not talking about blowing up ships and leveling enemy cities?"

"Because you're learning," answered Cole

"Sir?" said Rachel Marcos. She was standing in the doorway of the mess hall.

Cole, the only occupant, looked up from his coffee. "What is it?"

"We have a matter of some sensitivity," she said, approaching and sitting down across from him. "I don't know how widespread the knowledge of it may be, so I didn't want to discuss it from the bridge, where we could be overheard."

He stared at her curiously. "All right, what is it?"

"We have two men who may or may not be prisoners," she continued. "Nobody knows—or, rather, nobody but you."

"What the hell are you talking about, Rachel?"

"Mr. Brill and Mr. Dunyach, sir," she replied. "They've been confined to quarters since before we rescued the Octopus on Malagori V."

"Hell, I'd forgotten all about them," said Cole. "We've been a little busy in the interim. I promised to set them down on a neutral planet. We haven't come to one." He frowned. "In fact, the deeper into the Republic we go, the less likely we are to find one. I'll have to think about this."

"Maybe I can help," said Sharon's voice, and her image appeared a moment later.

"How?" asked Cole.

"I stopped by their cabins a couple of hours ago to make sure they were being fed on schedule and had been well treated. They asked me to ask you if they can remain on board. Their feelings haven't changed; they still want to do what they can to bring about the end of the Republic."

Cole looked at Rachel. "That'll be all, Rachel."

She saluted and left.

"So what are you going to do?" asked Sharon. "As you pointed out, it's going to be difficult to find a world where we can drop them."

"Difficult," he repeated. "Not impossible."

"They want to stay on the *Teddy R* and make war against the Republic."

"Damn it, Sharon!" he said, clearly annoyed. "They disobeyed a direct order from their Captain in the middle of enemy territory! There has to be a consequence!"

"All right," she said. "Then let's dump them on an agricultural world and be done with them—but you can't just keep them confined indefinitely for taking a stand on a matter of principle."

He stared at her image for a long moment. "How's Torres doing?"

"He seems fine," she said. "More than a little ashamed that he gave us the information, but physically he's just about recovered."

"So we did our worst, and he's fine," said Cole. "And if they'd had their way, he'd still be fine but eighty men would be dead."

"I'm not arguing that, Wilson," she said angrily. "Hell, I was an active participant! I'm just saying that we might not return to the Inner Frontier for a year or two, if then. You can't keep them confined to their cabins until then."

"All right," he said. "Let me think about it."

"If you want my opinion—"

"I know your opinion," he growled. "Now leave me alone."

She broke the communication, and Cole sat alone in the mess hall, considering his options. Finally he put through a call to Miguel Flores, whose ship was half a light-year away. They spoke for a few minutes, and then he ended the connection.

"Sharon?"

"Yes?" she replied.

"No sense doing this in front of the crew. Bring them down to my office."

"We'll be there in five minutes," she said, signing off.

He left his cup for the servo-mech to clean up, approached the air-lift, descended another level, got off, and walked to his office. The security system read his retina, weight, and bone structure and let him in.

He seated himself at his desk, ordered the door to remain open, and waited. Sharon arrived shortly thereafter, accompanied by Brill and Dunyach.

Cole studied the two men for a moment. They seemed none the worse for their confinement.

"I understand you two have a request," he said at last.

"Yes, sir," said Brill. "We're here because we agreed to go to war against the Republic. That hasn't changed." He paused, as if gathering his courage. "We would like to be allowed to remain on the *Teddy R* and return to our duties."

"What will happen the next time I give you an order you don't like?" asked Cole.

Brill met his gaze without blinking. "If it's the same order, you will get the same response."

Cole turned to Dunyach. "Is he speaking for you, too?"

"Yes, sir," said Dunyach. "I'm sorry, but you gave me an order that I could not obey."

"I respect you for that," said Cole. "And I wish it hadn't been necessary. But eighty lives were at stake."

"He might have talked anyway, sir."

"He might have," agreed Cole. "But we don't know that, and in my opinion, we couldn't take the chance. And the fact of the matter is that on this ship, it's my opinion that counts."

"Then will you be setting us down on a planet, sir?" asked Brill.

"Possibly," said Cole. "But as I told Colonel Blacksmith, I respect you for sticking to your ethical principles, and I also realize we need every man we can get in this crusade."

"Then we *can* go back to our jobs?" asked Dunyach, confused.

Cole shook his head. "No. You disobeyed a direct order, and you just told me if you receive another order that is contrary to your ethical precepts, you'll disobey it as well. I can't have you on the *Teddy R.*"

"Then I don't understand, sir," said Brill.

"I've contacted Mr. Flores, whose ship, *The Golden Dawn*, is a Class K, capable of holding a crew of twenty-two. He currently has only sixteen men and aliens aboard it. If you wish to remain a part of our team, he has agreed to take you on. Otherwise, we'll set you down on the next agricultural world we come to, though I can't guarantee they'll view a pair of insurrectionists with approval. That is your choice. We're in the middle of a war, we're in enemy territory, and I simply can't do any more for you."

Brill looked at Dunyach, who nodded his head.

"We'll go with Mr. Flores, sir," said Brill.

"All right," said Cole. "Return to your rooms and collect your gear." As they left he turned to Sharon. "Contact Flores and tell him to come over here and pick up his new crewmen."

"Thank you, Wilson."

"No need to. Security men are hard to come by."

"So are Captains," she said, kissing his cheek and leaving.

And hardest of all, he thought bitterly, *are Captains who will stick to their principles as doggedly as a pair of crewmen did.* A wistful expression crossed his face. *I wonder if I ever really was one.*

Cole had three chairs set up facing his desk in his small office. He wished he had room for Sharon, but the room felt cramped when he was alone in it.

At the appointed hour, Jacovic turned the bridge over to Braxite, and then he, Christine Mboya, and Val made their way down to Cole's office. When they were all seated, Cole spoke.

"Sharon is monitoring this, but she won't be speaking unless we ask her a direct question. I've called you here because you are my three senior officers, and it's time to take our next step in this campaign. We've made the Republic and the Navy aware of us, made them overreact, and stolen some prisoners out from right under their noses. It's time to escalate, without, of course, meeting them head-on. I have some thoughts, but I'd like your input first. Has anyone any suggestions?"

"Sir," said Christine, "I'm not qualified to discuss strategy. You want Mr. Sokolov, or perhaps Jaxtaboxl."

"I know who I want," said Cole firmly.

"We've proven that we can free our own people from a guarded sanctuary on Malagori V," said Jacovic. "What if we were to start attacking the prisons and freeing the prisoners out near the borders of the Republic? By the time word reached the Navy and they reacted, we could be a thousand light-years away."

"Not bad," commented Val.

"I don't know," said Christine. "It seems to me that you'd be freeing a few political prisoners and dissenters, but mostly you'd be freeing a bunch of criminals and crazies."

"So what?" said Val. "They could cause a lot of disruption."

"But it would be the kind of disruption that would have the people hoping the Republic would catch them and incarcerate them again," said Christine. "And I don't think we want to do anything that would make the Republic appear in a favorable light, which they would if they recaptured the felons before they could do any damage to the locals."

"She's right," said Jacovic. "I concede it. I should have thought more carefully before I spoke."

"What about the military prisons?" asked Val. "*They* sure as hell figure to hate the Navy."

Cole shook his head. "I don't think so. The mere fact that they're in a military prison to begin with implies that they lack discipline, and the fact that they may resent the Navy doesn't mean they'll want to overthrow the Republic."

"What then?" asked Jacovic. "We can't get much closer to Deluros without being spotted and drawing the attention of the Navy."

"I have no problem going out in a blaze of glory and taking as many of the bastards with us as we can," said Val, "but even I admit that won't get the job done."

Cole smiled. "I *knew* if I just talked sense to you for a couple of years it'd make an impression sooner or later."

"Save your compliments," snorted Val. "You called us here. You waited for everyone to say we don't have a plan. Now why don't you tell us yours, which you've obviously been sitting on all along?"

Cole looked at each of his three officers. "I think that there's no sense doing more of the same. We've threatened Susan Garcia and Egan Wilkie. We've freed some prisoners. It's time to do something completely unexpected."

All three leaned forward, trying to fathom what he had in mind.

"Governments thrive on propaganda," said Cole. "Usually they convince the media to collude with them in exchange for favorable treatment and status. And it almost always works." He paused. "But I don't think most governments, including this one, can withstand propaganda that is aimed against them, not from an exterior source, but from within."

"Sounds good in a lecture," said Val. "How does it work in practice?"

"I've been giving it some thought," began Cole.

"I'll bet you have," said Val with a grin.

"And I think I see a way that will put the Democracy's credibility in question, and quite possibly shatter it, without endangering any of us."

"And for your next trick, will you make Andromeda disappear?" asked Val.

Cole ignored her and looked at his Second Officer. "Christine, do you think you can find five abandoned worlds, all within the Republic, all farther out from Deluros than we are now?"

"Uninhabited worlds?" she repeated. "There are millions of them."

"I didn't say uninhabited," replied Cole. "I said *abandoned*. I want you to find five worlds that Man settled, built some structures on, and then left."

"Structures?" she repeated.

"Cities are good, but I'll consider anything that is clearly artificial."

"Does it matter what made them leave?" asked Jacovic. "It could be disease, war, diminishing natural resources, a natural disaster . . ."

"I don't care, as long as some structures remain," said Cole. He turned back to Christine. "Can you do it?"

"I don't know why not," she said. "In fact, if I can have Malcolm Briggs and perhaps Meloctin and Domak work around the clock in shifts, we can probably find a dozen or more worlds for you in a Standard day."

"Good," said Cole. "Start as soon as this meeting's over, and tell the other three that they're helping you. Have them check with me if there's any question about it." He looked at the Teroni. "You're suddenly smiling, Commander Jacovic."

"I think I see what you plan to do," replied Jacovic. "And I think it will work."

"I'm delighted to have the confidence of a leader with your experience."

"Well, *I* don't see it," said Val irritably. "Are we going to play guessing games, or are you going to confide in the rest of us?"

"Tell her, Commander," said Cole.

"If I have correctly deduced your plan, we are going to bomb a handful of abandoned worlds," said the Teroni. "We won't totally destroy them, because we'll want some of the structures to remain standing."

"Why?" asked Val, frowning.

"To *prove* these were inhabited worlds that we decimated," answered Jacovic.

"But they weren't," said Val.

Cole smiled. "I won't tell anyone if you won't."

Suddenly Val smacked her forehead with an open hand. "Of course!" she exclaimed. "We take credit for wiping out half a dozen planetary civilizations. Wilkie denies it. But we tell the media if they don't believe us, come and see for themselves—"

"—and when they come out, they see definite signs that a thriving civilization lived here prior to the attack!" concluded Christine.

"Right," said Cole. "Except that *we* don't take credit for it. We're just one ship, and we don't need the attention that will attract. We'll tell them that the Teroni Federation did it."

"They'll never believe it," said Val.

"Oh, I think they will," said Cole. "Especially if the one who reports it to them is a Teroni." He smiled and gestured toward Jacovic.

"Son of a bitch!" said Val. "Wilson Cole, you are one sneaky bastard!"

"Now, Secretary Willie will deny it, of course," continued Cole. "He may even convince most of the media that it's a ruse. But there's always some ambitious young reporter who will follow up on an interesting lead—and if no one does, then we'll broadcast the results of the carnage ourselves. Once we do that, you can be sure that private citizens will start checking out those worlds even if no one else does—and if it becomes Wilkie's word against that of a bunch of nonpolitical eyewitnesses who, unlike Wilkie, were *not* in charge of protecting all the people who lived on those worlds, who do you think the public will believe?"

"So who gets to blow these five worlds?" asked Val.

"We're just going to use one small ship," said Cole. "And we'll hit one every three or four days. If we hit them all at once, it's a single attack, and Wilkie can probably ride out the storm. But if we destroy one, and get word out that he couldn't protect the populace of that world, and while he's denying it, destroy another, and keep doing it . . . Well, I think it could snowball."

"And by the same token, I'll pick worlds that are hundreds, preferably thousands, of light-years from each other," said Christine enthusiastically. "As the Navy rushes to one to see what's happened, we'll be bombing another."

Cole turned to Jacovic. "You don't mind lending your face and voice to this enterprise?"

"I am no longer part of the Teroni Federation," he replied. "That does not mean I am a friend of the Republic."

"Any questions?" asked Cole.

Silence.

"All right. Christine, you might as well get started. Nothing gets done until you locate those worlds. This meeting is over."

The three officers filed out, and Cole leaned back on his chair as the door snapped shut.

"So what do you think?" he asked as Sharon's image appeared.

"I think you're going to drive Egan Wilkie crazy," she said. "You may even drive him from office. But we both know he'll be replaced by someone just like him. I don't see how this brings down the Republic."

"We don't want to bring it down," answered Cole. "We want to reform it. As many abuses as it's committed, it's still all that stands between Man and a frequently hostile galaxy."

"We're growing a strange crop of revolutionaries this year," she said.

"I'm not a revolutionary," he replied. "I served in this government's Navy my entire adult life. I don't want to *end* the Republic; I want to *fix* it."

"By attacking empty planets," she said with a smile.

"Why not?" he said, returning her smile. "I'd like there to be someone left alive after we win."

She stared at him thoughtfully. "You really do intend to win, don't you?"

"I wouldn't have left the Inner Frontier if I didn't," he answered.

Forli II was an oxygen world that had once been a small banking and trading center in the Wajima Sector. But as colonization spread in different directions, it was eventually abandoned, and it stood empty for almost three hundred years.

Five days after Cole announced his plan to his officers, Vladimir Sokolov bombed it, making sure to leave some of the ancient buildings standing.

And two days after that, Egan Wilkie explained to the populace at large via a galaxy-wide transmission that Forli II was a totally unpopulated world and no lives had been lost.

And a day after that, Jacovic—claiming that he was speaking from the flagship of the Fifth Teroni Fleet—explained to that same populace that Forli II was unpopulated *now*, and it was only the first world he planned to destroy.

Four days later, it was Buchanan IV. Wilkie denied, Jacovic bragged and promised more, and this time the media sent some people to see if there were any signs of civilization on that distant world.

Cole was feeling pretty good. He even allowed himself the luxury of both a beer and a dessert, and was sitting at his usual table in the mess hall with David Copperfield and the Platinum Duke, who seemed to have bonded simply because they were the only ones on the *Teddy R* without any duties.

"Those worlds are going to be tourist attractions after the Republic falls," the Duke was saying. "I'd love to have the gambling concessions on them."

"I thought you wanted to go back to Singapore Station," said Cole.

"That's my home," acknowledged the Duke. "But does that mean I can't have investments anywhere else?"

"Investments?" said Cole with a smile. "So you don't want a gift. You want to *lease* the gambling concessions?"

"Stop teasing me," said the Duke irritably. "You know perfectly well what I mean."

"Okay, they're yours," said Cole. "There's just one small obstacle we have to overcome."

"Oh?"

Cole nodded. "Overthrowing the Republic."

"That's all but done," said the Duke. "Wilkie can't survive something like this."

"Even if you're right, there'll be a next Wilkie, or someone just like him, and one after that, and one after that. I hope you didn't think this was going to be that easy."

"I have every confidence in you."

"And every hunger for five or six showplace worlds for tourists," said Cole dryly. He turned to David Copperfield. "You've been remarkably quiet, David."

"I'm thinking," said the little alien.

"Well, that's a step in the right direction," said Cole. "What are you thinking about?"

"I own a warehouse that seems to have slipped my mind until just now," said David. "And among other things, it possesses two paintings executed in the ancient way, with actual oils on canvas, by Bartholomew Miksis, the greatest artist of the twenty-sixth century AD, four hundred years before the dawn of the Galactic Era."

"And?" said Cole.

"As you know," continued David, "I have certain enemies on the Inner Frontier, evil men possessed of a totally unreasonable hatred of myself, and for that reason I have been loath to pass the word that some of these items, and especially the paintings, were available, since to purchase them the buyer would have to know where to deliver the money. I was thinking maybe I'll auction them here in the Republic, where my record is absolutely spotless."

"Why the hell don't you simply use an instantaneous transfer of money to a numbered account?" asked the Duke.

"I suspect our David has also annoyed his share of Inner Frontier bankers," said Cole with a smile.

"Absolutely not!" said David. He paused. "I have only offended relatively *few* of them—a mere handful."

"Then set up your account somewhere else," said the Duke.

"You don't understand the economics of the situation," said David.

"Let me take a guess," said Cole. "Since those paintings aren't legally yours, there's nothing to stop an unethical banker from keeping all the money—and you don't know any ethical bankers."

"Precisely," replied David. "Though of course the argument is based on a totally false premise: there are no laws on the Inner Frontier, and therefore nothing can be illegal—but bankers can be so unethical! Besides," he added, "I'm not a thief, I'm a fence—or I was, anyway. Which is to say that those paintings may or may not legally be stolen goods, depending on how they were obtained and whether they're in the Republic or the Frontier, but *I* didn't steal them. I simply bought them from the man who . . ." He paused, frowning. "From my source," he concluded lamely.

"That makes it all okay," said Cole, amused at the little alien's discomfiture.

"How did you two ever get together?" asked the Duke.

"We met during the *Teddy R*'s brief fling at piracy," said Cole.

"We found out that we were old school chums, Steerforth and I," said David, "and we've been inseparable ever since."

The Duke looked to Cole for a quick contradiction, but the latter merely shrugged and said, "I suppose that's as good a story as any."

They spoke for a few more minutes. Then David and the Duke left to play whist, and a moment later Sharon's image appeared over the next table.

"Yeah, what is it?" asked Cole.

"Gentry."

"Gentry to you."

"That's the name of the cargo ship pilot we've been carrying."

"Okay," said Cole. "What about her?"

"She wants to speak to you."

"Put her through."

"In person," said Sharon. He frowned and she continued. "She's not a prisoner or an enemy, just someone who was piloting the wrong ship at the wrong time."

"You know what this is about, I presume?"

"Yes."

"And you approve?"

"I do."

"All right," said Cole. "Send her down."

"Thank you, Wilson."

He had just finished his beer when Gentry arrived.

"Have a seat," he said, gesturing to the chair opposite him.

"Thank you, Captain Cole," she said, walking over and seating herself.

"My Security Chief tells me you have something to say to me."

She nodded her head. "Yes," she replied. "I've spent quite a bit of time thinking, and speaking to Colonel Blacksmith . . ." She paused awkwardly. "I've been apolitical all my life, but I had no idea of the abuses the Navy had committed, both here and especially on the Inner and Outer Frontiers." Another pause. "Captain Cole, I want to join the *Teddy R.*"

"You're aware that we're presently engaged in a military action against the Republic?"

"Yes."

"And what the odds are against our succeeding?"

"I'm aware of them."

"We have a pilot," said Cole. "He hasn't eaten or slept in maybe ten years, and he's as much a part of the ship as the cannons or the bulkheads, so clearly we're not in the market for another pilot. What other skills can you bring to us?"

"I can speak seven alien languages that aren't programmed into the standard T-Pack," she replied. "For example, I can speak to your Tolobite crewman in his own tongue."

"You can speak Slick's language?" asked Cole. "It's all clicks and growls."

"Yes."

"I'm impressed," he said. "Where the hell did you ever pick it up?"

"I was stranded on his planet for three months some years ago." She paused again. "They're a remarkable race, aren't they? And I like your name for him."

"Slick? Well, his second skin—that's the way I think of his symbiote—just *looks* slick and oily. He says it's intelligent, but I've never seen any evidence of it."

"The symbiotes can only communicate with their Tolobite hosts. It's a fascinating relationship."

"Yeah, the symbiote can let Slick maneuver in the cold of space without air for four and five hours at a time. He does all our external repairs, though we haven't needed him lately." He stared at her. "All right, Gentry, you're a member of the crew, and you have run of the ship. I'll leave it to Jacovic to figure out what duties to assign you, until we come to a race that our T-Packs aren't programmed for."

"Thank you, sir."

"By the way, is Gentry your first name or your last?"

"These days it's my only name," she replied.

"Sounds like there's a story there," said Cole. "Perhaps someday you'll share it." He opened communications to the bridge. "This is Cole. From this moment on, Gentry is a member in good standing of the crew of the *Teddy R*. Val, when Jacovic shows up to replace you, have him decide what her duties will be. Sharon, permanently kill the force field around her cabin." He turned to Gentry. "Okay, you're set— or you will be once Commander Jacovic wakes up. The Officers' Lounge is off-limits to you—you wouldn't like it anyway—and unless you have business in the engine room it would be best to keep away from it. Other than that, you have run of the ship."

"Will I be required to wear a uniform, sir?" asked Gentry.

"Only if you want to," he replied. "All we have are Navy uniforms from four years ago, and that's the same Navy you've just agreed to go to war against."

"Then I'll wear my own clothes, sir."

"Fine," said Cole. Then: "I just thought of another skill you bring to the ship. Well, knowledge rather than skill, actually."

"What is it, sir?" she asked. "I'll be happy to help in any way I can."

"You've been piloting cargo ships inside the Republic for the past four years," said Cole, "while we've been on the Inner Frontier for that same period of time. Things must have changed here and there—socially, economically, politically. I want you to sit down with either Christine Mboya or Malcolm Briggs and help them update our computers, since they're four years out of date."

"I'll be happy to, sir," said Gentry, "if someone will point them out to me."

"Christine is the black woman who's never five feet away from her computer. Briggs is—"

"*I'll* direct her," said Sharon's voice.

"Are either of them on duty right now?" asked Cole.

"No," said Sharon.

He turned to Gentry. "Okay, you might as well spend a few hours learning your way around the ship."

"Thank you, sir," said Gentry, getting up and heading toward the doorway.

"One last thing," said Cole.

"Yes?"

"Sooner or later—probably sooner—you're going to run into a gorgeous redheaded giant with a foul mouth and a certain lack of shipboard etiquette," said Cole. "Don't be put off by her. She's our Third Officer, and when the chips are down, there's no one you'd rather have on your side."

As if to emphasize what he had just said, Val's image suddenly appeared.

"Damn it, Cole!" she said. "I don't care what you say, I'm blowing up the next world! Why does that goddamned Russian get to have all the fun?"

The image vanished as suddenly as it had appeared.

"Your Third Officer?" asked Gentry.

"You guessed," replied Cole with a smile.

By the time they attacked the fourth world they were making galactic news, and the government, try as it would, couldn't keep it quiet. Experts were actually suggesting that the totally nonexistent death toll numbered in the tens of millions.

Cole decided that when Jacovic made his fourth appearance, he should not be standing alone and isolated. He selected a few crew members he'd picked up on the Inner Frontier, members who could not possibly be identified as being members of the *Teddy R*'s crew, put them in dress uniforms, and had them pretend to be going about their business in the background as Jacovic spoke.

The news transmissions went crazy. Were these humans turncoats working for the Teroni Federation? And it wasn't long before some of them spotted certain things in the bridge's structure that convinced them that it was a Navy ship, which immediately implied that some Navy ships had gone over to the enemy, and that made *every* Navy ship a potential turncoat, to be avoided, or lied to, or possibly even fired upon.

Cole knew what would come next, and recorded a message that was inserted into a probe and aimed at the Inner Frontier. Before it got there, someone had suggested that Jacovic was speaking from the bridge of the *Teddy R*. The probe then transmitted a holo of Cole, explaining that he *wished* his ship had been causing all the damage, but as Susan Garcia and others could testify, the ship was almost a century old, and it was now back in the Inner Frontier for reoutfitting. If they didn't believe it, all they had to do was trace the signal back to its source (which immediately self-destructed once the message was sent).

Within a week, Egan Wilkie's approval rating was in single digits, the lowest in the Republic's nineteen centuries of existence. He finally took to the galactic airwaves, admitted that serious damage had been done to a small handful of outlying planets, and laid the blame squarely at Admiral Garcia's feet. He demanded that she use all the resources at her command to find and capture or kill the saboteurs. (In one transmission, they were saboteurs; in another, insurrectionists; in a third, genocidal maniacs.) He explained that he had been elected to run the government; Susan Garcia was in charge of the Republic's physical safety, and it was her job to put an end to these attacks.

"Did you hear the latest?" asked Sharon as she burst into Cole's office.

"David's running a whist tournament?" suggested Cole.

"Be serious," she said. "I'm talking about the latest news."

"Probably not."

"I didn't think so, so I had Luthor capture it. Wait just a second." She gave Luthor Chadwick a brief order, then stepped back as Admiral Susan Garcia's face suddenly appeared above Cole's desk.

"We will do everything we can to apprehend these terrorists," she was saying, "but of course Secretary Wilkie misspoke when he said we would use the full force of the military to do so. He seems to have forgotten that we are in an all-out war against the Teroni Federation, and if I pulled every ship—or even a goodly number of them—back from that conflict to hunt for a small number of terrorists, the Republic would find itself overrun in a week. I would suggest that Secretary Wilkie stick to worrying about expenditures and taxation, and leave the security of the Republic to the Navy."

Susan Garcia's face vanished, and Sharon's sported a huge grin. "I think we've got them fighting with each other!"

"Stupid," said Cole. "She's the more competent of the two, but it's not a fight she can win. Eventually he'll call for her resignation. If she agrees to it, she's finished; and if she refuses, she's in open rebellion."

"If she *does* refuse, will the Navy side with him or her?" asked Sharon.

"I've been out of touch for four years," said Cole. "I just don't know."

"You've met her," said Sharon. "What was she like?"

"I disliked her personally," said Cole. "She was smug, self-centered, and abrasive—but she was a damned good admiral."

"Didn't she give you your last Medal of Courage—the one you won after you were transferred to the *Teddy R?*"

"Very reluctantly," said Cole with a rueful smile. "I was grateful that medals are bonded to the uniforms these days. If we'd been back in the days when they were affixed with pins, I honestly believe she would have stuck the point into my chest."

"And of course you were the personification of sweet reason," said Sharon, returning his smile.

"We didn't get along very well," said Cole.

"Somehow I think that you won't get along any better with Egan Wilkie."

"With any luck, he'll be history in a few more weeks."

"He must still be wondering what the hell's going on," she suggested.

"That's the purpose of the exercise," agreed Cole. "By the way, how's our newest crew member working out?"

"Gentry? There are no aliens for her to speak to—well, none that aren't programmed into our T-Packs—so I've got Bull Pampas teaching her the Gunnery section."

"She has no problem with that?" asked Cole.

"Should she?"

He shrugged. "It's easy to join a war when all you have to do is translate. It's a little different when you're expected to help shoot the enemy."

"She seems fine."

"Good," he said. "You know, I think there must be a few billion Gentrys out there—decent folks who would be repelled by some of the things the Navy does in the Republic's name, *their* names, and just want to get from one day to the next without hurting anyone or being hurt themselves." He paused and sighed. "That's a fair appraisal of human motivation. I wonder why it's such a faulty description of human history?"

"Sir," said Briggs's voice, "there's a Navy ship approaching. They're demanding we identify ourselves."

"We couldn't stay unseen forever," said Cole. "What class is the ship?"

"Class K, crew of twenty."

"Weaponry?"

"Checking . . . Unless it's been enhanced, this particular model carries two Level 4 burners and a Level 3 thumper."

"Okay," said Cole. "Give them a phony name and registration, and send Gentry to my office on the double."

"Yes, sir."

A moment later Gentry entered the office. "You sent for me, sir?" she asked.

"Yes," said Cole. "I need a face that's never been identified with the *Teddy R*. In a minute we're going to be contacted by a ship that's been trying to identify us. They'll think we might be the *Teddy R*, but they won't know for sure. They'll give us some orders, maybe want us to hold our position for boarding. You'll identify yourself as the Captain of the ship, claim that Admiral Garcia has ordered you to hunt this sector for saboteurs, and if they want to hinder us by making us stand still for a boarding, you will accede to their demands but will report to Garcia that they were responsible for delaying you. Do you think you can do that?"

"Just tell me what our ship's name is," she said.

"Listen to Mr. Briggs's reply," he said, right before it was piped throughout the ship. "*The Brave Bull*," said Cole, making a face. "He could have used a little more imagination." Then, on a private channel, he said, "Remember, Mr. Briggs—neither Sharon nor I can be seen."

"I understand, sir," replied Briggs.

"*Brave Bull*, I must speak to your senior officer," said a voice.

"I'll put you through, sir," said Briggs, and suddenly the image of a man wearing a Captain's insignia popped into view in the office.

"You are the Captain?" he said.

"That's correct," answered Gentry.

"You're not in uniform."

"When my ship is traveling incognito under express orders from General Garcia, I'll dress any way I please," she answered haughtily.

"We have no record of *The Brave Bull*, either by name or registration number."

Gentry smiled contemptuously. "What part of the word 'incognito' don't you understand?"

As she became more pompous and dismissive, the other captain became more and more defensive. Finally he conceded that she had the right to be in this sector, and he would now retreat and go about his business.

"Very nice," said Cole after the connection had broken. "Are you sure you haven't had any experience on the stage or in the holos?"

"None," said Gentry, suddenly collapsing on a chair. "I was *so* nervous!"

"You didn't show it," said Cole. "And you saved twenty lives."

"I did?" she said, surprised. "Whose?"

"The other ship. They had nothing that could breach our defenses. We have weapons that could have vaporized them."

"I know it sounds bloodthirsty," said Gentry, "but why *didn't* you fire on them? After all, they *are* the enemy."

"First, we don't know if they were in contact with any other ships, and we'd much prefer that the Navy think we're on the Inner Frontier."

"And second?" she asked.

"They could have fired, and didn't," said Cole. "They could have insisted on boarding us, and didn't. They're decent men and women who are just trying to protect other decent men and women. They're not the enemy, Gentry; they're working for the enemy."

"But you'd have destroyed them if you had to?"

"Without a second's hesitation," he replied.

"I believe you," she said, studying his face. She got to her feet. "I suppose I'd better get back to Gunnery."

When the door snapped shut behind her, he turned to Sharon. "She did a good job. Better than Moyer or one of the others we picked up on the Frontier would have done."

"I agree," said Sharon.

"Keep an eye on her," continued Cole. "She has qualities."

"I'm the one who told you she did."

"And I'm agreeing with you. I like her."

"Good," said Sharon. "And if you touch her, I'll cut your hand off."

"What do I care?" said Cole. "The Captain's not obligated to salute."

"I'm sure if I thought about it, I'd find other things to cut off," she replied.

"You old broads get so jealous."

"It's just to make you old geezers feel good."

"Let's go to my cabin," suggested Cole. "We can feel good a lot more comfortably down there."

It was six hours later that Val's voice woke them.

"I hope I'm interrupting you at an awkward moment," she said.

"No," said Cole. "You're waking us up before we indulge in another awkward moment."

"Perhaps you'd like to celebrate first," said Val, and now her face appeared with a huge grin.

"All right," said Cole. "I'm awake. Now what have you got to tell me?"

"You'll be interested to know that as of twenty minutes ago, Egan Wilkie demanded Susan Garcia's resignation."

"*That* fast?" said Cole.

"I've got a bigger surprise for you," continued Val. "As of five minutes ago, she gave it to him."

"You're kidding!" said Sharon.

"It's working!" laughed Val. "The fucking Republic is falling apart!"

Suddenly the ship shuddered.

"Well, all but the part that just started shooting at us," she added.

"Who the hell is it?" asked Cole, getting to his feet.

"Who else? The Navy," answered Val.

"Not that little ship that wanted to stop and board us earlier today?"

"No, they know better than to go up against us. But your pal Gentry's answers must not have satisfied them, because now they've got a Class L ship firing on us."

"Are there any other ships with it?" asked Cole.

"Not so far," said Val. "But then, they've only been shooting at us for maybe half a minute."

"Have you fired back?"

"Of course I fired back!" she said irritably. "They're shooting at *my* ship!"

"Cut and run," said Cole.

"If we cut and run, they'll know we have no business being here," said Val.

"If you fired on them, they know it already," replied Cole. "Cut and run."

"Where to?"

"Away from them and away from Deluros," said Cole. "No sense drawing even more of a crowd."

"Are we *ever* going to engage with one of these damned ships?" demanded Val.

"When the time is right," said Cole. "Put me through to Pilot."

Wxakgini's face appeared, his eyes still closed, his brain still attached to the navigational computer.

"Pilot, how far to the nearest hydra-headed wormhole?" asked Cole.

"There are none in this vicinity," replied Wxakgini, "but we are very close to the Sondermeyer Wormhole, which will let us out six thousand light-years from here in the neighborhood of the Tiznow Wormhole."

"And that one's hydra-headed?"

"At one end," confirmed Wxakgini.

"Entrance or exit?"

"With this approach, the exit."

"How many heads has it got?"

"Six," answered the pilot. "But two are unstable."

"Take us there, as fast as we can go."

There was a momentary pause, and then a brief shudder. "We are now inside the Sondermeyer Wormhole," announced Wxakgini.

"Good," said Cole. "I assume the Navy ship that was firing on us will follow. Now, once we emerge in normal space and we enter the Tiznow hole, can you navigate inside it—which is to say, can you choose which of the six exits we emerge from?"

"No, I cannot," said Wxakgini. "The hole will choose which exit it wants us to use."

"It's not always the same?"

"It is not."

"So if the Navy ship enters in hot pursuit a minute or two later, it won't necessarily come out through the same exit?"

"That is correct."

"How far apart are these six exits?"

"On average, two thousand light-years," answered Wxakgini.

"That'll do," said Cole. "Val, I assume you were listening?"

"Yes."

"Don't fire a shot until we come out of the Tiznow hole," continued Cole. "If they come out the same exit, we're all through running and we'll take them on."

"You mean it?" said Val excitedly.

"If we can't elude them, I don't see that we have any choice but to stand our ground and fight."

"We will emerge from the Sondermeyer Wormhole in less than four minutes," said Wxakgini.

"Good," said Cole. "One of these days we've really got to program the locations of all these damned wormholes into the computer."

"They are already in the computer," said Wxakgini.

"Oh?" said Cole, surprised. "I never saw them there."

"That is because *I* am in the computer, and I have encrypted them against detection."

"We're not the enemy, Pilot."

"I never thought you were," answered Wxakgini. "It is just a precaution."

"What if *you* die during combat?" demanded Cole.

"Then the *Theodore Roosevelt* will be without direction, and will be destroyed within seconds."

"He doesn't value himself too highly, does he?" said Val sarcastically.

"He's right, Val," admitted Cole.

The ship shuddered again as they returned to normal space.

"That was fast, even for a wormhole," remarked Sharon.

"They don't travel through normal space," said Cole. "If we could find the right one, we could conceivably reach the Andromeda galaxy in twenty minutes instead of two hundred years."

"One hundred eighty-seven," Wxakgini corrected him.

"Who cares about Andromeda?" said Meloctin, who was working one of the computers. "There are some really outré galaxies out there."

Cole turned to Sharon. "Do you get the feeling that my bedroom isn't as private as it was ten minutes ago?"

"Go be a hero," she said. "I'm off to Security."

"I'm not going anywhere," said Cole. "I've told Wxakgini where to take us, and if anyone starts shooting, Val's better able to defend the ship than I am."

"You're not going back to sleep while we're being chased through a wormhole by a Class L Navy ship?" she said incredulously.

"No," he said. "I'm awake now. But I think I'll take a shower and grab some breakfast—maybe some coffee and a couple of those awful Danishes."

"While we're under attack?"

"We're *not* under attack," he corrected her. "We're under pursuit. And the odds are that when it's over, we're going to be a few thousand light-years away from our pursuer."

"What if they sight us between the wormholes and start shooting while you're in the shower?"

"That's why I have competent subordinates," Cole replied. "The days of a captain standing on the bridge for two or three days at a time, tying himself to the wheel, are long gone."

"You just better hope the days of hanging captured captains from the mainmast are just as long gone."

"They got rid of all the mainmasts last year," he said with a smile.

"Damn it, Wilson—I'm being serious!"

"Leaving aside the fact that you love me and Val probably isn't your type, be honest now: which of us would you rather have protecting your ass when the chips are down?"

"You," said Sharon without hesitation.

"I asked for an honest answer, not an argumentative one," said Cole.

"That was an honest answer. She may be better in combat, but she'll never look for alternatives to killing or being killed, and you will."

"I'll consider that a compliment to my intellect rather than my lack of courage."

"Your lack of bloodthirstiness," she corrected him.

"Whatever," he said, walking toward the washroom. "You going to scrub my back?"

"I really don't think this is the time for it," she said. "I'll be in Security."

The ship shuddered again as he was showering, and he realized they had entered the Tiznow Wormhole. He was out, dried, shaved, dressed, and sitting in the mess hall when the ship shuddered one last time.

"We're out," Val informed him as he finished ordering his breakfast.

"Any sign of the Navy ship?"

"No, but it was a minute or two behind us."

"Keep me informed," said Cole. "And while I'm thinking of it, have Pilot find out just where the hell we are."

A moment later her face appeared again.

"Who did you kill?" asked Cole.

"No one," she said, puzzled. "Why?"

"Because you had such a happy smile on your face." He paused. "So do we know where we are, and has the Navy ship shown up?"

The smile returned. "Not yet, but I sure as hell hope it does."

"Oh?" said Cole. "Why?"

"Because this head of the wormhole spit us out on the Inner Frontier."

Cole entered the Officers' Lounge to find David Copperfield and the Platinum Duke engaged in an argument rather than a card game. It concerned the percentage of the break for the house in the alien game of *jabob*, and the argument made no sense since David had never played the game, but it didn't stop him from arguing his position passionately.

"Is the ship okay?" asked the Duke.

"Why shouldn't it be?" responded Cole.

"It shook a couple of times, even after we were beyond that Navy ship's firing range."

"We were entering and leaving wormholes."

"Good," said the Duke. "I thought for a minute it might be falling apart."

"You don't seem exceptionally worried."

"You tell me what good worrying will do when you're flung into space without a protective suit and I'll worry my ass off," answered the Duke.

"I assume we're safely away from that ship," said David. "Otherwise, you'd have told me to"—he searched for the right word—"*visit* my bulkhead."

"We're safe."

"Where are we?" asked the little alien.

"The Inner Frontier."

The Platinum Duke chuckled. "So we're back where we started!"

"Not for long," said Cole, sitting down on a chair that looked more comfortable than it felt, as did everything in the Lounge. "I'll give the

Navy a few hours to get discouraged and return home, and then we'll reenter the Republic, probably from a new direction."

"Well, I think you'll be doing it without me," said the Duke after a moment.

"Oh?"

"I came with you because the Navy might be attacking Singapore Station, or at least hunting for me on it. But enough time has passed now. Either they've gone, or at least they're not looking for me anymore."

"You don't know that," said David.

"I'm going stir-crazy on this ship," replied the Duke. "Singapore Station is more than my investment. It's my home, and as long as we're this close I'm going back."

"I can't chance sending a shuttle to the station in case the Navy's still there," said Cole. "But I can have one of the shuttles drop you off on a planet where you can find transportation the rest of the way."

"That'll be fine," said the Duke.

"I think you're stupid, going back to a station that may have a few hundred Navy men on it."

The Duke laughed. "Not as crazy as a man who thinks he can overthrow the Republic with eight hundred ships. In fact, do you still have that many?"

"Probably not," admitted Cole.

"Then why not come back to the station with me?"

"Because sooner or later the Navy will be back on the Inner Frontier, and when we try to drive them out, they'll attack Singapore Station in force."

"But you can't seriously think you have a chance to win."

"In a month's time we've gotten rid of Susan Garcia, and we've seen to it that Egan Wilkie couldn't be elected Chief Street Cleaner," Cole pointed out.

"Cosmetic," said the Duke. "The Republic's still there."

"It's a little different than it was yesterday," replied Cole. "I call that progress."

"I call it window dressing," said the Duke.

"No one's stopping you from going," said David Copperfield. "Why are you so bitter that we won't come with you?"

"*You'll* come," said the Duke with certainty. "At least they won't be shooting at you on the station."

"Englishmen are made of sterner stuff," said David. "I'm not deserting my friend Steerforth."

"You're *not* an Englishman," said the Duke. "You're not any kind of a man at all."

"Tell him, Steerforth," said David.

"If he says he's an Englishman, that's good enough for me," said Cole.

"You're both crazy!" said the Duke, getting to his feet. "I'm off to pack my gear. Let me know when and where the shuttle can take me."

He left the room and David turned to Cole.

"Thank you for vouching for me, Steerforth," said the little alien.

"*I* can deny we went to school together in nineteenth-century England," said Cole. "*He* can't."

"You are a true friend, Steerforth," said David.

"You want to make your true friend happy?" said Cole. "Start calling me by my real name."

"It *is* your real name," said David adamantly. "I don't put my life on the line for anyone named Wilson or Cole. That sacrifice is reserved only for classmates."

"Whatever you say," replied Cole wearily.

"Still no sign of 'em," announced Val's voice. "I think the hole dumped 'em somewhere else."

"Good," said Cole. "How far are we from Singapore Station?"

"How the hell should I know?"

"Ask Pilot."

"If I may make a suggestion, Steerforth?" said David.

"What is it?"

"Once our position is determined, have it transmitted here on a Tri-D cross section of the Frontier."

"Why?"

"It's possible you may have more friends than you know about," answered David. "Or at least more supplies."

"Val, you heard him."

"Coming up. Let me just speak to Wxakgini."

Cole muttered an obscenity. "How come everyone but me can pronounce his name?"

"Oh, names are easy," said David.

"Thanks."

"It's quantum mechanics that are difficult," continued the alien. "Why, it took me months to totally master them."

"I may put you ashore with the Duke," said Cole.

Before David could reply, Val's voice announced, "Coming at you!"—and an instant later the middle of the room was filled with a cross section of the Inner Frontier. A tiny blinking light represented the position of the *Teddy R*.

David studied the image for a moment, then moved his finger through it until it reached a large blue star. "Computer, is this Horatius?"

"Yes," answered the computer's voice.

David smiled and touched another star. "Then this would be New Macademia?"

"Yes."

David withdrew his hand and turned to Cole. "I know where we are now." He indicated a nearby yellow star. "See this? It's Nyerere, and the fifth planet circling it is Ngorongoro. I have a trading partner down there."

"A thief or a fence?" asked Cole.

"It depends on the day," replied David easily. "But he owes me a favor. I'm sure he'll be willing to transport the Platinum Duke to Singapore Station."

Cole stared at him. "David, you were one of the hardest-headed businessmen I ever met. No one owes you a favor. You'd never let it go uncollected."

"Semantics," said David.

"What?"

"A matter of tenses."

"What the hell are you talking about?"

"He *will* owe me a favor," explained David.

"How do you figure that?"

"You're still a Navy ship. I'll simply tell him that I will misdirect you away from Ngorongoro if he'll provide the Duke with transportation."

"If he's got half as good a security system as yours was, he'll know we're the *Teddy R*."

"And by now everyone knows that the *Teddy R* has teamed up with the Octopus, who is a thief and a cutthroat."

"Why don't we just offer him some money to transport the Duke, and save the threats for someone who doesn't figure to be on our side from the outset?" said Cole.

"Well, yes," said David. "I suppose we *could* do that."

"See to it before the shuttle leaves the ship."

"They taught you well in school, Steerforth," said David. "Of course I was just testing you."

"Of course."

"Well, that's that. Shall we go have some kidney pie and Yorkshire pudding?"

"In *our* galley?" asked Cole with an amused smile.

"All right," replied the alien. "Brisket of beef, then, with a good red wine."

"Later, perhaps."

"Fine," said David, getting up and walking to the door. "I'll check my records and see how to contact my friend."

"David, you didn't bring any records."

"All right," admitted the alien. "I'm going to check and make sure he's still in business. Not everyone has my survival instincts."

"I'll vouch for that," said Cole.

"Thank you for the compliment, Steerforth," said David, and left.

Sharon's image instantly appeared. "Have you ever wondered what would have happened if you'd said your name was Wilson Cole the first time you met?"

"He had nine bodyguards with their guns trained on me," answered Cole. "There's every likelihood that he'd have killed me."

"You really think so?"

"He's not always on speaking terms with the truth, but he was right about one thing: he has excellent survival instincts. That's the only way he could have stayed in business all those years. A lot of rivals tried to rob him or kill him, but he's still around and most of them aren't."

"So now that we're out here, what's our next step?"

"Well, Sokolov's still got another abandoned planet to bomb." He paused thoughtfully. "I think I'll have Christine find three or four more, and have each of them transmit a prerecorded message just before we hit them."

"What kind of message?"

"I think a panicky voice saying that the government promised to protect them, and they're being attacked right now, and where the hell is the Navy, and why won't the Republic protect them? *That* kind of message."

"And you'll make sure thousands of worlds hear it."

"Wouldn't be much point in just sending it to Deluros VIII, would it?" answered Cole.

"It's very effective, Wilson, but we can't just bomb abandoned planets forever."

"We don't intend to. But if we're going to throw the rascals out, as the saying goes, we want to make sure most of the populace agrees with us. All we're really doing now is shaping public opinion."

"So what else do you plan to do?" asked Sharon.

"It depends on conditions."

"What conditions."

"Various," said Cole.

"You can be an infuriating person to talk to!"

"So meet me in my cabin later and I promise not to talk."

"Maybe I'll meet you in your cabin, and unless you talk I'll cut off your supply of me."

"Whatever makes you happy," said Cole. "That Gentry's a fine-looking woman. I don't suppose you've noticed?"

"Men!" she snapped, and cut the connection.

"Val," he said, contacting the bridge, "who's working the main computer?"

"Idena."

"Let me speak to her."

Idena Mueller's image instantly appeared. "Yes, sir?"

"I want you to put me through to Lafferty," he said. "I'm pretty sure he's still in the Cicero asteroid belt. You'll find the coordinates and codes in your machine."

He waited almost two minutes, and then Lafferty's face popped into view above his desk.

"How's it going?" asked Cole.

"I was about to ask you the same thing."

"We're making some progress. Susan Garcia is no longer the Fleet Admiral."

"That's a step in the right direction," said Lafferty. "Whoever replaces her won't be as good. How'd you kill her?"

"We didn't."

"Who did—the Teronis?"

"She's still alive," said Cole. "She's just been relieved of command."

"Your doing?" asked Lafferty.

"I'd like to think so."

"One of my men who had to leave the Cicero system tells me you're also destroying millions of civilians."

"It's comforting to know the news is spreading," said Cole.

"Did you really have to kill that many?" asked Lafferty. "Our war is against the government and the Navy."

"I give you my word that we haven't killed a single civilian," said Cole.

Lafferty's image frowned. "Then how—?"

"I'll tell you when I see you. This is supposed to be a secure connection, but I'd prefer not to trust it if I don't have to."

Lafferty nodded his head. "Not a problem. And in the meantime, I'll accept your answer."

"So much for *our* progress," said Cole. "How about yours?"

"We've got our hands on one," answered Lafferty, making sure he wasn't explicit just in case the connection wasn't secure.

"How did you get it?"

Lafferty smiled. "I think we'll also save *that* answer for when we're face-to-face."

"How soon is it ready?" asked Cole.

"It won't be here for another day or two, and then it'll take at least four days to install it and check it out."

"Six days," said Cole. "Yeah, that'll be okay. What about ID?"

"We're blank on that."

"Okay, we've got six days to come up with something. You need anything else?"

"Not right at the moment."

"We'll see you then," said Cole, breaking the connection.

He got to his feet and began pacing, considering his options. He felt too confined, so he went down to the crew's quarters where he could walk with a little more freedom. Next he went up to the bridge, paced around it briskly with an expression that said he didn't want to be bothered, and finally he went to the mess hall, ordered some coffee, and sat staring at it for ten minutes.

After another five minutes had passed, David Copperfield came in.

"Someone told me you were here, Steerforth," said the little alien, "and that you looked troubled, so I thought I'd come and share my old friend's burdens."

"Hi, David," said Cole. "I was just about to pay you a visit in your room."

"You were?"

Cole nodded. "Yes, I was."

"What about?" asked David.

"How would you like to be the hero who helped win the war?" said Cole.

"You're teasing me, right?" said the alien nervously.

"Not this time, my old school chum."

"I'd hate it!" said David.

"But you'll do it for Crown and country."

"You're making my stomach hurt."

"David, if there was anyone else I could ask . . ."

"All right," said David unhappily. "But there had better be a knighthood for me in this."

"I'll speak to Queen Victoria," said Cole.

"You damned well better."

Cole sat down on a chair in the Platinum Duke's cabin. The Duke perched on the edge of the bed, and David Copperfield stood by the door, looking very unhappy.

"We'll go over this as often as necessary," Cole was saying, "though there's nothing very complicated about it."

"*Hah!*" said David bitterly.

"I have no idea what you have in mind," said the Duke. "All I know is that a few hours ago I was leaving alone and you were both going back into the Republic, and now suddenly I'm part of a mission and David's coming with me."

"All the more reason to listen instead of talk," said Cole.

"Why are we talking in my cabin?" demanded the Duke. "Are you afraid there are saboteurs or turncoats on board?"

"No. I just thought David would be more comfortable if we didn't discuss this where everyone could hear it."

"Why aren't we in *his* cabin, then?"

"You wouldn't like it," said Cole. "All those doilies . . ."

"All right, talk," said the Duke.

"You'll be taking the shuttle down to Ngorongoro. David will come with you. Braxite's coming along too."

"Braxite?" repeated the Duke. "Why?"

"Because as far as the contact is concerned, you and David are going to stay on Singapore Station, and someone has to bring the ship back to Ngorongoro."

"My friend may want one of his own men to pilot it," said David.

"Try to talk him out of it. And if you can't, Braxite goes anyway."

"Again, why?" said the Duke.

"Because if David's contact absolutely insists on his own pilot, someone's going to have to make sure the ship stays at the station until David is done with his job and is ready to return. If Braxite has to incapacitate the pilot so that David can complete his mission, he will—and we'll pay the contact enough money when it's done to make it all right."

"Okay, so David and I are taken to Singapore Station. Now what?"

"Now you go back to running the place, unless you feel the Navy may start using you for target practice. If that's the case, then hide as best you can until David's ready to come back, and come with him."

"I don't even know what David's coming along for!" said the Duke in frustration. "How can I help him if I don't know what he's going to do?"

"He's doing a little infiltration and a little sabotage."

The Duke stared at David. *Him?* he said with a laugh.

"Him," said Cole.

"Me," said David, his voice breaking.

"We need something, and I think he has the best chance of getting it without immediate repercussions."

"And what is that?" asked the Duke.

"We need the name and registration number of a Class M Navy ship. We can't make it up. It has to be one that Deluros will recognize and acknowledge."

"You don't need David," said the Duke. "I can get that easy enough. Every ship that's docked has to use its name and registration."

"And you can check it?"

"If I want to," said the Duke. "I almost never do, but the mechanism's there."

"Can anyone on the station access this information?"

"No, only about half a dozen employees—though if you just want the name, go out on the docking arms and look. Navy ships are never shy about displaying their names in big bold letters."

"So only six or seven of you can access it," said Cole. "That implies you each have a code or a password."

"Yes."

"Different ones?"

"Yes, of course."

"That's why *you* can't get the information for us. You plan to stay on the station, and so do your employees. That puts you at risk. Do all the paperwork required to make David one of your employees, and give him his own password. Since he's leaving the station with the name and registration, it doesn't matter if they know *he* took it."

"Seems awfully complicated," muttered the Duke.

"I'm just trying to protect your ass," said Cole. "After what we do to the ship, the Navy's going to be out for blood. Now, if you'd rather it was your blood than David's . . ."

"When you put it that way . . ." said the Duke.

"I thought you might see reason," replied Cole with a smile.

"Why are they going to be out for blood?"

"Because David has volunteered to disable their ship."

The Duke looked at David again. "You?"

The little alien smiled a sickly smile.

"So he's going to blow up a ship right on my dock, and they're not going to blame *me*?"

"He's not going to blow it up. That wouldn't serve our purpose."

"How can destroying a Class M ship not help your cause?" asked the Duke.

"If it's destroyed, it will be reported," said Cole, "and we don't want Deluros or anyone else to know that the ship they see isn't what it's supposed to be."

The Duke's eyes widened. "You're going to swipe the name and registration and give it to Lafferty's ship!"

"That's right."

"It may do some damage, but you can't bring the Republic down by attacking it with one misidentified ship, not even a Class M."

"We don't intend do," said Cole.

"Then what *do* you plan to do?"

"You'll stay healthier a lot longer if you don't know," said Cole. "Anyway, David is going to be instructed in the subtle art of sabotage by some of the best—Bujandi, Moyer, and of course Val—and then he's going to find a way to disable the ship, not permanently, but for three or four weeks. And he's going to make it look like some kind of malfunction, nothing to report or get alarmed about."

"And then what?"

"And then he's going to take the ship back to Ngorongoro, and we'll pick him up there in the shuttle and bring him back to the *Teddy R.*"

"And you really think he'll do it?"

Cole stood up, walked over to David, and placed a hand on the little alien's shoulder. "He risked his life for me once before, in your casino. Now he'll be risking it for a cause that's far more important than any single life."

"Including his own," said the Duke.

"Don't *say* that!" snapped David.

"So when do we go down to Ngorongoro?"

"Tomorrow," answered Cole. "David's still got to be instructed in the art of disabling a ship. And you could save a little time if you decide on a password with him on your way down to Ngorongoro."

"I've got a question," said the Duke.

"What is it?"

"What if there aren't any Class M ships docked at Singapore Station?"

"You're not going to like the answer," said Cole.

"Oh?" said the Duke apprehensively. "What *is* the answer?"

"You do whatever it takes to lure a Class M to the station."

Cole paced the ship like a caged animal. He was in a foul mood. When he spoke, he growled. When he slept, which was rarely, he awoke every hour. When he ate, he left half his food on the plate. He snapped at Jacovic, which he hadn't done since the Teroni had joined his crew. He actually had Christine in tears. Nothing intimidated Val, but she left him completely alone.

When he wasn't stalking through the ship he stayed in his office. Finally, after four days, Sharon went down to the office and entered it.

"Any word?" asked Cole anxiously.

"No, Wilson," she said. "And if there was, it would come to you from the bridge."

"I know," he said.

"How long are you going to be like this?"

"Until I find out what's happening on the station."

"You don't expect to hear for another two days," she said.

"I know."

"Then don't you think it's time you stopped behaving like this?"

"Damn it, Sharon—I shamed him into it! The little bastard's no more fit for sabotage that I'm fit to box or wrestle with Bull or Val. I had no business asking him to do it."

"Why don't you wait and see what happens before you mourn him?"

"There was no one else I could send," said Cole. "He's the only member of his race anyone's ever seen, and if they've been there before they know he spent time at the station. He's not at war with anyone, he's not allied with the Teronis, and if he's with the Duke and we're somewhere else, he's not part of the *Teddy R.*"

"I know. That's why he was the proper choice."

Cole shook his head. "He was shaking like a leaf when I walked him down to the shuttle."

"But he went," she noted. "And if he hadn't been willing to go to Singapore Station, someone on Ngorongoro would have contacted us and told us to come and get him."

"Do you know how well protected a Class M ship is?" said Cole. "Even Four Eyes would have said to forget it, and he was the best damned saboteur I ever knew."

"I don't know exactly what you have in mind, but I know you need that ID and registration, and I know you feel that the ship has to be incapacitated for a few weeks. This is war, and in war you sometimes have to take chances when all the odds are against it."

"I know all that," said Cole. "It doesn't make me feel any better. I took the most cowardly being I know, stuck him down in the middle of a war he has no part of, and sent him off on an impossible mission."

"He risked his life for you once before, when a would-be warlord had you at his mercy."

"That was different."

"How?"

"That was *his* decision," said Cole. "This was *mine*."

Sharon grimaced in frustration. "You're going to be like this until you hear something, aren't you?"

"Probably."

"Then do yourself and your ship a big favor."

"What is it?"

"Stay in this damned office and don't talk to anyone," she said. "That way you won't have to spend all next week apologizing."

He stared at her and made no reply. She waited for a moment, then turned on her heel and left.

Cole took her advice. He no longer paced the ship. He had his meals delivered to his office, primarily so he could toss what he didn't want into the trash atomizer without anyone looking at him reproachfully or telling him to eat more. After two more days he decided that David had failed, the Duke hadn't had the courage to notify him, and he was no closer to carrying off his plan than he'd been a month ago.

He was just about to go down to the shuttle bay and take it to Ngorongoro where he would rent or buy a ship, find some way to disguise himself, and do what he felt he should have done in the first place, when Jacovic's voice broke the silence of his office:

"Captain Cole to the bridge, please."

"What's up?" he asked, leaving the office and heading to the airlift.

Sharon's voice broke in. "We have a hero who would like to report personally to you."

Cole ran the last few steps to the airlift, took it up to the bridge, and a moment later was confronting David Copperfield—who looked incredibly proud of himself and very little the worse for wear—in the flesh.

"I did it!" said the little alien. "Me, Steerforth! I did it!"

"I always knew you could," lied Cole. "Tell me about it."

"I had the name and the registration within three hours of arriving on the station," said David. "It was as easy as the Platinum Duke said it would be."

"And the rest?"

"I couldn't gain access to the ship," answered David. "It was too heavily guarded, so I wasn't able to do any of the things I learned from Mr. Moyer or Bujandi or Val." He paused. "But I'd had a feeling I might not be able to get onto the ship, so before I left the *Teddy R* I had Mr. Briggs prepare an undetectable virus that should eat away the memory of the navigational computer. He showed me how to transmit it in such a way that the Bdxeni pilot wouldn't be aware of it for at least three days. It also destroys just enough of the hardware so that the computer can't receive a transmission of the missing memory. This particular hardware will take at least two weeks to replace, including delivery time, and since it doesn't come from the same source as the computer code and memory, it will have to be installed before the memory can be transmitted."

Cole turned to Briggs. "You never told me about this."

"You never asked, sir," answered Briggs. "Besides, I assumed you had approved it."

"I wish I'd thought of it," admitted Cole.

"What do you want done with the ship's name and registration?" asked David, who clearly enjoyed being the center of admiring attention.

"Give them to Mr. Briggs, who will transmit them to Mr. Lafferty. How's the Duke doing?"

"He announced two full days of free drinks and meals for the Navy, and they're all friends again," answered David.

Cole looked at the little alien with an almost fatherly pride. "You did well, David."

"Thank you, Steerforth."

"Even Mr. Creakle would agree, however reluctantly."

David's chest puffed out.

"Who is Mr. Creakle?" asked Sharon.

"Our old headmaster," said Cole as David grinned happily.

Val came onto the bridge. "I heard you were back," she said to David. "Get the job done?"

"Yes," answered the alien.

"Good," she said, then turned to Cole. "So we're ready for the next phase of the war?"

"Absolutely," said Cole.

"When do we attack?" she asked.

"We don't attack."

She frowned. "What *do* we do?"

"Surrender," answered Cole.

The *Teddy R* entered the Cicero system and made its way to what the crew had dubbed Lafferty's Asteroid. It was easy enough to find. Contrary to the belief that Man had held when he was still Earthbound that asteroid belts were like incredibly busy meteor showers, asteroids were generally so far apart that seeing a handful, spread out over thousands of miles, broke the boredom of the approach.

Cole chose the *Kermit*, as usual, and selected a landing party consisting of himself, Jacovic, Idena Mueller, Bull Pampas, Jaxtaboxl, and Gentry. A few minutes later they were standing in front of the Class M ship.

"Looks good, doesn't it?" said Lafferty, who greeted them in his protective space suit.

"Looks new," said Cole. "I think I'd better have the Platinum Duke send me some holos of the ship whose identity we're borrowing, and we'll have Slick match any markings it's got."

"Markings?" repeated Lafferty. "You mean name and numbers?"

Cole shook his head. "We already know those. But the fact that a Class M ship is still functional doesn't mean it hasn't seen some serious action, either against the Teronis or elsewhere, and it could be showing the scars of battle, or just simple collisions with some minor space debris. If so, I want Slick to duplicate them."

"What kind of weaponry does it carry?" asked Gentry, stepping forward.

"Standard," said Lafferty. "Eighteen cannons, ten of them Level

5—half pulse, half laser. The wild thing is that it even has a pair of screechers."

"That doesn't make any sense," said Cole. "You can't use sonic weapons in space where there aren't enough molecules to vibrate, and a ship like this never enters a planetary atmosphere."

"Maybe they know something we don't know," said Jacovic. "The fact that I've never seen a sonic cannon on a starship, and neither have you, doesn't mean they can't carry them. Maybe there's some innovation that lets the sound waves go directly to the enemy ship and not dissipate in space."

"Maybe," said Cole. "It makes no difference, though. If we have to fire *any* of this weaponry, we're dead meat. I just want to make sure it's carrying what it's supposed to be carrying if someone checks it out."

"Want to inspect the inside?" asked Lafferty.

"That's what we're here for."

Lafferty led them to the ramp that lifted them and drew them to the main hatch, and a moment later they were inside the ship.

"Wow!" said Idena. "I knew these things were big, but I had no idea!"

"Ceiling's got to be nine or ten feet high," noted Pampas. "You'd never feel trapped or claustrophobic in this baby."

"How many does it hold?" asked Jaxtaboxl.

"I can answer that," said Jacovic. "According to our information, a Class M starship holds a crew of ninety-six."

"Not this one," said Lafferty. "Oh, it's got room enough to carry a couple of hundred, but as far as I can tell, there are only forty-two duty stations. You wouldn't believe how many functions have been mechanized."

"Just tell me that it's got a powerful tractor beam," said Cole.

"Of course," answered Lafferty. "But so did the older models." He smiled suddenly. "Maybe not the antiques like *your* ship—you know, the ones that still ran on steam or fossil fuels."

"Let's see the rest of it," said Cole, ignoring the older man's comment.

Lafferty led them through the Gunnery section, which sported a truly impressive array of cannons and other weaponry, then up to the bridge.

"Have you ever seen a bridge like this?" asked Pampas in awe-struck tones.

"Admiral Garcia had a bigger one on her flagship," said Cole. "Still, it's impressive." He walked over to the pilot's hanging ham-mock-chair. "Same setup?" he asked. "The pilot sits up there and ties in to the navigational computer?"

"Right," said Lafferty. "Assuming he's a Bdxeni, of course—and these days just about all of them are."

"Well, let's see how the communication system works." He acti-vated it. "David, are you there?"

"Right here, Steerforth," said David Copperfield, his image sud-denly appearing.

"Let me speak to Val for a minute."

The redhead instantly appeared. "What do you want?"

"Take a shuttle, or transfer to one of the small ships," said Cole, "go out a few hundred miles, and see if you can intercept the transmissions David and I are sending to each other."

"On my way," she said, and vanished. "I'll be in the *Alice*."

"Okay, David," said Cole, "just talk for a few minutes until we find out how secure this connection is."

"Certainly," said the little alien, who immediately fell silent.

"David, you have to keep talking," explained Cole. "She can't try to intercept a message or a conversation if you remain quiet."

"I'm thinking," said David. "But nothing's coming."

"Tell me the details of your adventure at Singapore Station," said Cole.

"I already did."

"Tell me again."

"I'm uncomfortable in the spotlight," said David.

"You'll be a lot more uncomfortable in the sights of a Level 5 thumper that homed in on you because we didn't know it was able to capture our transmission."

Suddenly David began talking a blue streak. Finally Cole told him he'd spoken long enough, and sent a message to the *Alice*. "Did you pick up any of it?"

"No," answered Val. "I couldn't even tell that you were signaling to each other."

"Fine," said Cole. "You can go back to the ship now."

He broke the connections, first to Val, then to David. "All right," he said to Lafferty, "it looks like the codes work." He looked around once more. "I hope to hell this galley is better than the *Teddy R*'s."

"You ever see a Navy galley with good food?" asked Lafferty with a grin.

"No," admitted Cole. "Not on any ship I've ever been on. But allow me to hope."

"Hope all you want," replied Lafferty. "But given its defenses, you're more likely to die of hunger or food poisoning aboard the *Sabine Nova* than of enemy fire."

"That's its name—the *Sabine Nova*?"

"Commanded by Captain Tucker Marchand," said Lafferty, surprised. "Didn't you know that?"

"I told David to transmit the information to you," answered Cole. "I figured I'd find out when I got to the Cicero system."

"We programmed in its registration numbers and its Navy code, and your Mr. Briggs has told us how to program all of your private codes, so it's ready to go."

"Not quite ready," Cole corrected him. "I still want the Duke to transmit some holos to us, and then I want Slick to match any marks, scars, *anything* that the real *Subine Nova* has."

"Who is this Slick you keep referring to?"

"A Tolobite."

"Damn!" said Lafferty. "I wish we had one! It would have made working on the ship's exterior a lot easier."

Cole turned to the crew that had come over with him. "I want you to go through the ship, learn where everything is, and make sure it's all in working order."

"Including the weaponry?" asked Pampas.

"Everything *but* the weaponry," answered Cole. "Then, when you're done, go back and send over six more crew members, and keep rotating six new ones every time the previous batch returns. I want every member of the *Teddy R* to know the inside of this ship by this time tomorrow." He turned to Jacovic. "Contact the Duke and tell him about the holos I want."

Jacovic nodded and began walking through the ship, as did the others.

"I don't understand," said Lafferty. "You want to make sure the climate control and the toilets and the airlift are working, but you don't care about the weapon systems?"

"That's right."

"Why not?"

"Because if we have to fire a shot, we're in deep trouble," answered Cole.

Lafferty frowned. "Just how far into the Republic do you plan to go?"

"All the way to Deluros."

"Without firing a shot?"

"Correct."

"You're crazy, you know that?" said Lafferty.

"Perhaps," said Cole easily.

"Definitely," insisted Lafferty.

Cole smiled. "Did you ever hear the story of the Trojan Horse?"

"Now here's the way it's going to work," said Cole, speaking to the entire ship through the communications system. "We're going to leave a ghost crew on the *Teddy R*, just enough so if it becomes necessary they can prove that the ship can defend itself. I need six volunteers, preferably human since the Navy knows that was the bulk of our crew. I'll want one ranking officer to remain on board in case any command decisions are required, and it can't be Commander Jacovic since there are no Teronis in the Navy."

He paused, giving them time to digest what he was saying. "Pilot is going to be transferred to the *Sabine Nova*, and will tie in to its computer, just as he's tied in here. Anyone who's joined us since the mutiny four years ago will go to the *Sabine Nova* without question; I don't want anybody on board the *Teddy R* that the Navy hasn't got a record of."

"I'll stay on board the *Teddy R*, sir," said Christine. "If Jacovic has to leave, then it comes down to Val and myself, and if you're going to face any danger, she'll be more use to you than I would be."

"Thank you, Lieutenant Mboya," said Cole. "And of course your logic is impeccable."

"Also," added Christine, "she joined us after we reached the Inner Frontier, so I'm really the only choice."

"I've gotten so used to her that I forgot," Cole admitted. "All right," he continued. "As for those who are transferring ships, you all know what the plan is. The only way we can approach Deluros is if we pose as the ship that has finally captured the *Teddy R*, and a Class M ship is the most likely to have done so. The *Sabine Nova* will be towing the *Teddy R*, and if we're lucky we'll tow it all the way to Deluros VIII itself. You can be sure Secretary Wilkie and his cronies are going to want to have a show trial and brag about how they nailed us, and I'm betting they'll feel they can control things better on Deluros than some other world. Therefore, I am ordering all personnel on both ships not to fire a shot except on my direct orders. Even a Class M ship like the *Sabine Nova* can't get within a thousand light-years of Deluros if the Navy decides to stop it. Christine, even if some local system sends out a few ships to take a few potshots at the *Teddy R*, you can't fire back."

"Can we activate our defenses?" she asked.

He gave it a moment's thought. "I don't see why not," he said. "The fact that the *Sabine Nova* didn't blow you apart means that your defenses are working. And of course the Captain of the *Sabine Nova* would never begin towing the *Teddy R* until he'd deactivated all its weapons systems. In fact, he'll probably *want* the defenses activated; he can't present the government with the *Teddy R* as a trophy if someone blows it away. So yes, you can protect yourself—but you can't fire back, not a single shot. And I don't want you communicating with anyone except the *Sabine Nova*, and only on channels and in codes that won't show up on the most sophisticated Navy surveillance computers."

"Understood, sir."

"All right," said Cole. "I want the volunteers who are remaining on the *Teddy R* to report to Jacovic. If there are more than six or seven, he'll choose who stays and who doesn't. The rest of you, pack all essential gear and head down to the shuttle bay, where we'll start transferring you to the *Sabine Nova*. Pilot's going to put the *Teddy R* in orbit. Then we'll take him down to the *Sabine Nova*, and when everyone's aboard, including any of Lafferty's men who want to come along, we'll take off and start towing the *Teddy R* to Deluros. It won't be long before we're spotted by some Navy ship or other. We'll simply report that we've captured the *Teddy R* and are taking our prize to Deluros."

"What if they order us to stop?" asked Jaxtaboxl.

"We'll explain, with all due courtesy, that we will only respond to that order if it comes from Fleet Admiral Garcia," said Cole. "We've been chasing the *Teddy R* on the Inner Frontier, we don't know she's been replaced, and we won't believe it if we're told."

"I have a question, sir," said Gentry.

"You always ask intelligent ones," replied Cole. "What is it this time?"

"If word gets out that the *Sabine Nova* captured the *Theodore Roosevelt*, I would imagine that the real *Sabine Nova* will hear of it shortly. What's to stop them from warning the Navy what's happened? Even if the Navy doesn't believe them, they're nonetheless going to have to board and inspect us before we get near Deluros."

"Very good question," said Cole. "Mr. Briggs, would you like to answer it?"

"Part of the virus we introduced into the *Sabine Nova*'s computer destroyed its ability to receive any communications after two Standard days," replied Briggs. "This allowed them to report their problem and to order replacement parts, but right now they can neither send nor receive any communications, and we've also contacted the Platinum Duke and told him to shut down his public communications systems until he receives another coded message telling him to activate them again."

"Does that answer your question?" said Cole.

"Yes, sir, it does," replied Gentry.

"Are there any other questions?" asked Cole. He waited a moment. "No? Okay, start gathering your gear and heading down to the shuttles."

He looked for Pampas and finally spotted him. "Bull, get the medic and help him unhook Pilot, then carry him to the shuttle, cart him into the *Sabine Nova*, and stick with him until the medic attaches him."

"Carry him, sir?" asked Pampas.

"Bull, he hasn't been out of that sling in fifteen or twenty years. His muscles have got to have atrophied."

"Yes, sir."

"All right," said Cole. "Let's get moving."

The crew dispersed and went to their cabins, and Cole caught Sharon's eye.

"What is it?" she asked, approaching him.

"Are you ready to stop pretending we sleep in separate cabins?"

"Well, it's hardly a secret," she said with a smile.

"Okay. When you get down to the *Sabine Nova*, hunt up the captain's suite and move your stuff in."

"*Suite?*" she repeated.

"This is a Class M ship," he replied.

"A real suite!" she repeated happily. "If we have a fight and break up, I'm keeping it."

"Don't be such an optimist," said Cole. "We're not breaking up. We're much more likely to be hanged for treason."

"They don't hang people anymore," said Sharon.

"They don't?" said Cole in mock surprise. "Hell, if I'd known that, I'd have mutinied ten years sooner."

The *Sabine Nova* had been towing the *Teddy R* for more than a Standard day when a Navy ship finally spotted it.

"Please identify yourself," demanded the ship, a Class L.

"Just voice," Cole ordered Briggs. "No holo."

"Yes, sir."

"This is the *Sabine Nova*," answered Cole, "three hundred and four days out of Spica VI, registration number HVT678939QW2, Tucker Marchand commanding, destination Deluros VIII."

"And your companion ship?"

"It is not a companion," answered Cole. "It's a trophy that we're presenting to Secretary Egan Wilkie."

"A trophy?" said the voice at the other end. "Explain yourself, please."

"The ship we are towing is the *Theodore Roosevelt*."

"That's Wilson Cole's ship?" said the voice excitedly. "You really got him?"

"We really got him," answered Cole.

The voice gave out a holler of triumph. "Good for you, *Sabine Nova*! We're going to ride shotgun for you until you've passed through our sector."

"We'd be proud to have you," said Cole, ending the transmission.

"Proud?" said Val contemptuously.

"What do you think he'd have done if we told him to leave us alone?" asked Cole.

"We could have blown him to bits," she said. "In fact, we still can. He's a bigger target now."

"We're not on the Frontier or the outskirts of the Republic any longer, Val," said Cole. "He's got to be in constant contact with other ships."

And no sooner had he said it than two more ships, each on its normal patrol route, contacted him and volunteered to help escort him to Deluros.

"We're going to be quite a parade if we keep picking up help in each sector," remarked Sharon after Cole had thanked them for their offer.

"Just as well," replied Cole. "Then no outraged patriots will take any potshots at the *Teddy R.*"

Within three hours Briggs found a galaxy-wide newscast concerning the daring capture of the notorious Wilson Cole and his rebel ship. One politician after another made self-congratulatory speeches, and at least three of them suggested that when the whole truth came out it would show that Cole was in the employ of the Teroni Federation.

"They may trample each other getting to the microphone to take credit for it," remarked Sharon as she and Cole took dinner in the sitting room of their suite. "I never thought much of our government, but suddenly I think even less of it."

"At least Susan Garcia's not coming out of retirement to claim that *she* planned our capture," said Cole with a smile.

"What are we going to do when we finally get there?" asked Sharon. "The media is going to want to take endless holos of the triumphant crew."

"Then I guess we'll let them."

She stared at him curiously. "Are you going to tell me what you have in mind?"

"It would be more fun if you seduced it out of me," he answered. "But what the hell. They want a triumphant crew? We'll give them one. We have eleven crew members, like Moyer and Gentry, who never served on the *Teddy R* when it was in the Navy, men and aliens we picked up on the Inner Frontier . . . and Lafferty's got over a dozen or more. We'll make sure they're wearing some of our old Navy uniforms—I'll give one of mine to Lafferty; we'll have to take it in a bit, but I trust him to come up with the right answers—and they can meet the press."

"Including Val?" asked Sharon.

Cole shook his head. "I need her with me." Suddenly he smiled. "Besides, can you imagine the answers she'd give to their questions?"

"I assume from the way you worded that, you're planning on leaving the ship?"

"That shouldn't come as a surprise," he said.

"You and Val alone?"

"No, I'll need more than that. It's a shame I can't take Jacovic, but we can't let a Teroni show his face on Deluros."

"Am *I* coming?" she asked.

"I haven't decided yet," he told her.

"I'd like to."

"I know."

"You wouldn't say no just to protect me?" she persisted.

"I'm taking those I think best fit the mission," he said. "If it fails, we're all dead anyway."

Sharon opened a line to the bridge. "Commander Jacovic, what's our ETA on Deluros VIII?"

"If we use the Kominsky Wormhole and no one hinders us along the way, Wxakgini says we will arrive in forty-three Standard hours," answered the Teroni.

"That fast!" she said after breaking the connection. "The most heavily guarded planet in the galaxy, probably in the history of the galaxy, and we're actually going to do it, aren't we, Wilson?"

"We're actually going to make it to Deluros," he replied. "But that was always the easy part."

"Easy?" she repeated incredulously.

He nodded his head. "Compared to what comes next."

They docked in one of the six thousand orbiting hangars under the watchful eyes of the local authorities, the system authorities, the sector authorities, the Navy, and the media.

Cole was standing just outside Engineering, his hands in glowing manacles.

"You're sure?" he said.

"Absolutely," said Mustapha Odom. "Try them."

Cole flexed his muscles and tried to pull his hands apart. At first he thought the experiment was a failure, but then he felt the manacles break apart, and a moment later they shattered and the pieces fell off his wrists.

"I *told* you," said Odom, annoyed that Cole hadn't taken his word for it.

"All right," said Cole. "I'm going to be sending some of the crew down here. I want those manacles on each of them."

"I made up a dozen pair, just as you told me."

"I know. But we won't need that many."

Odom frowned. "Then why——?"

"Because the others may also be a little dubious about being able to break out of them when the time comes," replied Cole. "And if each of them needs to try them out, so be it. I don't want any of them having doubts when the chips are down."

"Send your crew," said Odom. "I'm ready for them."

"Soon," promised Cole, walking to the airlift.

A moment later he was on the bridge. "Val, get down to Engineering, and don't fight whatever Mr. Odom does to you. He'll explain it all." He looked around. "You too, Braxite. You're our only Molarian, and since most of the Men we're going to see today can't tell one Molarian from another, you can pass for Four Eyes."

"That will be an honor," said Braxite, accompanying Val to the airlift.

"Put me on the ship's intercom," Cole told Jacovic.

"Done."

"Mr. Pampas, get down to Engineering, on the double. Mr. Sokolov, you too. Right now." He considered the final name for a long minute, then shrugged. "Colonel Blacksmith, report to Engineering immediately."

He joined them a moment later, waiting until the other five were manacled, then had Odom affix another set to his wrists.

"You five, down to the shuttle bay. That's the way we'll leave the ship. Remember, you are prisoners, and no one breaks out of his manacles until I do."

He waited until they'd gone, then went back on the intercom. "Mr. Lafferty, take the five members of your crew that you've decided upon and report to the shuttle bay. Gentry and Mr. Chadwick, you too."

He went down to the shuttle bay and waited until they were all assembled.

"Mr. Lafferty, from this moment on you are Captain Marchand. Right this second they want to see who and what's on the *Teddy R*, but the second they see my face, and assume that Braxite is Four Eyes, they'll turn their entire attention on us. Be a little arrogant, explain that you know how big the reward is, and that you're not sharing it with anyone else. They've already announced that there will be a special shuttle to take us down to the Secretary's Mansion. Insist that no one from that shuttle except you, your crew, and your prisoners enters the Secretary's Mansion, and once we're there, demand that we be marched directly to Wilkie's office. I can't imagine he isn't there, ready to take his bows to the press."

"What if some of his security team wants to come with us?" asked Lafferty.

"I'm sure they will, and I'm sure they won't permit you to enter the office without at least some of them in attendance."

"So . . . ?"

"So let them accompany you, and the second the door's closed try to get the drop on them. I promise we won't be a hindrance." He looked at his team. "Are we ready?"

There were a few nods and grunts of assent.

"Okay. Open the hatch."

Lafferty walked out onto the enclosed dock first, tall and dignified in one of Cole's old uniforms. He gruffly demanded that the press keep their distance, and then he had Luthor Chadwick, burner in hand, grab Cole's arm with his free hand and yank him forward until he was a few feet clear of the shuttle.

Suddenly there was an excited buzzing among the media.

"It's him! It's really him!"

"It's Wilson Cole!"

"It's Cole and that Molarian, Forrice!"

"It's really Wilson Cole! We finally caught the bastard!"

"Who's the giantess—the one with the red hair?"

A patrol of local gendarmes and a squad of Navy Special Police were waiting for them. The leader of the Navy group approached Lafferty and saluted.

"Captain Marchand?"

"That's right," said Lafferty, returning a lazy salute. "And I believe you know this gentleman?"

"I've been studying his poster for four years," replied the Navy man. "How did you finally capture him?"

"It's a long story," said Lafferty. "I'll be happy to tell it to you over a beer or two, but first I want to deliver Mr. Cole and his cohorts so I can collect my reward."

"That's *Captain* Cole," snapped Cole.

"You lost that title when you committed mutiny," said Lafferty harshly. "Now shut up and follow these men." He nodded to the Navy man, who turned and began leading them to another shuttle, one with the Secretary's seal on it.

The flight down to Deluros VIII was both fast and uneventful. Each of the six prisoners spent the ten minutes staring down the barrel of a burner or a screecher. Not a word was spoken, and as quickly as they landed they were ushered out.

Cole looked around. He was on a rooftop. He'd never been on the roof of this particular building before, but Deluros VIII was not unknown to him. It was a huge planet, far larger than Earth, but through some fluke of position and rotation, it possessed an almost identical gravity and atmosphere. It had enough room for endless expansion that Man had all but abandoned Earth and moved the seat of government here, to the larger and more convenient location. The planet was covered by a single city, which sprawled hundreds of miles in every direction, covering deserts, burrowing through mountain chains, submerging beneath the oceans, totally interconnected, a proper capital world for the galaxy's dominant race.

"Where are we?" asked Lafferty, who had never been on Deluros VIII before.

"We're on the roof of the Knight's Castle," answered the leader of the Navy squad.

Lafferty frowned. "I don't believe I've heard of it before."

"It's the media's name for the Secretary's Mansion," was the reply. "Follow me, please."

The man led them to a raised structure that had a large door in it. It sensed their approach and opened.

"Some security!" snorted Lafferty, trying to appear impatient and officious, and doing a reasonably good job of it.

"It read my retina, bone structure, and ID chip"—the Navy man placed a finger to the side of his neck, where a small scar indicated the chip was embedded—"or it wouldn't have opened."

Lafferty nodded sagely and tried not to look as silly as he felt.

"This way, sir."

The Navy man entered the enclosure and waited on a cushion of air until Lafferty, Cole, two of Lafferty's men, and four police officers were inside the structure. They then descended four levels, stepped off, and waited while the next batch of prisoners and guards were brought down. After the third trip they were all assembled once again, and the Navy man led them down the brilliantly lighted corridor, past a holo of Johnny Ramsey, who was universally considered to be the greatest of all the Republic's Secretaries, and finally came to a door that had four armed, uniformed Security men on each side of it.

"Secretary Wilkie's office," he announced.

"Just how big is the damned thing?" demanded Lafferty.

"Pretty big."

"That's no answer. These are dangerous men, even manacled as they are. I'm not going to have them cause any trouble in a crowd and then make a break for it—or, worse still, go for the Secretary."

"You can't enter alone, sir," said one of the Security men. "By your own admission, these are dangerous men, and there are only eight of you."

"We *caught* the bastard, which is something no one else in the damned Republic could do for four years," said Lafferty, feigning anger. "We can take care of him."

"It's against the Secretary's own rule for anyone to enter the office until some of us also enter."

"All right," said Lafferty, frowning as if considering his options. "Choose some of your men and we'll accept it." He turned to the Navy man. "You and your team got us here safely from the shuttle, but we *are* here now, and in these gentlemen's hands. Thank you for your service."

"Will you be coming back, sir?"

"Eventually. We left a skeleton crew on the *Theodore Roosevelt*, just to make sure it's still functioning. They're under guard, of course, and now that we're here we'll unload them and turn them over to whoever will be in charge of them." He paused and pugnaciously jutted his chin forward. "But not until we get our reward."

The Navy man saluted, turned, and motioned his men to return to the airlift.

"Let's get started," said Lafferty, heading to the door.

"One moment, sir," said a guard.

"What is it?" demanded Lafferty.

"Just a precaution, sir," said the guard, pulling out a personal scanner and running its beam over every inch of Cole's body from a distance of about five feet. "Last month we caught a man trying to come in here with a tiny explosive device inside a false molar. Others have hidden weapons and explosive in their shoes, in their clothes, even inside their bodies." He turned the scanner off. "You're clear," he said to Cole. "Commander Forrice next." Braxite stepped forward for examination.

It took another five minutes, but finally the man announced that all the prisoners were clean.

"All right, sir," he said, ordering the door to open, and a moment later Cole and his five associates were brought, manacled and at gunpoint, to the desk of the most powerful man in the Republic, quite possibly the most powerful man who had ever lived.

"Captain Cole," said Egan Wilkie, getting to his feet, "you have no idea how much I have longed for this moment, how I have planned for it and plotted for it and even prayed for it." He allowed himself the luxury of a triumphant smile. "You will be given a fair trial, you will be fairly judged, and"—the smile became broader—"you will be fairly executed."

"I don't think so," said Cole.

"I admire your audacity, Captain Cole," said Wilkie, "but your grasp on reality leaves a little something to be desired."

Cole nodded his head almost imperceptibly, and an instant later Lafferty's five men, Chadwick, and Gentry all had their weapons out and aimed at the guards.

"Is my grasp on reality getting any more secure?" asked Cole, tensing and breaking out of his manacles. The other five prisoners followed suit.

Cole turned to the guards. "Mr. Pampas here is going to disarm each of you in turn. If you offer no resistance, you won't be harmed. If you resist, or cause any problems before we leave, I have absolutely no compunction about ordering your deaths. Bull, collect their weapons, please."

Pampas went from one guard to another, disarming them. The very last one backed up a step and reached for his weapon. Val, who had posed as a member of Lafferty's team, drilled him squarely between the eyes with a beam of solid light, and he collapsed to the floor.

"He was warned," said Cole. "I want each of you to walk to the far end of the office. Gentry, did you bring that tape I asked for?"

She nodded and held up two rolls of tape.

"Mr. Pampas and Mr. Sokolov, take the tape from her, and bind each of our prisoners' hands and feet—you'll need knives or scissors to cut it; Gentry will supply them. And you might as well cover their mouths while you're at it." Sokolov seemed about to ask a question.

"It's all right, Mr. Sokolov," said Cole. "I know it's light in weight, but even Val couldn't break free of it."

Pampas and Sokolov went to work, while a couple of Lafferty's men pitched in and helped. The job was done in less than three minutes, and Cole turned his attention back to Wilkie.

"Are you all through with empty threats and false claims of victory, Secretary Wilkie?" he asked.

"What do you want?" growled Wilkie.

"I should have thought that would be obvious," said Cole. "I want amnesty for every man, woman, and alien serving under me, I want your pledge to keep the Navy out of the Inner Frontier, and"—he paused briefly—"as a public show of contrition for all the abuses of your administration, I want your resignation and that of your cabinet and advisors."

"Never!" said Egan. "I am the duly elected representative of the people!"

"I'm sure you are," said Cole. "I'm even sure it was an honest election. Well, as honest as elections get to be. But that in no way alters the fact that you are a disgrace to your office, and your continued presence in it is no longer tolerable."

"Says the mutineer!" said Wilkie contemptuously.

"Did Susan Garcia ever explain the conditions surrounding my act of mutiny?" asked Cole.

"No. Why should she?"

"No reason that I can think of," said Cole. He shrugged. "It's ancient history anyway. We're not here to rehash it, but to make some new history. I want you to summon your top three advisors. There's no sense having you resign if your successor is just going to carry out the same policies. We'll want a mass resignation."

"You go to hell!" said Wilkie.

"I don't think you understand your position, Mr. Wilkie—or ours, for that matter. If we walk out any of these doors while your government is in place, the very best we can hope for is a quick and painless death. Therefore, we're not going to do that."

"Do your worst!" snapped Wilkie. "I'm not resigning!"

"I want you to consider what our worst entails, Mr. Wilkie," said Cole. "You already know that we can't leave this office while you remain the Secretary of the Republic. The choice is yours: you can resign, or you can be removed in a more permanent way."

Wilkie glared at him and made no reply.

"I'm going to ask you again: will you tell your top three advisors to report here?"

"I will not."

"I think you've made a very unwise decision," said Cole.

"I can live with it."

"For about thirty more seconds," said Cole. "Val, will you come over here, please?"

The Valkyrie walked over until she was standing at Cole's side.

"The reason I asked for you rather than one of the others is because Mr. Wilkie has seen that your burner works. I wouldn't want him to make a foolish decision on the assumption that this was a ruse. Please point your burner at him."

Val raised her weapon and aimed it at Wilkie.

"I want you to count to ten," said Cole. "If he hasn't agreed to summon his assistants by then, fire the weapon."

Val began counting. On "six" Wilkie seemed to slump into himself.

"All right," he said.

"Damn!" muttered Val.

"Keep it trained on him," said Cole. "If the first three people to show up aren't his advisors, use it." He turned to Wilkie. "All right, Mr. Wilkie. A galaxy is waiting."

Wilkie touched three spots on his desk. "I need the three of you," he said. "Right now!"

"Colonel Blacksmith?" said Cole.

"Yes?" said Sharon.

"You're the security expert. Did that seem legitimate to you? No hidden signals, no codes?"

"It looked normal."

"Mr. Wilkie, what door will they come through?"

"Two will use the door you entered through," said Wilkie. "The third will use that one," he continued, pointing to a different door.

"I hope you're right," said Cole.

All three advisors arrived within two minutes. Cole had them stand behind Wilkie's desk, where Val and the others could watch the four of them, and then explained the situation.

"If you resign willingly, we have no further business with you," Cole concluded. "There will be no trial, no jail time, nothing but a complete retirement from public life."

"And just who do you think will replace us?" demanded one of them. "Yourself?"

"No," said Cole.

"So you'll hold an election?" continued the man. "Well, we *won* the damned election! You don't like our policies? I'm sorry about that, but you can't be so dumb as to think every policy in the Republic gets made in this room! Good God, man—we're governing sixty thousand worlds and fighting four wars!"

"Four?" said Sharon, surprised.

"You think the Teroni Federation is the only power that's opposed to the Republic? Where the hell have you been?"

"Where you couldn't reach us," said Cole.

"So you've taken it upon yourself to get rid of Secretary Wilkie and us," said the man. "What about his other advisors? One of them might have given the particular advice you object to. You'd better get rid of them all. Same with his cabinet. And of course you'll have to dissolve parliament. They might pass a bill you don't like."

"Who *is* this man?" demanded Val angrily.

"I'm Aloysius Chang, and I'm sorry if you don't like what I'm saying, but the truth is often uncomfortable." He turned to Cole. "You want to depose Secretary Wilkie? Maybe kill him? And you think that will change everything?" His face contorted in a sneer. "It'll change *nothing!* It'll just be a case of the king is dead, long live the king. You don't change something like the Republic by getting rid of one man— or four, as the case may be."

"You're right," agreed Cole.

"Well, then?"

"We have to start somewhere," said Cole, "and it makes more sense to start at the top than at the bottom."

"Do you think you'll live to see any noticeable change?" asked Chang.

"I'm the most wanted man in the Republic, standing here in the Secretary's office on Deluros VIII. I may not live out the afternoon."

Chang smiled. "Well, you're honest anyway, Captain Cole," he said. "But you're not realistic. The Republic is too damned big and far-flung for any change to have a major effect in one mere lifetime."

"You make a lot more sense than Wilkie does," said Cole. "Why aren't *you* the Secretary?"

"Come back in five years," said Chang with a smile.

"I think not," said Cole.

"Then leave now. I'll guarantee you safe passage out of the Republic."

"The hell you will!" snarled Wilkie.

"Shut up, Egan," said Chang, "and maybe I can save your ass." He turned back to Cole. "What do you say, Captain Cole?"

"You can do that?" asked Cole.

"In the Secretary's name, yes," said Chang. "Take my offer, Captain. You can't beat the odds."

"You had the Navy hunting us for four years and we beat those odds," said Cole. "Mr. Wilkie is in the best-protected office on the best-protected planet in the galaxy, and we beat those odds, too. Now you tell me it's a million-to-one against our effecting a change. Maybe you're right, but we're going to have to find out for ourselves."

"I bear you no ill will, Captain Cole," said Chang. "In fact, you are precisely the kind of man who explored the stars and created the Republic in the first place. But you are making a serious mistake, and I will do everything in my power to stop you."

"Well, *I* bear him plenty of ill will," said Wilkie, "and if we survive this episode, I plan to prove it."

Cole glanced at Wilkie, then leaned over and said, making no effort to hide the contempt in his voice, "How do you stand it?"

"If I wasn't here, things would be much worse," answered Chang just as softly.

"Wilson?" said Sharon suddenly.

"Yes?" said Cole. "What is it?"

"Wilkie has glanced very furtively at his watch two or three times in the last couple of minutes."

"Well, Mr. Wilkie?" said Cole. "Who are you expecting, and when?"

"No one," said Wilkie.

"Oh, for God's sake, Egan, don't be an ass!" snapped Chang. He turned to Cole. "We're due to have a meeting with the leaders of the parliament in about ten minutes."

"Here in this office?" asked Cole.

"Yes."

"You fucking traitor!" yelled Wilkie.

"Use your brain, Egan!" snapped Chang. "They've got eight men and women with their weapons out, and they're in enemy territory. If they don't know who's coming, they'll kill anyone who walks in through that door."

"How many are we expecting?" asked Cole.

"Six," replied Chang. "There's time to cancel it. I won't tell them you're here."

"No, let them come," said Cole. "We might as well have some un-impeachable witnesses to Wilkie's resignation."

"They'll claim it was at gunpoint and isn't valid."

"I think the leader of the opposition will take a different view of it," said Cole.

Chang shrugged, then checked his own timepiece. "We'll know soon enough."

Suddenly the building seemed to shake.

Cole frowned. "A quake?"

"We've never had one before," said Chang.

There was a massive explosion a mile to the north, the building shook again, and the air outside the window turned black with smoke.

"That's no quake!" exclaimed Val. "That was a bomb!"

"Planted?" asked Sokolov.

"Hell, no!" she said as five more explosions followed in rapid order. "Somebody got through the planet's defenses!"

Cole walked over to the window and looked out.

"A *lot* of somebodies," he said, as the massive court building across the plaza took a direct hit and collapsed in a pile of rubble.

"This has got to be their number one target," said Val. "We're sitting ducks here. We'd better try to get back to the ship."

"Forget it," said Cole.

"We can't just stay here!" said Lafferty nervously.

"Try to remember where you are," said Cole as another explosion rocked the building. "This office is the only place on the whole damned planet where you won't be shot on sight."

"I've got to contact the Navy and find out what's going on!" said Wilkie. "The Teronis weren't supposed to be within thirty thousand light-years!" He reached for a panel on his desk.

Cole grabbed his hand. "I don't trust you, Mr. Wilkie."

"Damn it, I have to know what's happening!" said Wilkie as a nearby explosion shook the building again.

"Mr. Chang, you contact whoever you need," said Cole.

Chang walked swiftly behind the desk and began touching various hot spots, asking terse questions, getting disjointed answers. After a moment he looked up, a puzzled frown on his face. "It's not the Teronis," he said.

"Who *is* it?" asked Wilkie.

"We don't know. But they're here in numbers, and they have formidable weaponry."

"Why didn't we have any warning?" demanded Wilkie.

"I don't know, Egan," replied Chang. "This is the first minute of a surprise attack. We're not going to get all the answers immediately."

A corner of the parliament building crumbled.

"You may not live long enough to get any answers at all," said Cole, looking out the window.

"How bad is it?" asked Val.

"The sky is black with ships, and they sure as hell don't look like the Navy's."

A light flashed on the desk.

"What's that?" asked Cole sharply.

"The parliamentary leaders," said Chang.

"Mr. Chang, go to the door and let them in one at a time. No Security personnel can enter. Val, if Mr. Wilkie tries to summon help from the corridor or anywhere else, kill him."

"I could kill him right now and save a lot of bother," she said.

"Just do what I say. Bull, you and Vladimir stand guard by the door. I think Mr. Chang is a reasonable man, but I won't bet your lives on it. If any Security personnel, or anyone besides the people we're waiting for, try to enter, or take a shot from outside the office, kill them."

Pampas and Sokolov accompanied Chang to the door. It split open, he quickly ushered in seven men and women, and it snapped shut again.

"Do we know who's attacking us?" asked one of the women.

"No," said Chang.

She suddenly noticed Cole and his team, and the bound Security men.

"What's going on here, Aloysius?"

"I'll explain it later," said Chang. "Right now we and Captain Cole seem to have an enforced truce while we're dealing with the greater danger."

As he spoke a bomb left a huge hole in the adjacent street, and the weapon-proof glass in the windows shattered.

"Captain," said Chang, "you've got a ship up there. Two ships, in fact. Can either of them give us a clearer picture of what's happening?"

"I'll have to see if either of them still exist," said Cole, pulling out a communicator. He decided to send it coded and scrambled, on the assumption that if Deluros survived the attack, he still had a planetful of enemies.

"Are you all right, sir?" said Christine's voice. Her image appeared and surveyed the room. "Who *are* all these people?"

"Forget that," said Cole tersely. "What's going on up there?"

"A fleet of maybe a thousand ships just appeared out of nowhere, sir," she said. "It looks like they're doing heavy damage to the planet."

"They're not bothering you or the *Sabine Nova*?"

"Not so far. Most of the Navy has flown to meet them. I don't think they're concerned with a pair of ships that are docked in orbit."

"*Stay* docked," ordered Cole. "This isn't our battle."

"Yes, sir."

"If I don't check in every hour, assume we're dead. Make one final attempt to contact me, Val, or Lafferty, and if you can't, then get the hell away from Deluros whenever you think the coast is clear."

"I won't leave you, sir."

"If I'm dead, I won't mind," said Cole. "Just follow my orders, damn it!"

"Yes, sir," she said miserably, and broke the connection.

"You're wrong, Captain," said Chang.

"It wouldn't be the first time," said Cole. "What do *you* think I'm wrong about?"

"You're a Man. This *is* your battle."

"We know who our enemies are, Mr. Chang," said Cole. "These guys don't even know we're here. If they kill us, it'll be by accident."

"You'll be just as dead."

"Spare me your moralizing. If they leave this whole planet in ruins, all that means is that the Republic can set up shop somewhere else and make a fresh start."

The light on the desk began flashing, and this time Wilkie responded to it, while Val kept her burner trained on him. He spoke in short sentences and low tones, and finally looked up. "The *Xerxes* has been destroyed," he announced.

"Wasn't that Susan Garcia's flagship?" asked Lafferty.

"It was the *Republic's* flagship," said Wilkie. "Susan Garcia is no longer aboard it." He frowned. "Fleet Admiral Bolinski was aboard it. His second and third in command were also killed."

"So who's in charge?" asked one of the politicos.

Wilkie shrugged. "The *Xerxes* was supposed to be impregnable. Most of our senior command was aboard it."

"So no one's directing our response?" asked another.

"*Someone* must be trying, but there's no reason for the others to accept his or her authority. They're probably all acting on their own now."

"So much for the greatest Navy ever assembled," snorted Val contemptuously.

Wilkie seemed shell-shocked. He moved his hands in meaningless frantic gestures. "This wasn't supposed to happen," he said at last.

"Yeah, I'll bet that's what every beaten general says," she replied.

"I think, Egan," said another woman, "that you had better call Admiral Garcia back."

"Don't be foolish, Anya," said Chang. "She's half a galaxy away, and besides, her ship has just been demolished."

"It's not *her* ship," said Wilkie petulantly as the remainder of the parliament building collapsed.

"It's not anyone's ship, not anymore," said Chang.

"Are you blaming *me* for that?" demanded Wilkie. "Do you think Susan could have defended it any better than Bolinski?"

"We'll never know now," said an advisor.

The light flashed again, and this time it was Chang who began whispering with the voices at the other end of the transmission. Finally he looked up. "We're in *big* trouble."

"You're just figuring that out?" said Val.

"There's no central authority. The Navy's like a snake without a head. It's thrashing about with no direction."

Wilkie glared at Cole. "This is *your* fault!"

"*I'm* not bombing your damned planet," said Cole.

"But if it wasn't for you, half the ships we had in reserve against the Teronis wouldn't be crisscrossing the galaxy looking for the *Theodore Roosevelt*, and I wouldn't have had to fire Susan Garcia." A tear, whether of regret or frustration or terror, rolled down his cheek. "She was the greatest military mind of her era."

Another bomb hit nearby, and the building literally swayed.

"I have an idea," said Chang. He looked at Cole. "I need to pull a more powerful communication device out of his desk drawer. May I?"

Cole signaled Val to walk around to the side of the desk where she could see exactly what Chang was doing. "Go ahead," he said.

"Thank you," said Chang, opening a drawer, pulling out a complex communicator, and putting it on the desk. He programmed in a complex code, and a moment later Susan Garcia's face—gaunter than Cole remembered it, but every bit as arrogant—appeared.

"Why are you disturbing me?" she said coldly.

"Deluros is under attack by an unknown foe," said Chang.

"Not the Teronis?" she asked as another bomb shook the building. "No."

She smiled. "You do seem to have your work cut out for you."

"The *Xerxes* has been destroyed," said Chang.

"That's a shame," she said. "That ship was my home for eleven years."

"Admiral Bolinski has been killed. So have Admirals Palatine, Burstein, and Ngima."

"I'm very sorry to hear it," said Susan Garcia. "They were all good friends. But I don't know what you expect *me* to do about it."

"You know damned well what we want!" said Chang.

She uttered a cold laugh. "I admire your audacity, Aloysius. Was this *his* idea?"

"It was mine."

"You can guess my answer."

"You didn't hear my offer yet."

"Oh?" she said. "You mean there's more than simply the chance to die in glorious battle for the government that publicly humiliated me?"

"A lifetime appointment as Fleet Admiral, which can't be rescinded," said Chang.

"I thought I had that," said Susan Garcia. "What Wilkie gives, Wilkie can take away. You know the old saying, Aloysius: fool me once, shame on you. Fool me twice, shame on me."

"What if Wilkie resigns his office conditionally upon your accepting our offer?" said Chang.

"*What?*" bellowed Wilkie.

Chang turned to him. "Your office won't be worth two credits if we can't repel this invasion."

"Never!" said Wilkie.

"It's all right, Aloysius," said Susan Garcia. "I wouldn't have accepted anyway." Her image looked directly at Wilkie. "I hope you don't die instantly, Egan." She reached a hand out and broke the connection.

"Nice try," said Cole.

"I can't say that I blame her," replied Chang.

Another explosion, and two nearby buildings burst into flame.

"No vaporizer," noted Val. "Just thumpers. Level 3 or 4, or we'd just be a hole in the ground."

"It's not a suicide attack," said Cole. "I haven't seen any ships plunge down."

"You say that as if it means something," said the woman named Anya.

"It means they didn't come here to die," said Cole. "And that means they probably can't conceive of anyone having a more powerful pulse cannon than their own. If they could defend against a Level 5 cannon, they could create one, and clearly they haven't."

"You sound like you know what you're talking about," said Anya.

"He served in your Navy with distinction for almost twenty years," said Sharon proudly.

Chang stared at Cole for almost a full minute, studying him.

"Don't look at me like that," said Cole. "I have even less reason to love your Navy than Susan Garcia has."

Chang continued to stare at him.

"I came here to overthrow your government," continued Cole. "Now someone's doing it for us. I have no serious problem with that."

"Do you have a problem with eleven billion innocent men and women dying?" asked Chang.

"Innocent of what?" said Val sarcastically. "They all work for the Republic."

"Can you let them all die?" persisted Chang.

This time it was Cole's turn to stare. Finally he said, "If I agree to what you want, I'll ask a lot more than Susan Garcia did."

Chang looked out the window at his city in flames, then turned back to Cole. "List your demands."

"First, amnesty for every man, woman, and alien under my command," said Cole.

"Agreed."

"Second, complete control of the Navy for the duration of the battle. I don't want any freelancers, and I don't want anyone questioning my authority."

"Done—at least to the best of our ability."

"Third, a Security patrol to escort us to the shuttle that will take us up to the *Theodore Roosevelt*. I suspect that most of the people in this building are sure we're responsible for what's happening."

"All right," agreed Chang.

"Fourth, I want the entire government to resign. Not just Wilkie, but all his advisors including yourself, as well as his cabinet and the parliament."

"*Never!*" shouted Wilkie.

"Shut up, Egan," said Chang. He turned to the politicians. "Will you consent to Captain Cole's demand?"

Another explosion, and the ceiling began caving in.

"Have we got a choice?" said Anya grimly, and the others nodded their consent.

"Yes, we do," said Chang. "But it's not a very palatable one."

"The rest of you can do what you want," said Wilkie doggedly. "I'm not resigning."

Chang turned to another advisor. "Mr. Berkmeyer, write up a brief statement of resignation and have everyone in the room sign it."

"I'm not signing anything!" said Wilkie.

"Captain Cole, you have my word that your conditions will be met," said Chang. "I think you'd better make your way back to your ships while you still have ships to return to."

"What about *him?*" said Cole, indicating Wilkie.

"He'll sign it."

"And if he doesn't?"

"We are on the thirty-seventh floor. If I have to throw him out the window, I will."

"You're out of shape," said Val. "I'd be happy to do it for you."

The ceiling crumbled a bit more.

"I'm going to trust you, Mr. Chang," said Cole. "Get us a Security squad to escort us to the shuttle, have a pilot waiting, and get the word to the fleet before we reach our ships."

"I will."

Cole waited until Chang informed him that the squad was outside the door, and then he and his crew left the office. There wasn't much visible damage in the corridor, but when they took the airlift to the roof the damage was extensive. The shuttle that had brought them down from the docking station was a twisted piece of metal, buried in the rubble of a collapsed air vent.

"We're not going anywhere in that thing," said Val as the Security squad withdrew, their job done.

They stood there for a moment, then realized that their position was totally exposed to enemy fire, and began returning to the airlift when a shuttle rose up above the edge of the roof. A panel opened and the pilot gestured for them to approach.

"I can't land," he said. "The roof won't hold the weight. Just come to the edge and you should be able to get in."

When they were all aboard, the shuttle took off to the east, and only after it had gone a quick fifty miles did it begin climbing.

"The whole planet's one enormous city," said the pilot. "If they're bombing the court and the parliament, they're familiar with the design of the city, so it made sense to get out of the line of fire. I'll signal ahead and find out which docking station you're at. They try to make them orbit at the exact speed of the planet, so it's always the shortest route down to your destination and back up, but they haven't got it perfected yet."

They reached the required altitude, and the pilot frowned. "Half of the docking stations have been blown to hell and gone." Another few seconds passed. "If yours is still there, it's not answering."

Cole pulled out his own communicator. "Christine, are you there?"

"Yes, sir," she said. "But the *Sabine Nova* was hit. We managed to transfer the crew to the *Teddy R*, but I don't think you can get the *Nova* running again."

"That's okay. We'll be there in a couple of minutes. Have someone standing by to open the shuttle bay."

"Yes, sir."

Cole turned to the pilot. "You know which station we want?"

"Yeah, I've got it programmed here," he said, patting his control panel.

"Then let's go."

As the shuttle jumped ahead Cole turned to his crew and Lafferty's men.

"I assume you all heard that?" he said.

A general nodding of heads.

"It means that a century-old ship that should have been decommissioned eighty years ago is about to become the flagship of what's left of the Republic's Navy," he continued. "The very same Republic that we came here to destroy." An ironic smile crossed his face. "As I remarked once or twice to the late Commander Forrice, we seem to live in interesting times."

They made it safely to the *Teddy R*. The shuttle elected to stay docked in orbit, on the reasonable assumption that *any* location was safer than the surface of Deluros VIII.

"Where's Jacovic?" asked Cole as he walked onto the bridge.

"His shift finished a few hours ago," answered Christine.

"Get him up here. He's had more experience at this kind of thing than any of us. I'm going to want his expertise."

"Yes, sir."

"Val, take a nap."

"The hell I will," she said. "If we're going to get blown apart, I want to see who did it so I can hunt them down in hell."

"Your logic is impeccable," said Cole, "but there's every chance we *won't* get blown apart in the next eight or ten hours, and I want you fresh and alert when Jacovic starts fading."

"Well, I'll grab a beer and a sandwich," she said, heading off to the airlift. "But I'm not sleepy."

"Christine, as difficult as this will be for you to believe, the *Teddy R* is now the flagship of the Republic's Navy. I don't have codes, IDs, or even positions for any of the ships, so you're just going to have to broadcast whatever orders we have for them and hope the attackers don't speak Terran."

"I speak English, sir," said Rachel, who was at one of the stations.

"And I speak Swahili," added Christine.

"There *might* be a few people on the receiving end who speak one or the other, but we can't count on it." He lowered his head in thought for a moment. "Contact Aloysius Chang—he'll be in the Secretary's office—and tell him we really need the codes, IDs, everything. We have to have some safe channels."

"Will he respond, sir?" she said. "I mean, we came here to depose his superior."

"He's a sensible man," said Cole. "He'll respond—and Egan Wilkie isn't superior to anyone."

"I'll get right on it, sir."

Cole walked over to Jacovic. "You've been watching the ships?"

"Yes," said the Teroni.

"Ever see anything like them?"

Jacovic shook his head. "They're very similar in outline to the Molarian Class XB," he replied. "But that may not mean anything."

"They didn't fire any Level 5 thumpers or burners, at least that I could tell from my vantage point," said Cole. "Is it possible they're holding back?"

"I don't think so," said Jacovic. "This is a surprise attack, and it caught Deluros off guard. But the Republic *does* have more than three million ships. Probably ninety-five percent of them are engaged against the Federation and can't be relocated, but that still leaves well over one hundred and fifty thousand ships that the attackers can't account for. You and I know that most of them are patrolling their own sectors, and probably a few thousand are in the Inner and Outer Frontiers, but *they* don't know that. It makes sense that they'd hit Deluros with everything they have and then leave before reinforcements arrive. Clearly this isn't a war of conquest, not with only a thousand ships."

"So we shouldn't wait for reinforcements," said Cole. "They figure to do their damage and run."

"That would be my conclusion, yes, sir," said Jacovic.

"Rachel, capture an image of one or two of those ships, and see if the computer can identify them," said Cole.

"I've been trying, sir," she replied. "That was the first thing I thought of when they flew by and started attacking. But so far I haven't had any luck."

"Okay, don't bother anymore," said Cole. "If the computer can't find them in its data banks in a minute or two, they're not there." He turned back to Jacovic. "If all they've got are Level 3s, we ought to be able to move with impunity. If they have Level 4s, how many hits do you think we can take? Twenty? Thirty?"

"I believe we'll have to check with Mr. Odom, sir," said the Teroni.

"Do that, please," said Cole. "Where's Mr. Briggs?"

"I think he's sleeping, sir," said Rachel.

"Wake him up. I need him here."

"Yes, sir."

Cole walked over to the main viewscreen and watched it, hands on hips. There were perhaps two hundred enemy ships, swarming like bees, over the section of Deluros VIII he'd just left. He couldn't spot a single Navy ship.

"Sir," said Jacovic, walking up to him, "Mr. Odom says it will depend on the proximity of the other ships, and the angle of attack, but our defenses can take a minimum of twenty Level 4 pulse strikes before any portion of the *Teddy R* loses its structural integrity."

"How about Level 4 burners?"

"Unless the pulse attacks weaken the shields and screens, we should be practically immune to Level 4 laser cannons."

Cole grimaced. "I distrust that word 'practically.'"

Jacovic looked at the viewscreen. "We could safely withdraw from this position now, sir. Have you any instructions for Wxakgini?"

Cole shook his head. "Where would we go? We're probably safer here than as a moving target. We need to devise some sort of strategy before we show ourselves."

"As you wish, sir."

"I don't suppose you ever found yourself in an analogous situation?"

"One ship, momentarily safe, surrounded by perhaps a thousand enemy ships?" said Jacovic. "No, never."

"Somehow I'm not surprised," said Cole.

Malcolm Briggs came onto the bridge, rubbing his eyes. "Welcome back, sir. I'm glad to see you're all unharmed."

"I'm sorry to wake you, Mr. Briggs," said Cole, "but we need your expertise."

"What would you like me to do, sir?"

Cole looked around the bridge. "Christine and Rachel are at the main computer stations. Take the small one in the corner, or go down to my office and use mine."

"And do what, sir?" persisted Briggs.

"You and Christine are my two best computer operators, and I'm going to keep her busy for the next few hours. I want you to try to capture any enemy messages—they're acting in concert, so they must be communicating with each other—and see if the computer can make any sense out of them. If not, tell Mr. Aloysius Chang that you're acting on my behalf—Christine will give you the contact information—and get permission to tie in to the Master Computer down on Deluros. Maybe *it* can translate them if our own computer can't."

"Yes, sir," said Briggs. "If you don't mind, I'll use your office. There will be fewer distractions."

"Fine," said Cole.

"Ground crews are firing up at the ships, sir," noted Jacovic when Briggs had left, "but they're too far away. They've only made two hits in the last few minutes." He paused. "On the other hand, the ships have moved their center of operations some four hundred miles to the west."

"Rachel?" said Cole.

"Sir?"

"This is clearly not a war of conquest. It's more like the kind of punishment party the Navy sent up to Singapore Station, maybe a little larger but the same principle. Have the computer scan all the news reports for the past five years—and not just the local ones. Let's see if it can figure out who would be mad enough to try to destroy Deluros VIII."

"And who has the technology to avoid detection," added Jacovic. "After all, they just suddenly appeared. As far as I know, no one reported seeing them approach, and no one tried to stop them."

Cole frowned. "You have a point. We've been so busy ducking we forgot to ask the operative question: how the hell did they get here?"

"They had to use a wormhole, sir," said Jacovic. "It's the only way they could get this far undetected."

"Pilot," said Cole, "is there any wormhole that would let a ship out within the Deluros system?"

"Infrequently," answered Wxakgini.

Cole frowned. "What do you mean: infrequently?"

"The Stutz Wormhole is extremely unstable. It occasionally exists in the Deluros system, between Deluros II and III."

Cole and Jacovic exchanged looks. "That explains it," said the Teroni. "All of the Navy's defenses were geared to stopping an invasion from outside the system, not from within."

"Just a minute," said Cole. "If Pilot knows it, and damned near every ship in the Navy has a member of his race on it, why didn't they all know it?"

"I told you," said Wxakgini. "The Stutz Wormhole is unstable."

"How often does it exist inside the Deluros system?"

"It exists for an average of thirty hours once every seventeen years," answered Wxakgini. "This time frame is only an estimate. The interval has been as short as fourteen years and as long as thirty-four."

"That's your answer," said Jacovic. "You don't build your defenses around a weakness that occurs one day every seventeen years."

"That's a long time to hold a grudge," remarked Cole.

"How long have you held yours?" asked Wxakgini.

"Not quite that long," said Cole. "But I'm young yet. Relatively speaking."

"How much longer will the Wormhole remain here?" asked Jacovic.

"Twenty-seven hours, eleven minutes, and sixteen seconds," answered Wxakgini.

"Where does the other end let out?"

"I don't know," said the pilot. "It has never been charted. Well, not by any member of the Republic, which is where the navigational computer draws its information."

"Wonderful," muttered Cole.

"Sir?" said Christine.

"Yes?"

"I have most of the codes and contact information you requested, sir."

"Good. Send a message to our ships right now. Tell them if they're within twenty-five hours of the Deluros system to get here as fast as they can. Tell them that they'll be taking their orders from the *Teddy R*, and if they have any problems with that, to check with the Secretary's office."

"Right away, sir."

"Summoning all those ships isn't going to help much," Cole confided to Jacovic. "The enemy will deliver its ordnance and get the hell out of here. They're not going to stick around till the last minute."

"I know."

"Can you mine a wormhole, I wonder?"

Jacovic shook his head. "I wouldn't think so, sir. Normal time and space don't exist in wormholes. I wouldn't think explosives do, either."

"Ships work in them."

"Ships cannot accelerate in a wormhole," replied Jacovic. "The momentum is supplied by the wormhole, not the ship." He paused thoughtfully. "It's entirely possible that a ship does not produce oxygen or water for the crew in a wormhole, but we traverse them so quickly we don't notice because we're not inside them long enough to run out."

"I know," said Cole. "I'm just grasping at straws."

"I beg your pardon, sir?"

"I'm hoping for a solution, other than the obvious one."

"The obvious one, sir?"

Cole nodded. "If we can't find out where they're from in the next hour or so, we're going to have to enter the hole before it moves. And if *we* know that the hole leads to their home system, or at least near it, they know it too."

Jacovic nodded his agreement. "And if they have this many ships here, on a surprise mission, how many ships will they have protecting their home when they know the Navy will be able to find it by traversing the wormhole?"

Cole went down to his office, where Briggs was working at the computer.

"Any luck?"

"I've captured a few messages," said Briggs. "The problem is that they're not anything the computer recognizes."

"Even the Master Computer on Deluros VIII?" said Cole, frowning. "That doesn't make any sense. These people didn't choose Deluros out of a hat. They clearly have a grudge against the Republic. That means at some time in the past they *must* have spoken to them."

"The Master Computer is down, sir," said Briggs. "I don't know if it's been destroyed, or has merely lost its power source—something that big and that powerful must take a lot of power. But whatever the reason, I can't access it."

"These messages," continued Cole. "Audio or transmitted in code?"

"Code, sir."

"Then keep working on it. The ship's computer may not be able to translate growls and snorts and clicks, but if we feed it enough written or coded transmissions, sooner or later it'll start to make sense of them."

Cole left the office and wandered to the mess hall, where he sat as his usual table and ordered a coffee. Sharon appeared in the doorway a moment later.

"Want a little company?" she asked.

"Sure."

"You look troubled," she said. "Or at least preoccupied."

"I'm missing something," he said, "and I haven't been able to put my finger on what it is."

"I'm sure you'll think of it before the Navy ships start arriving—and you really can't do anything until then."

"I think that's what's bothering me," he said. "We won't be at anything near full strength for almost a Standard day, and I think the enemy will be long gone by then. Hell, the first of our ships will be arriving in an hour; I don't even know if the enemy will stick around that long."

"I don't know what you can do about it," insisted Sharon. "There are hundreds of them, possibly a few thousand. You can't do battle against them alone."

"I know."

"So we just sit it out until our ships start arriving," she concluded.

He shook his head. "Not good enough."

"Wilson," she said, "the *Teddy R* can't stand against a fleet of these ships, even if they don't have Level 5 weapons."

"We can't just stay here doing nothing," replied Cole.

"This isn't like you," she said. "I've never known you to take foolish risks before."

"If I look troubled, it's because I'm about to take the most foolish risk of all."

"Why don't I like the sound of that?" she said with a failed attempt at flippancy.

"Because *I* don't like the sound of it," said Cole. "But I don't see any alternative." He frowned. "No, we have to do it." He got up from the table. "And the sooner the better."

He walked briskly to the airlift, and a moment later was back on the bridge.

"Pilot," he said as he approached Wxakgini, "take us into the Stutz Wormhole."

"Are you sure?" asked Jacovic. "We don't know what's waiting for us at the other end."

Cole looked at Wxakgini. "Do we?"

"No," confirmed the pilot. "As I said, it's never been mapped by the Republic."

Cole frowned. "If it was just the *Teddy R* I'd wait," he told Jacovic, "but it's not. We're the flagship now. I can't ask a few thousand Navy ships to go through that hole if the enemy's ships have all returned and I don't even know who or where the enemy is. We've got to find what's at the other end of that wormhole." He turned to Christine. "Send a coded message to our ships, that if we're not here when they arrive we haven't deserted them, that we're scouting the enemy and will be back shortly."

"Yes, sir."

"Okay, Pilot—let's go."

The *Teddy R* burst out of cover and began racing for the wormhole. A few ships spotted it and took up pursuit.

"Who's in Gunnery?" asked Cole.

"Mr. Pampas and Mr. Braxite, sir," said Christine. "And I believe one of Mr. Lafferty's men, who has weaponry experience, is with them."

"Put me through to them."

"Done."

"Bull, this is Cole. We're being pursued by a half dozen enemy ships. They have nothing but Level 3 and 4 weaponry, and probably can't do us much harm. Take them out before we pass Deluros V."

"Yes, sir."

"Pilot, what's the transit time within the wormhole?"

"I don't know exactly where the hole leads," answered Wxakgini. "A guess would be twenty-five to thirty-five minutes."

"Damn!" muttered Cole.

"What it is, sir?" asked Jacovic.

"I wanted to get in and out fast," said Cole. "Identify the location and the alien culture, see how they've positioned their ships, and get the hell out of there."

"There's no reason why we can't do that, sir," said Jacovic.

"I'm not so sure," said Cole. "After we've done a quick survey, we want to come back here so we can inform our ships what's waiting for them, what to look out for." He grimaced. "But if we're coming back in, say, an hour, we could run right into the enemy in the wormhole." He turned to Wxakgini. "I don't suppose we can fire a weapon inside the hole?"

"You can," replied the pilot. "But you would probably outrun it and end up killing yourself. Or it might not fire at all; remember, the laws of time and space do not necessarily apply to the interiors of wormholes."

"You want to expand upon 'not necessarily'?"

"They *may* apply," said Wxakgini. "Or they may selectively apply."

"You are not the most helpful guy I ever met," said Cole.

"Being helpful is not my function," replied Wxakgini. "I pilot the ship. ETA for the Stutz Wormhole is ninety-three seconds."

"Got the last of them!" cried Pampas's triumphant voice. "Take a look!" An image of a blazing fireball appeared, then vanished as the fire sputtered out and the debris scattered through space.

Cole stared at the viewscreen. He'd spent his entire adult life in space, and he still couldn't get used to the fact that even though he knew a wormhole was dead ahead he couldn't see it. In fact, he could see right through it, see all the stars behind it, could see no hint of an entrance, no warping of space.

"Here it comes," said Rachel.

"You actually see it?" asked Cole.

"No, sir," she replied. "I was checking my watch."

There was a sudden shudder, and then the *Teddy R* was inside the wormhole. And, as always, the viewscreens ceased to work.

"All right," said Cole. "When we emerge, Bull and Braxite will man the weapons from Gunnery, and Jacovic will work the auxiliary weaponry, if needed, from the bridge. Christine, I want you and Rachel to have your computers pinpoint our position, because if this war lasts more than thirty hours after we launch our invasion, we need to know where we are and how to get home—and I also want you to capture any images that we can transmit to the rest of our ships. If the enemy's home planet isn't obvious, then you're going to have to run an analysis on every planet within five light-years, as well as determining their position." He paused. "Correction: make that oxygen worlds only."

"Are you sure, sir?" said Rachel. "I mean, there *are* chlorine breathers."

"I know," said Cole. "But when you hit them, they don't burst into flames the way the ones Bull and Braxite hit did. You need oxygen for that." He paused. "I don't know if they'll have any ships guarding the other end of the wormhole, but it would be foolish to assume they won't, so I want a couple of you without express duties to perform at that time to get down to Gunnery and see if there's any way you can assist Bull and Braxite. That includes your people too, Mr. Lafferty. There are more than two stations down there—but under no circumstance do we fire unless we're fired upon. If we can just sneak in and sneak out unseen, maybe they won't have a welcoming committee when we return here with our Navy. Christine, put me through to Briggs."

"Yes, sir."

"Mr. Briggs," said Cole. "Any luck yet?"

"Not much, sir," answered Briggs. "The computer says it's a logical language, but it knows none of the reference points, so it may take as much as two days to translate it."

"That's not going to be much help," said Cole. "Can you just order the computer to keep working, or do you have to be there?"

"I can program it, sir."

"Good. Then do so, and come back up to the bridge. I'm going to put you at that small computer station you hate. I need all the data we can gather when we emerge from the hole. You, Christine, and Rachel can divide it up any way you want, but I want the area blanketed."

"Yes, sir."

"Once you're done, I promise you can go back to sleep until we're ready to invade them," added Cole.

"I'm wide awake now, sir," said Briggs. "I'll be on the bridge shortly."

Cole turned to Jacovic. "Am I forgetting anything?"

"Not that I'm aware of, sir."

"Okay," said Cole. "We've got about twenty minutes to go. Take over while I finish what's left of my coffee."

He went back down to the mess hall. Sharon was still sitting at the same table.

"I thought you'd be back," she said. "I know how you dislike the bridge."

"It brings up images of heroic captains standing by the wheel, sword in hand, the salt spray in their faces. That's not me."

"It's closer to you than you think."

He made a face. "Any order I can give on the bridge I can give from right here."

"I take it we have absolutely no idea who or what we're up against?" she asked.

"Not yet."

"Let me ask you a question, Wilson," said Sharon.

"Go ahead," replied Cole.

"Has it occurred to you that we should be joining them rather than fighting them? After all, we both went to Deluros with the same target in mind."

"Not for a second," said Cole. "They're bombing and killing indiscriminately, just like the Navy has been doing on the Inner Frontier. And this is just a hit-and-run. If its existence was threatened, the Republic would sign a truce or a cease-fire with the Teroni Federation and pull three million ships back to defend Deluros. At least if we pull this off, we can choose more reasonable leaders for the Republic."

"*Are* there more reasonable leaders?" she asked.

"We spent years living in the Republic, and more years defending it," said Cole. "They're not all bad. Hell, most of them are just like you and me; they just want to get through the day without hurting anyone or being hurt. This Chang seems like a reasonable man; surely there are others."

"All right," said Sharon. "I just wanted to make sure you'd thought it out." A self-deprecating smile. "I should have known you had."

"ETA in six minutes," announced Jacovic's voice.

"Damn!" said Cole. "I wish Briggs had broken their language or code or whatever the hell it is. If we take any prisoners, I don't know how the hell you're going to question them."

"It depends who you capture," said Sharon. "They have to have had *some* contact with the Republic. With ten billion planets in the galaxy, they didn't choose Deluros VIII by chance. What they speak to each other is one thing; maybe some of them will speak or understand Terran, or possibly Teroni."

"Five minutes," announced Jacovic.

"I'd better get up there," said Cole, getting to his feet.

"You've already explained to me why you don't have to."

"Under normal circumstances, I can avoid the bridge for a week," he said. "But these aren't normal circumstances."

"Come on, Wilson," she said. "The truth?"

"All right," he said. "They deserve to see their captain on the bridge, sharing the danger with them."

"Strapped to the wheel, sword in hand," she said with a smile.

"You know, Rachel and Gentry are looking better by the minute," growled Cole as he left the mess hall.

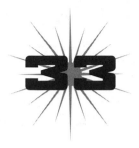

"We should be out of the wormhole in about twenty seconds," said Jacovic.

They kept their eyes on the viewscreen, and finally the *Teddy R* emerged into normal space.

"No ships, sir," said Christine.

"I agree, sir," said Rachel.

Cole turned to Briggs. "Mr. Briggs?"

"Nothing, sir."

"All right. Rachel and Briggs, start surveying those planets, and see which ones have an oxygen atmosphere and can support carbon-based life. Christine, try to figure out where the hell we are." He paused. "Jacovic, just keep an eye out for visitors."

After a minute Christine spoke up. "This would be a lot easier if we could move a few light-years ahead, sir. There are a lot of red and blue giants that are obscuring what's beyond."

"Not unless we have to," said Cole. "I don't want anyone to know we're here."

"They have to know the wormhole works in both directions," said Christine.

"If the Navy had ever used it, these people—whoever they are—would be a Republic colony by now. And if they thought someone *might* use it, they'd have been waiting for us when we came out of it."

"It does imply that they will be easier to meet in battle than an enemy that prepares for all eventualities," offered Jacovic.

"Sir!" said Rachel excitedly. "I think I've got them!"

"Where?"

"Fifth planet circling the type G star two light-years away, she said. "If you look at the viewscreen, it's on the left side, toward the bottom."

"This one?" asked Cole, indicating a star.

"Yes, sir. Oxygen world, considerable neutrino activity, and I'm picking up planetary transmissions."

"Mr. Briggs, see what you can do about narrowing things down," said Cole.

"I beg your pardon, sir?" said Briggs.

"I'm sure Pilot won't mind your tying in to the navigational computer. I think we can assume no enemy planet or empire could exist within twenty thousand light-years of Deluros, so why don't you have the computer check every populated non-Republic oxygen world that's the fifth planet circling a G-type star?"

Briggs looked up a minute later. "There are thirty-two of them in the galaxy, sir."

"Well, that's a start. Christine, you're on the best of our computers. Have it chart all the stars within, say, ten light-years and see if it can narrow it down further."

"Checking . . ." she said, whispering instructions to the computer that only she and the machine understood. "We've narrowed it down to two planets, sir."

"Only one, sir," said Rachel a moment later.

"Explain," said Cole.

"The eighth planet of the Tamerlaine system has eight moons. The eighth planet of *this* system has six. Therefore, this has to be the Rubino system.

"Very good," said Cole. "At least we should be able to figure out how to get home if we survive. Have we got anything on the Rubino system?"

A moment later Christine turned to face him. "Rubino V is what we want, all right. Five centuries ago they had an empire of twenty-seven planets. They tried to assimilate a few of the Republic's worlds, the Republic warned them off, they ignored the warnings, and the Republic destroyed almost their entire fleet in a single afternoon. They also brought about half of the Rubino empire into the fold. As far as I can tell, Rubino V seems to have disappeared from galactic history thereafter. It was a little planet that flexed its muscles once too often, got slapped down, and hasn't been heard from again."

"That is one hell of a long time to plan your revenge," said Cole. "It makes me feel better, though, that we're not fighting a world or an empire that's just trying to break away from the Republic and gain its freedom. Do we know what the Rubinos look like?"

"I doubt that they're called Rubinos, sir," said Christine.

"They are until someone gives me a better name."

"They're humanoid, sir," said Rachel. "Erect bipeds, two arms, two legs, the usual senses. I can't find out whether or not they're mammals."

"Any word on how many planets they control today?" asked Cole.

"No, sir," said Christine. "We have almost nothing on them for the past five hundred years."

"So we know, or can assume we know, that Rubino V is their headquarters world, but we don't know for a fact that we won't face reinforcements from other worlds. I almost said other nearby worlds, but I suppose we don't know that, either."

"No, sir."

"And we don't know if the two thousand ships they sent through the wormhole was an attack team or their entire Navy."

"That's correct, sir."

"How far is Rubino from Deluros?"

"Forty-seven thousand light-years, sir," said Christine.

"That's a long walk home from the battlefield," commented Cole. He turned to Jacovic. "Is there anything I should be asking that I've missed?"

"There are things we won't know until the battle begins, and there are things you have to decide, sir, but there's no question that you have neglected to ask."

"Okay. Pilot, get us the hell out of here," said Cole. "Same way we came."

"There's every likelihood we'll meet the returning ships after we emerge from the hole," noted Jacovic.

"Better to meet them at that end than this," said Cole. "Pilot, the second we're out of the hole, get to the far side of the star, inside the orbit of Deluros I." He turned to Jacovic. "That's the safest I can make us. We'll see if it works." The ship shuddered as it entered the Stutz Wormhole. "Come down to my office with me."

The Teroni accompanied Cole to the airlift, and a moment later was sitting opposite him, with the desk separating them, in the office.

"You wished to speak privately with me, sir?" said Jacovic.

"Yes," said Cole. "I wish I could offer you a drink, but you don't and I probably shouldn't."

"I am not thirsty, sir."

"I know," said Cole. He leaned forward. "I just want to make sure we're on the same page, or if not, what page I need to be on."

"I do not understand, sir."

"Slang," said Cole. "You said there were things we couldn't know before the battle begins. I can think of a few. Let's compare notes."

"First, you cannot know the size of their fleet," said Jacovic. "Second, you cannot know if they have weaponry on the planet that is superior to the Level 3 and 4 cannons in their ships. Third, you cannot know if they will be supported by any allies."

Cole nodded. "I also don't know if their allies are oxygen breathers," he said. "I'd hate to fly by a planet with a chlorine or methane atmosphere, pay no attention to it, and have them attack our flank once the battle's started."

"True," said Jacovic. "Some races are so outré that it is all but impossible to discern their presence until they leave their planet."

"How much attention we pay to that possibility will depend on the size of the fleet we assemble. Remember, we've got to come back here within a Standard day or the mouth of the wormhole will be somewhere else."

"I know," said Jacovic. "And that leaves you even less time to make your decision."

"I know," said Cole. "Do we punish them or annihilate them?"

"It is the kind of decision that makes me glad I am no longer a Fleet Commander," said the Teroni.

The *Teddy R* emerged into normal space in the Deluros system.

"Sir, the Rubino fleet is approaching from Deluros VIII," announced Christine.

"Tell Pilot to do what I told him to do," said Cole. He turned to Jacovic. "They've got to be on their way home. They couldn't know we were going to come out of the wormhole. I don't think they'll follow us."

"I'd better get back up to the bridge," said Jacovic. "Just in case."

"Yeah, go ahead. The crew needs to see someone in authority."

The *Teddy R* shot between Deluros I—a small, unwelcoming ball of rock—and its sun, and soon positioned itself on the far side of the star as the Rubino ships entered the Stutz Wormhole in a tight formation.

"The last of them has entered the wormhole, sir," said Christine some fifteen minutes later.

"Okay," replied Cole. "Have Pilot take us to fifty thousand miles from the hole and hold that position."

"Yes, sir."

"Now see if you can connect me to Aloysius Chang."

Chang's image appeared a moment later.

"Good to see you," said Cole. "I half expected you'd be dead by now."

"Our ground batteries destroyed about fifty of their ships," said Chang, "and when they found out that part of the Third Fleet was racing to Deluros, they decided they'd done enough damage and retreated." He frowned. "Where were you? I tried to contact you three different times."

"Visiting their home system," said Cole. "If I told you they were from Rubino V, would that mean anything to you?"

Chang frowned. "Rubino V," he said. "Rubino V." He shook his head. "I don't think I've ever heard of it. What did we ever do to them to precipitate this attack?"

"Nothing lately," said Cole. "This particular wound has been festering for half a millennium." He paused. "Before we get into the next phase of this thing—did Wilkie ever sign that paper?"

"No."

"Let me speak to him."

"I'm afraid you can't," said Chang.

"You didn't really throw him out the window?" said Cole.

"Of course not," said Chang noncommittally. "That would be illegal. He was merely a victim of the battle." He paused. "Anya Kranchev is the Secretary now, but she'd already signed, and says she'll honor it even though her position has changed."

"Then we're still in business," said Cole. "How many ships am I expecting in the next few hours?"

"Only about four thousand," said Chang. "We can't take any more away from the front." He smiled. "It might interest you to know that more than thirty of them have already checked to make sure that they are taking their orders from you. I think the last four years have conditioned them not to like you very much."

"They'll have to live with it," said Cole, declining to comment on the idiocy of a front that encompassed half the galaxy. "How many Class Ms and Class Ls have we got?"

"I have no idea."

"All right," replied Cole. "We'll have to make do with whatever shows up."

He cut the transmission, then went to his cabin. A moment later Sharon's image appeared.

"Am I seeing this correctly?" she said incredulously. "You're actually lying down on your bed?"

"You'd prefer I lie down on the floor?"

"Damn it, Wilson!"

"Why not take a nap?" asked Cole. "We won't be entering the hole for a few hours, and I may not get another chance for the next couple of days."

"I don't know how you can sleep at a time like this!"

"I can't," he replied. "Not while you keep talking to me." He ordered the lights to dim. "Wake me in about three hours."

She broke the connection, and woke him about eighty minutes later.

"I said three hours," he complained, staring at his watch.

"I know, but we need you now," said Sharon.

He sat up instantly. "We're under attack?"

"No," she said. "But Chang told the Navy that they're taking their orders from you, and some of them refuse to listen to Mr. Jacovic."

"Shit!" said Cole, getting to his feet. "I should have thought of that. Most of them have been fighting the Teronis since they joined the service. Have Christine patch me through to all the Navy ships."

"Comb your hair while I'm doing it," said Sharon. A brief pause. "You're connected."

"This is Wilson Cole, the Captain of the *Theodore Roosevelt*. As you've been told by Aloysius Chang or one of his surrogates, there have been some changes in your chain of command. Deluros VIII has just undergone a devastating attack, and we will be going to Rubino V, the attackers' home world, to mete out retribution for their actions and make sure such an attack never happens again. The *Theodore Roosevelt* will serve as the flagship of this section of the Third Fleet, and you will take your orders from us. My second command is Commander Jacovic, a Teroni. When he issues an order, it is done with my full knowledge and approval, which means that you will be expected to obey it. The fleet that attacked Deluros is neither human nor Teroni. They are currently half a galaxy away, but they can be reached through an unstable wormhole that will only remain in this system for another day. Have your pilots program Rubino's location into their navigational computers. *That* is our destination."

"Captain Mellinara of the *Silver Flame* here, Captain Cole," said a voice. "What kind of weaponry and defenses have they?"

"We know they didn't use Level 5 cannons against Deluros," answered Cole. "But that doesn't mean they don't have any. We also don't know anything about their planetary defenses. We do know that our ground batteries destroyed about fifty ships in the air above Deluros VIII, so their defenses are not up to our Class Ms and Class Ls—at least, not the ones we shot down."

"Commander Bainshank here," said another voice. "Are we just going after their fleet, or their home world as well?"

"We'll start with the fleet, and any ground units," said Cole. "We're not here to kill civilians if it can be avoided. If it can't be avoided, we'll worry about it when the time comes."

"I notice they didn't have any such compunction about killing *our* civilians," said another captain.

"Our missions are different. If you don't feel you can obey my orders, stay behind."

"Why are we taking orders from you anyway?" continued the captain. "We've been hunting you for four years."

"Because circumstances change. A century ago the Molarians were your enemies; now they're your allies. Today the Teronis are your enemies; next month or next year or next century they'll be your allies."

"So who *are* we fighting?"

"The natives of Rubino V," said Cole.

"Where the hell is that?"

"Just beyond the exit of the Stutz Wormhole, which we'll be entering in a few hours, when we're up to strength."

There were no further questions, and four hours later almost all of the ships had arrived. Cole divided them into eight groups, lettered A through H, put a ship in charge of each group, and had Christine program the eight group leaders into her computer. He noticed that she was almost falling asleep at her station, and he summoned Domak to replace her.

"But I don't want to leave!" she protested. "This is my post!"

Cole stared at her. "You really want to stay on duty?"

"Absolutely, sir!"

"All right. Report to the infirmary, and get yourself a shot of adrenaline and some kind of pep pill that won't affect your judgment. I'll see you back here when the doctor assures me you can function rationally and responsibly."

"Thank you, sir," she said, heading off to the infirmary.

Cole gave orders to put him through to the entire makeshift fleet.

"This is Wilson Cole again. We're still missing a few ships, but the Stutz Wormhole is unstable and I don't want to waste any more time. The area around the wormhole's exit was totally unprotected when the *Theodore Roosevelt* visited it a few hours ago. I don't imagine that will change, but be prepared, just in case they do anticipate an attack."

He paused, ordering his thoughts. "We know that Rubino V possessed a small empire of just under thirty planets about five hundred years ago. Some may still be allies, so we will have to be aware of that possibility. Also, since they've had spaceflight for at least that long, and we know there are other inhabited planets within their reach, there is every likelihood that commerce exists between the planets. I want you to make sure you are only attacking military ships. Passenger and cargo ships are *not* targets. We will begin by softening their military, and when we know the extent of their strength, we'll decide upon our next steps."

Cole waited for questions. There weren't any.

"All right," he said. "The *Theodore Roosevelt* will go first, followed by Groups A through H in that order. The time for talking is over. Let's go to work."

He nodded to Wxakgini, and a moment later the *Teddy R* plunged into the mouth of the Stutz Wormhole.

There were no Rubino ships waiting for them when they emerged. Cole waited until his entire fleet was out of the wormhole, then contacted his eight appointed leaders.

"Rubino V is about two light-years from here. If anyone has trouble finding it, let me know now."

There was no response.

"We're going into this blind," he continued. "We *think* they don't have Level 5 thumpers or burners, but we don't know it for a fact. We think they are not expecting us or we'd already be targets, but we don't know that for a fact. All the ships that attacked Deluros VIII were of the same general design, but that doesn't mean they don't have bigger and better ships they didn't want to risk, and it doesn't mean they don't have allies positioned all the hell over the area.

"For that reason, we're not going to attack in full force, at least not at the start. Groups A, B, C, and D, I want you to approach Rubino V. When they see that you've got two thousand ships and recognize that you're from the Republic, they're not going to wait or offer to talk. They'll start shooting. You have eleven Class L ships between you. I want them to make the closest approach, because they should be able to stand up under anything that Rubino can throw at you, at least for a short period. Once you analyze the strength of their weapons, you can go on the offensive. We'll try to pinpoint all ground batteries and feed them to your ships, but most of your battle is going to take place against their fleet. I have no idea whether it's in orbit around the planet, or possibly in orbit around one of the moons or another planet in the system. Once they show themselves, and they'll do it before you fire a weapon, we'll have a better idea of what we're up against.

"Group E will target any ground batteries that are harassing us during the battle and take them out. Groups F and G will remain in high orbit as backups until we know we're facing their entire military, and will then fill in at any spot where they're needed."

"What about Group H?" demanded the leader of that group.

"You stick with the *Theodore Roosevelt*," answered Cole.

"Doing what?"

"It will depend on things we can't know now."

"We came here to fight!" growled the leader.

"You came here on my orders, and you're still subject to them," replied Cole. "Group H stays in formation behind the *Theodore Roosevelt*. I promise you'll see your share of action."

There were no further comments or questions.

"All right. Groups A through D can begin their approach. Remember: I want those Class L ships out well ahead of you."

Two thousand ships began approaching the Rubino system.

"Any sign of activity there yet?" asked Cole.

"No, sir," said Christine, who had returned from the infirmary and replaced Domak.

"Figures. It won't come from the planet. What's the point of having a fleet of space ships if they're not in space?"

"Got them, sir!" said Briggs. He frowned. "Well, some of them. Maybe twelve hundred. They were orbiting the second moon. But there should be more."

"There will be," said Cole.

The Rubino ships began gathering in a defensive formation between the planet and the Navy ships, but they didn't move out to meet them. The eleven Class L ships accelerated ahead of the rest, and when they got within range the Rubino ships began firing.

"This is Bainshank," came a group leader's voice. "So far they haven't got anything we can't handle—or, rather, that the Class Ls can't handle."

"Let 'em know it," said Cole. "Don't fire back. Just keep moving and let them see they can't harm you. Maybe we can convince them it's not worth the effort."

"Right," said Bainshank. "We're within about ten thousand miles now and—"

Suddenly there was a brilliant flash of light on the viewscreen.

"What the hell was *that*?" asked Cole.

"I don't know," said Jacovic. "Some form of pulse torpedo, but nothing I've ever seen before."

"I can't raise Captain Bainshank," said Christine. "Do you suppose that was his ship?"

"Probably," said Cole. "Broadcast this to all of them: We've just lost Group Leader Bainshank to an unfamiliar weapon that instantly destroyed his ship. Go on the offensive immediately. Don't wait for them to prove it wasn't a fluke. If any of you can spot anything that will help us identify which ships are carrying that particular asset, let us know instantly."

"There can't be too many of them," said Jacovic. "Otherwise, they'd have used it on Deluros."

"Let's hope you're right," said Cole.

The Navy opened fire, and the results were devastating. More than one hundred Rubino ships were destroyed in the first three minutes. Then there was another brilliant explosion, and another Class L ship vanished.

"I've spotted the source of that weapon," said Mellinara's voice. "It's on the second moon, but we can't break through to get to it yet."

"How the hell can they shoot so accurately if their ships are shielding the weapon from your attack?" asked Cole.

"I saw that energy bolt or torpedo or whatever it was," said Mellinara, "and crazy as it sounds, it seemed to thread its way through the Rubino ships. There's got to be something in or on their structure that repels it . . . well, that sidesteps it, at least. I've sent the coordinates to you."

"Got them," said Christine.

"We'll take it from here," said Cole. "Mr. Briggs, feed those coordinates to the leaders of Groups F and G, and tell them to attack from opposite directions, get this weapon in a crossfire and hit it with everything they've got."

"Just F and G, sir?" said Briggs. "Not Groups E and H as well?"

"Just do what I tell you," said Cole.

"Yes, sir."

"I wish to hell I knew where the bulk of their fleet is," said Cole.

"Watching," answered Jacovic.

"Why aren't they fighting?"

"Why aren't your Groups E and H fighting?" replied the Teroni. "They're doing the same thing we planned to do: testing your strength and your defenses with that weapon. It's kept us occupied. We haven't fired a single shot at the planet."

"You're not suggesting this is a ruse?" said Cole, frowning.

"No, sir. But I have a feeling that once we destroy this weapon, as I'm sure we will, they'll find other ways to draw our attention away from the planet, to lead us where they want us to go."

"Where do you suppose that is?"

"I don't know," answered Jacovic. "But wherever it is, that's where we'll find the rest of their fleet."

"I agree," said Cole. Then: "Let's not play in their ballpark."

"I beg your pardon, sir?" said Jacovic, looking confused.

"Let's choose our own battlefield and make our own rules of engagement," said Cole. "Christine, get me the leader of Group E."

"Captain Gimanji here," said a strong female voice.

"This is Cole. Don't wait for the forces on the planet to shoot. Pick a couple of legitimate targets on the surface, either military or something showing major industrial activity if you can find them, and take them out. If you draw any fire, and I'm sure you will, then go after the weaponry."

"Yes, sir."

"We destroyed the weapon, sir!" announced Rachel excitedly.

"If they could make one, they could make more," said Cole. "Let me think." He was silent for a few seconds. "All right. Have Groups F and G start searching for more weapons on the moon. With the instruments they have, and a thousand ships sharing the job, we should know what's there inside five minutes. If there *is* another one, coordinate their efforts and take it out. If not, have them report to me." He turned to Jacovic. "There won't be any, not there. If they wanted to draw us farther away from the planet, they wouldn't do it by giving us a reason to keep searching that moon."

"Sir," said Rachel, "the planet is firing Level 5 lasers at Group E."

"All from one location?"

"So far."

"Christine, put me through to Gimanji."

"Done, sir."

"Gimanji, this is Cole."

"You didn't tell me they had Level 5 burners," she said.

"I didn't know."

"We'll turn them into rubble in about ninety more seconds," she promised.

"Good. Once you do, disperse your group around the planet. Fire at any likely target, and see what fires back. If it's anything above Level 2, report its location and knock it out."

"Will do."

He broke the connection, then concentrated on the battle around the moon. They hadn't been fired on by anything similar to the weapon that had destroyed Bainshank's ship, and their superior numbers were grinding the Rubino fleet down.

"They have to show up soon," said Cole.

"They may not like what they've seen," suggested Jacovic.

"That would make sense at Deluros, or the Inner Frontier," replied Cole. "But Rubino is their home. They won't stand by while we blow it apart. I just wish I knew what's keeping them."

"They're retreating to the vicinity of Rubino VII, sir," said Mellinara's voice. "Do you want us to pursue them?"

"Absolutely not," said Cole. "Hold your position, and tell the other groups to do the same."

"Yes, sir."

Cole looked at the screen, which was filled with the rubble of dead spaceships floating aimlessly, occasionally colliding with each other or still-living ships.

"What are our losses?" he asked.

"I can't be totally accurate, sir," replied Briggs, "but I'd estimate we've lost two hundred ships and they've lost, oh, it must be close to seven hundred."

"And nothing's taken off from the planet?"

"No, sir."

"Have Groups F and G finished hunting for another weapon on that moon?"

"Yes, sir. Results negative."

"Get me Mellinara." Cole waited a few seconds for the connection to be made. "Are they still retreating toward the seventh planet?"

"Yes, sir, they are," said Captain Mellinara.

"Okay. I want Groups A, B, C, and D to approach Rubino V. If no one tries to hinder you, ask Captain Gimanji what targets she's picked out and give her a hand with them. Try to hold collateral damage to a minimum."

"We're on our way, sir."

"Groups F and G," said Cole. "Take up orbit around the moon you've been searching. Those Rubino ships aren't going to stay away when they see we aren't following them. When they return, engage them."

The next five minutes consisted of reports from Groups A through E, which were hitting selected industrial areas on the planet and demolishing any ground batteries that fired on them.

"Here they come, sir!" Briggs suddenly announced.

"From the outer planets?"

"Yes, sir."

"How many?"

"Six thousand, seven thousand," he answered.

"Captain Mellinara, Captain Gimanji, you're about to get some company," said Cole. "The rest of their fleet is on the way. Groups F and G will meet them out by the moon, but they're badly outnumbered and they're going to need some help. I want groups B through E to withdraw from the planet and support our forces out by the moon."

"What about us, sir?" said a voice. "Captain Ramos, Group A, sir."

"Keep pounding industrial sites and ground batteries," said Cole. "I'll let you know if we need you at the moon."

"Seven thousand of them, a little less than three thousand of us," noted Jacovic.

"It'll be a fair fight," said Cole.

"Our weaponry is a little better, and so are our defenses," said Jacovic. "But the numbers . . ."

"Weapons don't mean that much in these quantities. What counts is that we refused to play their game, and we've forced them to play ours."

"Could you explain that, sir?" said the Teroni.

"They wanted us to follow them; we didn't. We wanted them to reveal their full strength and come back to Rubino V; they did."

"Sir!" said a harsh voice.

"Who is this?"

"Commander Kristoff. I'm the leader of Group H. Are you *ever* going to use us?"

"When the time comes," said Cole.

"When is that?"

"I'll let you know." He signaled Christine to cut the connection, then turned to Jacovic. "I admire his enthusiasm, if not his discipline."

"When *are* we going to use them, sir?" asked Briggs.

"When the need arises," said Cole. "It shouldn't be long now." He walked over to Wxakgini. "Pilot, take us inside the orbit of Rubino V."

"How far inside?"

"Halfway to Rubino IV. What's that—about twenty million miles?"

"Eighteen million," Wxakgini corrected him.

"Mr. Briggs, make sure Kristoff and his group follow us."

"What are you expecting, sir?" asked Rachel.

"I'm not sure, but that was pinpoint bombing we saw on Deluros VIII. The whole planet is one single city, but they knew exactly where to hit the parliament and the court, and where the Secretary's office was. What does that say to you?"

"They had previously scouted out the territory," she said.

"Right. And if they scouted it out, they had to know how massive and powerful the Republic's military engine is."

"Maybe they thought the wormhole would move before the Republic could mount a counterattack," suggested Briggs.

Cole shook his head. "The Republic has three and a half million ships. They control a sizable portion of the galaxy. They didn't *need* the wormhole. It's convenient, but it's not necessary. They could mount a massive retaliation without it, and I can't believe the Rubinos weren't aware of it."

"What are you driving at, sir?" asked Christine.

"That whatever they've got in reserve, we haven't seen it yet. And if it wasn't on the outer planets, it's either coming from the inner planets or a nearby system . . . and it can get here a lot faster if it starts within the Rubino system."

"The fact that they tried to draw us to the outer planets would seem to support that," agreed Jacovic.

"We'll find out soon enough," replied Cole. "That's why I wanted Captain Ramos to keep bombarding the planet. If we *all* went out to meet their fleet, they might wait to see the outcome before calling in the reserves. I think this will encourage them not to hold anything back."

"I am now holding our position," said Wxakgini.

"Fine," said Cole. "It shouldn't be long."

Three minutes later Briggs announced that a small fleet, numbering no more than fifty ships, was approaching from the direction of Rubino II.

"We've got to find out what they have, and quick," said Cole. "Clearly they don't plan to overwhelm us with numbers."

"One ship seems much larger than the others, sir," said Briggs. "It's almost as big as a dreadnought."

"A dreadnought, even the *Xerxes*, wouldn't turn the tide of battle," said Cole. "It's something else."

"I'm getting an image, sir," said Briggs.

Soon everyone on the bridge could see the glowing mechanism that was larger than any ship on either side, but seemed to be more weapon than ship.

"It's not flying," noted Jacovic. "It's being towed."

"Five will get you ten it's the big brother of the one we destroyed on the moon," said Cole. "Run the image by the groups that destroyed it and ask if it looks familiar."

The reply was almost instantaneous. It looked identical, but was twelve to fifteen times larger.

"Why don't they have hundreds of them?" asked Rachel.

"I don't know," said Cole. "Maybe they have a limited supply of whatever it is that they fire. Maybe they just invented it, and the one we destroyed was a prototype for this baby. After all, they could have attacked any time in the past five centuries if they felt safe. Clearly they think it's all they need to defend the planet. Put me through to Kristoff."

"Kristoff here," came the reply a few seconds later.

"I think we're ready to unleash you, Commander Kristoff. Do you see that huge weapon that's being towed by the four Class J ships?"

"Is that what it is?"

"That's what it is," said Cole. "Destroy it and the battle's as good as over."

"We'll be happy to!"

"And don't underestimate it. I have a feeling that neither you nor I have ever seen a weapon as powerful as this one. Spread your group out, try to englobe it, and do it fast. Believe me when I tell you that you can't withstand it for even a fraction of a second once it fires at you."

"What the hell is it?"

"Powerful," said Cole. "Now get to work."

Cole could hear Kristoff giving orders to the five hundred ships in his group. They instantly spread out, shooting off in different directions, and within a minute they had the Rubino ships and the weapon englobed. The Rubino ships began firing, the Navy ships returned their fire, and after another minute had passed some twenty-six of the Rubino ships and eleven Navy ships floated dead in space.

Then the weapon joined the battle. What looked like a series of lightning bolts shot out, and where each hit a ship—and every single one of them hit a target—the ship exploded and briefly became a fireball, just as the ship had during the initial encounter by Rubino V's moon.

"Those blasts are like heat-seeking missiles," remarked Cole, staring at the screen. "Once they've chosen a target, they keep after it even if it's changed directions."

"They're decimating H Group, sir," said Jacovic. "It's not fighting like a weapon that's in any danger of running out of ammunition."

"I agree," said Cole. "We've got to think of something soon, before all of H Group is a pile of ashes floating in space."

"More ships, perhaps?" suggested Jacovic without much conviction.

Cole shook his head. "More firepower usually just makes for more confusion and more collateral damage. You win most battles by using your brain." He muttered a curse. "Mine doesn't seem to be functioning."

"We've hit it fifteen or twenty times, but we're not doing it any damage," reported Kristoff. "Maybe the damned thing will run out of ammunition; I can't see any other way to stop it."

"It won't run out of ammunition," said Jacovic. "If there was a chance of it, they wouldn't have put their planet at risk."

"You'd better think of something quick," said Kristoff. "I've lost about fifty ships to it already."

"Kristoff," said Cole. "You've got a Level 5 thumper on your ship. Have you used it on the weapon?"

"Didn't make a dent, sir."

"Okay, thanks," said Cole. He broke the connection. "No sense using ours. It'll just make the damned weapon concentrate on the *Teddy R.*" He stared at the viewscreen as the devastation continued—and suddenly he peered forward intently. "I can follow those pulse blasts with my eye."

"I don't follow you, sir," said Jacovic.

"They're not going at light speeds, or anywhere near," continued Cole. "Either they can't, or they won't do it until they have to."

The Teroni merely stared at him.

"That implies that a ship could outrun the blast, at least for a few seconds."

"All right, it can outrun the blast for a few seconds," said Jacovic, still puzzled. "So what?"

"Get me Pampas."

"Done," said Christine.

"Bull, get down to the shuttle bay on the double. Program the *Archie* to leave the ship, approach the weapon, fire a laser blast at it—"

"It won't do any good, sir," said Pampas. "All the shuttles have are Level 2 weapons. That won't make a dent in it."

"Then stop interrupting and listen," said Cole. "The *Archie* goes without a pilot or crew. I want you to program it to take evasive action the instant it fires at the weapon. Got it?"

"Yes, sir," said Pampas, as he got off the airlift and raced to the shuttle bay.

"I don't understand what you're doing, sir," said Briggs.

"I think I'm beginning to," said Jacovic.

"Ready, sir," said Pampas.

"Turn it loose," said Cole.

They all watched on the viewscreen as the *Archie* shot out of the ship, made a beeline for the Rubino superweapon, fired a laser blast, and then began evasive maneuvering. The weapon responded, the lightning bolt spurted out and closed in on the *Archie*, matching it move for move, and turned it into a fireball a few seconds later.

"It *could* work," said Jacovic.

"I'm still in the dark," said Briggs.

"Me, too," agreed Rachel.

"Mr. Briggs, instead of Bull programming the *Kermit*, can you fix it for me to control it from up here?" asked Cole.

"Yes, sir," said Briggs. He manipulated his computer for a moment, then stood up. When you touch this spot"—he indicated a place on the terminal—"a holographic panel will appear. It won't have any solidity, of course, but it will be identical to the controls on the shuttle, and as you touch them the *Kermit* will respond as if you were inside it at its controls."

"Let me give it a try," said Cole. "Bull, open the shuttle bay again."

"No crew on the *Kermit*, sir?"

"None."

"All right, you're ready to go, sir," said Pampas.

Cole touched the spot Briggs had indicated, then held his hands just above the holographic panel. He moved the *Kermit* out into space, and put it through two minutes of maneuvers until he was comfortable with it.

"Put me through to Kristoff," he ordered.

"Kristoff here."

"Commander, withdraw your ships. You're not making any progress, and we're going to try something different."

"Yes, sir," said Kristoff, making no attempt to keep the reluctance and disappointment out of his voice.

Cole waited until Kristoff's group began clearing the area.

"Okay, here goes," he said. He turned the *Kermit* to face the Weapon—Cole thought of it with a capital W now—and fired a totally ineffective laser blast at it. As he did so, he simultaneously pushed the *Kermit* to near light speed, darted well to the left of the Weapon and below, then turned and plunged directly toward it. The lightning pulse caught up with the shuttle a microsecond after it crashed against the Weapon, and the Weapon itself exploded in the biggest fireball of all.

Cole turned to his crew. "We destroyed it with the only thing strong enough to destroy it," he said. A satisfied smile crossed his face. "I just had a feeling it might work."

"This is Kristoff," said a voice. "What the hell happened?"

"I'll explain later," said Cole. "Right now I want you to ride shotgun for me while I approach Rubino V." He broke the connection. "Mr. Briggs, how is the conflict going out by Rubino's moon? I need a damage report."

"It's continuing, sir. I can't give you an exact count—there's too much debris obscuring parts of the battle—but we seem to be getting much the better of it." A pause. "The reports are starting to come in, sir. Group B has lost twenty-seven ships, Group C sixty-two, Group E thirty-nine . . ."

"What about Group D?"

"I can't contact them, sir. I suspect their leader has been destroyed. Group F had lost one hundred seventy-one ships and Group G one hundred sixteen, but those two groups did bear the brunt of the attack. Enemy damages number upwards of three thousand."

"Good," said Cole. "Pilot, get us to Rubino V and put us in orbit."

Once the *Teddy R* was circling the planet, Cole walked over to Christine's station. "I want to send a message to the president, premiere, secretary, king, whatever he is. Can you do that?"

"I don't have his code or coordinates," she replied. "But I can broadcast your message to the entire planet. It's sure to reach him, and we'll sort out which reply is his."

"Fine," said Cole. "Do it."

"Ready," she replied in a few seconds.

"Leaders of Rubino V," he said, "this is Wilson Cole, Captain of the *Theodore Roosevelt*, which is the flagship of this response to your unprovoked attack on Deluros VIII. We have destroyed your weapon, and we are currently decimating your fleet. We can continue the battle until your last ship has been destroyed, and then land and hunt down the members of your government one by one—and if you don't surrender we will do just that. If, on the other hand, you *do* surrender, there will be no further hostilities, now or in the future. Our collective memories will extend no farther back than this moment, and you will be invited to participate in a galaxy-wide government."

"There isn't one," came the reply.

"Wait," he promised.

Within ten minutes the government had agreed to a cease-fire.

Cole and his senior officers stood in the Secretary's office on Deluros VIII, facing Aloysius Chang, Anya Kranchev, and half a dozen other members of the parliament.

"We have all signed that paper," said Chang, pulling it out of his pocket. "I now present it to you. Not everyone in this government has as low a regard for the truth as our most recent Secretary."

"I hope you're not expecting me to tear this up as a gesture of goodwill," said Cole, folding the paper and placing it in a pocket. "There have been too many abuses committed in the name of the Republic. Maybe the people in this room didn't support them, but you didn't do anything to stop them either."

There was no response, and Cole continued. "I think the Republic has outlived its usefulness. It was necessary when Man made his first tentative steps into a galaxy that was frequently hostile to him, but that time is passed. You need a government that encompasses all the sentient life-forms on equal footing—including the Teronis and the Rubinos."

"I won't even argue it with you," said Chang. "In fact, we have discussed it among ourselves, and we would be honored if you would accept the Secretaryship of this new government."

"Me?" said Cole, surprised.

"Yes."

"I hate politics, and with all due respect, I hate politicians even more. I respectfully decline your offer."

"Are you quite sure?" said Anya.

"I am. But when you form your government, I do have a recommendation."

"Oh?"

He put an arm around his First Officer's shoulders. "Commander Jacovic is the most honorable being I have ever known. I think you would be well advised to offer him a position of some authority."

"But he's a Teroni!" blurted Anya.

"Who better to negotiate a peace treaty with the Teronis?" said Cole. "You can't build a true galactic democracy without them."

The politicians whispered among themselves for a moment. Then Chang approached Jacovic.

"Commander Jacovic, would you consider joining our government's leadership?"

"I would be empowered to negotiate with other races on behalf of the government?"

"That goes without saying," replied Anya.

"When you're dealing with politicians, nothing goes without saying," interjected Cole. "Will all of you sign a statement agreeing to these conditions?"

They didn't even bother conferring this time.

"Yes, we would," said Chang. "Commander, once again: will you join us?"

"I would be honored," replied the Teroni.

Chang turned to Cole. "And what will *you* do?"

"The *Teddy R* still has a few years and a few voyages left," answered Cole. "The Democracy will probably be better than the Republic, especially with Jacovic in it, but to tell the truth I think we're sick of *all* governments. There's a big galaxy out there, and there are still a lot of things to be seen for the first time."

And so saying, Wilson Cole and his crew went off to see them.

APPENDIXES

Appendix One

THE ORIGIN OF THE BIRTHRIGHT UNIVERSE

t happened in the 1970s. Carol and I were watching a truly awful movie at a local theater, and about halfway through it I muttered, "Why am I wasting my time here when I could be doing something really interesting, like, say, writing the entire history of the human race from now until its extinction?" And she whispered back, "So why don't you?" We got up immediately, walked out of the theater, and that night I outlined a novel called *Birthright: The Book of Man*, which would tell the story of the human race from its attainment of faster-than-light flight until its death eighteen thousand years from now.

It was a long book to write. I divided the future into five political eras—Republic, Democracy, Oligarchy, Monarchy, and Anarchy—and wrote twenty-six connected stories ("demonstrations," *Analog* called them, and rightly so), displaying every facet of the human race, both admirable and not so admirable. Since each is set a few centuries from the last, there are no continuing characters (unless you consider Man, with a capital M, the main character, in which case you could make an argument—or at least, *I* could—that it's really a character study).

I sold it to Signet, along with another novel titled *The Soul Eater*. My editor there, Sheila Gilbert, loved the Birthright Universe and asked me if I would be willing to make a few changes to *The Soul Eater* so that it was set in that future. I agreed, and the changes actually took less than a day. She made the same request—in advance, this time—for the four-book Tales of the Galactic Midway series, the four-book Tales of the Velvet Comet series, and *Walpurgis III*. Looking back, I see that only two of the thirteen novels I wrote for Signet were *not* set there.

When I moved to Tor Books, my editor there, Beth Meacham, had a fondness for the Birthright Universe, and most of my books for her—not all, but most—were set in it: *Santiago, Ivory, Paradise, Purgatory, Inferno, A Miracle of Rare Design, A Hunger in the Soul, The Outpost,* and *The Return of Santiago.*

When Ace agreed to buy *Soothsayer, Oracle,* and *Prophet* from me, my editor, Ginjer Buchanan, assumed that of course they'd be set in the Birthright Universe—and of course they were, because as I learned a little more about my eighteen-thousand-year, two-million-world future, I felt a lot more comfortable writing about it.

In fact, I started setting short stories in the Birthright Universe. Two of my Hugo winners—"Seven Views of Olduvai Gorge" and "The 43 Antarean Dynasties"—are set there, and so are almost twenty others.

When Bantam agreed to take the Widowmaker trilogy from me, it was a foregone conclusion that Janna Silverstein, who purchased the books (but moved to another company before they came out) would want them to take place in the Birthright Universe. She did indeed request it, and I did indeed agree.

I recently handed in a book to Meisha Merlin, set—where else?—in the Birthright Universe.

And when it came time to suggest a series of books to Lou Anders for the new Pyr line of science fiction, I don't think I ever considered any ideas or stories that *weren't* set in the Birthright Universe.

I've gotten so much of my career from the Birthright Universe that I wish I could remember the name of that turkey we walked out of all those years ago so I could write the producers and thank them.

Appendix Two

THE LAYOUT OF THE BIRTHRIGHT UNIVERSE

The most heavily populated (by both stars and inhabitants) section of the Birthright Universe is always referred to by its political identity, which evolves from Republic to Democracy to Oligarchy to Monarchy. It encompasses millions of inhabited and habitable worlds. Earth is too small and too far out of the mainstream of galactic commerce to remain Man's capital world, and within a couple of thousand years the capital has been moved lock, stock, and barrel halfway across the galaxy to Deluros VIII, a huge world with about ten time's Earth's surface and near-identical atmosphere and gravity. By the middle of the Democracy, perhaps four thousand years from now, the entire planet is covered by one huge sprawling city. By the time of the Oligarchy, even Deluros VIII isn't big enough for our billions of empire-running bureaucrats, and Deluros VI, another large world, is broken up into forty-eight planetoids, each housing a major department of the government (with four planetoids given over entirely to the military).

Earth itself is way out in the boonies, on the Spiral Arm. I don't believe I've set more than parts of a couple of stories on the Arm.

At the outer edge of the galaxy is the Rim, where worlds are spread out and underpopulated. There's so little of value or military interest on the Rim that one ship, such as the *Theodore Roosevelt*, can patrol a couple of hundred worlds by itself. In later eras, the Rim will be dominated by feuding warlords, but it's so far away from the center of things that the governments, for the most part, just ignore it.

Then there are the Inner and Outer Frontiers. The Outer Frontier is that vast but sparsely populated area between the outer edge of the Republic/Democracy/Oligarchy/Monarchy and the Rim. The Inner Frontier is that somewhat smaller (but still huge) area between the inner reaches of the Republic/etc. and the black hole at the core of the galaxy.

It's on the Inner Frontier that I've chosen to set more than half of my novels. Years ago the brilliant writer R. A. Lafferty wrote: "Will there be a mythology of the future, they used to ask, after all has become science? Will high deeds be told in epic, or only in computer code?" I decided that I'd like to spend at least a part of my career trying to create those myths of the future, and it seems to me that myths, with their bigger-than-life characters and colorful settings, work best on frontiers where there aren't too many people around to chronicle them accurately, or too many authority figures around to prevent them from playing out to their inevitable conclusions. So I arbitrarily decided that the Inner Frontier was where *my* myths would take place, and I populated it with people bearing names like Catastrophe Baker, the Widowmaker, the Cyborg de Milo, the ageless Forever Kid, and the like. It not only allows me to tell my heroic (and sometimes antiheroic) myths, but lets me tell more realistic stories occurring at the very same time a few thousand light-years away in the Republic or Democracy or whatever happens to exist at that moment.

Over the years I've fleshed out the galaxy. There are the star clusters—the Albion Cluster, the Quinellus Cluster, a few others, and a pair that are new to this series, the Phoenix and Cassius clusters. There are the individual worlds, some important enough to appear as the title of a book, such as Walpurgis III, some reappearing throughout the time periods and stories, such as Deluros VIII, Antares III, Binder X, Keepsake, Spica II, some others, and hundreds (maybe thousands by now) of worlds (and races, now that I think about it) mentioned once and never again.

Then there are, if not the bad guys, at least what I think of as the Disloyal Opposition. Some, like the Sett Empire, get into one war with humanity and that's the end of it. Some, like the Canphor Twins (Canphor VI and Canphor VII) have been a thorn in Man's side for the better part of ten millennia. Some, like Lodin XI, vary almost daily in their loyalties depending on the political situation.

I've been building this universe, politically and geographically, for over a quarter of a century now, and with each passing book and story it feels a little more real to me. Give me another thirty years and I'll probably believe every word I've written about it.

Appendix Three

CHRONOLOGY OF THE BIRTHRIGHT UNIVERSE

Year	Era	World	Story or Novel
1885	A.D.		"The Hunter" (*Ivory*)
1898	A.D.		"Himself" (*Ivory*)
1982	A.D.		*Sideshow*
1983	A.D.		*The Three-Legged Hootch Dancer*
1985	A.D.		*The Wild Alien Tamer*
1987	A.D.		*The Best Rootin' Tootin' Shootin' Gunslinger in the Whole Damned Galaxy*
2057	A.D.		"The Politician" (*Ivory*)
2403	A.D.		"Shaka II"
2988	A.D. = 1 G.E.		
16	G.E.	Republic	"The Curator" (*Ivory*)
264	G.E.	Republic	"The Pioneers" (*Birthright*)
332	G.E.	Republic	"The Cartographers" (*Birthright*)
346	G.E.	Republic	*Walpurgis III*
367	G.E.	Republic	*Eros Ascending*
396	G.E.	Republic	"The Miners" (*Birthright*)
401	G.E.	Republic	*Eros at Zenith*
442	G.E.	Republic	*Eros Descending*
465	G.E.	Republic	*Eros at Nadir*

522	G.E.	Republic	"All the Things You Are"
588	G.E.	Republic	"The Psychologists" (*Birthright*)
616	G.E.	Republic	*A Miracle of Rare Design*
882	G.E.	Republic	"The Potentate" (*Ivory*)
962	G.E.	Republic	"The Merchants" (*Birthright*)
1150	G.E.	Republic	"Cobbling Together a Solution"
1151	G.E.	Republic	"Nowhere in Particular"
1152	G.E.	Republic	"The God Biz"
1394	G.E.	Republic	"Keepsakes"
1701	G.E.	Republic	"The Artist" (*Ivory*)
1813	G.E.	Republic	"Dawn" (*Paradise*)
1826	G.E.	Republic	*Purgatory*
1859	G.E.	Republic	"Noon" (*Paradise*)
1888	G.E.	Republic	"Midafternoon" (*Paradise*)
1902	G.E.	Republic	"Dusk" (*Paradise*)
1921	G.E.	Republic	*Inferno*
1966	G.E.	Republic	*Starship: Mutiny*
1967	G.E.	Republic	*Starship: Pirate*
1968	G.E.	Republic	*Starship: Mercenary*
1969	G.E.	Republic	*Starship: Rebel*
1970	G.E.	Republic	*Starship: Flagship*
2122	G.E.	Democracy	"The 43 Antarean Dynasties"
2154	G.E.	Democracy	"The Diplomats" (*Birthright*)
2239	G.E.	Democracy	"Monuments of Flesh and Stone"
2275	G.E.	Democracy	"The Olympians" (*Birthright*)
2469	G.E.	Democracy	"The Barristers" (*Birthright*)
2885	G.E.	Democracy	"Robots Don't Cry"
2911	G.E.	Democracy	"The Medics" (*Birthright*)
3004	G.E.	Democracy	"The Policitians" (*Birthright*)
3042	G.E.	Democracy	"The Gambler" (*Ivory*)

3286	G.E.	Democracy	*Santiago*
3322	G.E.	Democracy	*A Hunger in the Soul*
3324	G.E.	Democracy	*The Soul Eater*
3324	G.E.	Democracy	"Nicobar Lane: The Soul Eater's Story"
3407	G.E.	Democracy	*The Return of Santiago*
3427	G.E.	Democracy	*Soothsayer*
3441	G.E.	Democracy	*Oracle*
3447	G.E.	Democracy	*Prophet*
3502	G.E.	Democracy	"Guardian Angel"
3504	G.E.	Democracy	"A Locked-Planet Mystery"
3504	G.E.	Democracy	"Honorable Enemies"
3719	G.E.	Democracy	"Hunting the Snark"
4375	G.E.	Democracy	"The Graverobber" (*Ivory*)
4822	G.E.	Oligarchy	"The Administrators" (*Birthright*)
4839	G.E.	Oligarchy	*The Dark Lady*
5101	G.E.	Oligarchy	*The Widowmaker*
5103	G.E.	Oligarchy	*The Widowmaker Reborn*
5106	G.E.	Oligarchy	*The Widowmaker Unleashed*
5108	G.E.	Oligarchy	*A Gathering of Widowmakers*
5461	G.E.	Oligarchy	"The Media" (*Birthright*)
5492	G.E.	Oligarchy	"The Artists" (*Birthright*)
5521	G.E.	Oligarchy	"The Warlord" (*Ivory*)
5655	G.E.	Oligarchy	"The Biochemists" (*Birthright*)
5912	G.E.	Oligarchy	"The Warlords" (*Birthright*)
5993	G.E.	Oligarchy	"The Conspirators" (*Birthright*)
6304	G.E.	Monarchy	*Ivory*
6321	G.E.	Monarchy	"The Rulers" (*Birthright*)
6400	G.E.	Monarchy	"The Symbiotics" (*Birthright*)
6521	G.E.	Monarchy	"Catastrophe Baker and the Cold Equations"

6523 G.E.	Monarchy	*The Outpost*
6599 G.E.	Monarchy	"The Philosophers" (*Birthright*)
6746 G.E.	Monarchy	"The Architects" (*Birthright*)
6962 G.E.	Monarchy	"The Collectors" (*Birthright*)
7019 G.E.	Monarchy	"The Rebels" (*Birthright*)

16201 G.E.	Anarchy	"The Archaeologists" (*Birthright*)
16673 G.E.	Anarchy	"The Priests" (*Birthright*)
16888 G.E.	Anarchy	"The Pacifists" (*Birthright*)
17001 G.E.	Anarchy	"The Destroyers" (*Birthright*)

21703 G.E.   "Seven Views of Olduvai Gorge"

Novels not set in this future

Adventures (1922–1926 A.D.)
Exploits (1926–1931 A.D.)
Encounters (1931–1934 A.D.)
Hazards (1934–1939 A.D.)
Stalking the Unicorn ("Tonight")
Stalking the Vampire ("Tonight")
Stalking the Dragon ("Tonight")
The Branch (2047–2051 A.D.)
Second Contact (2065 A.D.)
Bully! (1910–1912 A.D.)
Kirinyaga (2123–2137 A.D.)
Kilimanjaro (2235–2241 A.D.)
Lady with an Alien (1490 A.D.)
A Club in Montmartre (1890–1901 A.D.)
Dragon America: Revolution (1779–1780 A.D.)
The World behind the Door (1928 A.D.)
The Other Teddy Roosevelts (1888–1919 A.D.)

Appendix Four

WORMHOLES

I f you've been reading the *Starship* books, you know that the quickest way to traverse the galaxy at many multiples of the speed of light is by the use of wormholes.

A science fiction invention, you say?

Guess again.

The term "wormhole" was actually invented in 1957 by John Wheeler, an American theoretical physicist. The concept predated him by thirty-six years, and was theorized by Hermann Weyl, a German mathematician.

So do they break Einstein's laws of the universe?

Well, Einstein didn't think so. He and a colleague named Nathan Rosen came up with Einstein-Rosen bridges, which are bridges between areas of space that get around the limitations posed by Einstein's special theory of relativity . . . and for the record, they inspired what have come to be known as Schwarzschild wormholes and Lorentzian wormholes.

There has even been some interesting cross-pollination.

Carl Sagan, old "Billions and Billions," was writing his first novel, *Contact* (science fiction, of course), in 1985, and asked cosmologist Kip

Thorne to devise a wormhole that was traversable, at least in theory—and Thorne and his partners proceeded to do just that. The traversable wormhole is now known as the Morris-Thorne wormhole. (A side effect was that the science behind these wormholes allowed Thorne to make a legitimate, scientifically sound proposal for a time machine.)

Are there wormholes in space?

Almost certainly.

Can we travel through them.

The obvious answer is no.

The optimist's and the science fiction writer's answers are: not yet . . . but stick around.

Appendix Five

ETHICS

I hope the *Starship* books are fun, but like most science fiction, they also deal with serious human problems. *Starship: Mutiny* examined the question of when (and if) you must refuse a legitimate order, regardless of consequences. *Starship: Pirate* explored the unwritten rules of engagement for someone who is forced to operate outside the law. *Starship: Mercenary* considered when (and if) you must refuse a job in your chosen field due to moral considerations. *Starship: Rebel* was concerned with the reaction to serious abuse when it is committed not to yourself but to someone else, and what (if anything) must be done about it.

For *Starship: Flagship*, the question was in this week's headlines (as I write this in late May of 2009), and it concerns the debate over the harsh interrogation of prisoners. At what point, the American people are being asked to decide, is harsh interrogation justified? At what point does it become torture? And is torture itself ever justified?

Well, of course, every civilized person's first response is to say that no, of course torture is never justified.

Okay. We now know that waterboarding revealed the existence of a planned attack on a bank tower in Los Angeles, a plan that was thwarted only because the victim of the waterboarding, who had refused to cooperate with his interrogators for months prior to that, gave them all the vital details after his experience.

Unjustified?

I think a good many people's initial reaction would be yes.

Now let's pretend that my wife works in that building, and would be instantly killed when a plane rammed into it.

Still unjustified? I don't think so any longer.

So we come to the crux of it: Is torture acceptable under rigidly defined extreme circumstances, like saving five thousand Angelinos who would be in that tower? Or—everyone's favorite example—if it is the only way to find out where a bomb (possibly a nuke) has been hidden before it explodes?

But there's another consideration, too. Everyone will grant that waterboarding and similar methods are harsh methods of interrogation indeed. But *are* they torture?

After all, the terrorist who revealed the information about the tower was perfectly healthy the next day. He suffered no ill effects, and waterboarding him may have saved a few thousand lives. (Of course, it may not have saved them; we'll never know what continued gentler methods might have achieved.) But the fact remains that, unlike the torture American soldiers suffered at the hands of the Japanese in World War II, this man emerged none the worse for wear. Indeed, our US Navy Seals undergo waterboarding routinely to prepare them for it should they fall into enemy hands; no one has ever died or been permanently disabled by it.

Still, many feel that it is opposed to the principles outlined in the Constitution. There is an argument, perhaps valid, that using such methods makes us no better than our enemies. And there is another argument that until you *know* there is a hidden bomb set to explode in three hours, you apply all legitimate methods of questioning on the assumption that sooner or later you'll get the answers you need.

I realize there are two sides to the question, and each side is sure it has the morally correct position.

Which made it a perfect problem for Wilson Cole to come to grips with.

Appendix Six

THE BALLAD OF WILSON COLE

John Anealio

Music

In the time of the Ga-lac-tic E - ra in the year of Nine-teen Six-ty - Six,
Com-man-der Cole had to wrest-le con - trol from the Pol-o- noi run-ning the
ship. And de - spite his four med- als of cour - age they court-mar-tialed
him an - y- way, The men of his crew came to his res - cue and em-barked on their
own deep in space. Yes they say Wil-son Cole was a he - ro
and the Cap-tain of the Ted - dy R. He kept up the fight
and he did what was right as he led his fleet through the stars.

Lyrics

Verse 1
In the time of the Galactic Era
in the year of 1966
Commander Cole had to wrestle control
from the Polonoi running the ship.
And despite his four medals of courage
they court-martialed him anyway.
The men of his crew came to his rescue
and embarked on their own deep in space.

Refrain
Yes they say Wilson Cole was a hero
and the captain of the *Teddy R.*
He kept up the fight and he did what was right
as he led his fleet through the stars.

Verse 2
Then it came to 1967
after the ship's mutiny.
They made a deal with David Copperfield
and they allied with the Valkyrie.
And he didn't make much of a pirate
Wilson has an honest man.
He went and retrieved *A Tale of Two Cities*
and decided that he'd change his plan.

Refrain

Verse 3
Then they became mercenaries
the year was 1968.
Their destination was Singapore Station
so they met at the Platinum Duke's Place.
Then they met the Teroni Jacovic
who became the ship's Third Officer.
Cole marshaled one thousand ships against a lunatic
Csonti retreated then went berserk.

Refrain

Verse 4
The Navy murdered First Officer Forrice
at a brothel on Braccio II.
Cole went and avenged the death of his best friend
killing the *Endless Night* and its crew.
Then the Navy laid waste to the planet
and Wilson searched for volunteers.
He gathered a fleet that would never retreat
as it defended the Inner Frontier.

Refrain

Verse 5
And then in 1970
Cole infiltrated Deluros VIII.
He aimed his gun at the Admiral just as the sky
filled
with enemies set to invade.
Wilson Cole led the *Theodore Roosevelt*
and the ships of the Republican Fleet.
The enemy was defeated and the Secretary ceded
Cole's mission was finally complete.

Refrain

JOHN ANEALIO writes songs about science fiction and fantasy. Alternate-tuned acoustic guitar picking, soaring synthesizers, and catchy pop hooks power his odes to androids, princesses, starship captains, and vampires. You can download "The Ballad of Wilson Cole" and many other original songs for free at http://scifisongs.blogspot.com.

ABOUT THE AUTHOR

Locus, *the trade journal of science fiction, keeps a list of the winners of major science fiction awards on its Web page. Mike Resnick is currently fourth in the all-time standings, ahead of Isaac Asimov, Sir Arthur C. Clarke, Ray Bradbury, and Robert A. Heinlein. He is the leading* award-winner among all authors, living and dead, for short science fiction.

* * * * * *

Mike was born on March 5, 1942. He sold his first article in 1957, his first short story in 1959, and his first book in 1962.

He attended the University of Chicago from 1959 through 1961, won three letters on the fencing team, and met and married Carol. Their daughter, Laura, was born in 1962, and has since become a writer herself, winning two awards for her romance novels and the 1993 Campbell Award for Best New Science Fiction Writer.

Mike and Carol discovered science fiction fandom in 1962, attended their first Worldcon in 1963, and sixty science fiction novels into his career, Mike still considers himself a fan and frequently contributes articles to fanzines. He and Carol appeared in five Worldcon masquerades in the 1970s in costumes that she created, and they won four of them.

Mike labored anonymously but profitably from 1964 through 1976, selling more than two hundred novels, three hundred short stories, and two thousand articles, almost all of them under pseudonyms, most of them in the "adult" field. He edited seven different tabloid newspapers and a trio of men's magazines, as well.

In 1968 Mike and Carol became serious breeders and exhibitors of collies, a pursuit they continued through 1981. During that time they bred and/or exhibited twenty-seven champion collies, and they were the country's leading breeders and exhibitors during various years along the way.

This led them to purchase the Briarwood Pet Motel in Cincinnati in 1976. It was the country's second-largest luxury boarding and grooming establishment, and they worked full-time at it for the next few years. By 1980 the kennel was being run by a staff of twenty-one, and Mike was free to return to his first love, science fiction, albeit at a far slower pace than his previous writing. They sold the kennel in 1993.

Mike's first novel in this "second career" was *The Soul Eater*, which was followed shortly by *Birthright: The Book of Man*, *Walpurgis III*, the four-book Tales of the Galactic Midway series, *The Branch*, the four-book Tales of the Velvet Comet series, and *Adventures*, all from Signet. His breakthrough novel was the international bestseller *Santiago*, published by Tor in 1986. Tor has since published *Stalking the Unicorn*, *The Dark Lady*, *Ivory*, *Second Contact*, *Paradise*, *Purgatory*, *Inferno*, the Double *Bwana/Bully!*, and the collection *Will the Last Person to Leave the Planet Please Shut Off the Sun?* His most recent Tor releases were *A Miracle of Rare Design*, *A Hunger in the Soul*, *The Outpost*, and the *The Return of Santiago*.

Even at his reduced rate, Mike was too prolific for one publisher, and in the 1990s Ace published *Soothsayer*, *Oracle*, and *Prophet*; Questar published *Lucifer Jones*; Bantam brought out the *Locus* best-selling trilogy of *The Widowmaker*, *The Widowmaker Reborn*, and *The Widowmaker Unleashed*; and Del Rey published *Kirinyaga: A Fable of Utopia* and *Lara Croft, Tomb Raider: The Amulet of Power*. His current releases include *A Gathering of Widowmakers* for Meisha Merlin, *Dragon America* for Phobos, and *Lady with an Alien, A Club in Montmarte*, and *The World behind the Door* for Watson-Guptill, *Hazards* and *Kilimanjaro* for Subterranean Press, and *Stalking the Unicorn, Stalking the Vampire, Stalking the Dragon*, and the Starship series for Pyr.

Beginning with *Shaggy B.E.M. Stories* in 1988, Mike has also become an anthology editor (and was nominated for a Best Editor Hugo in 1994 and 1995). His list of anthologies in print and in press totals forty-eight, and includes *Alternate Presidents, Alternate Kennedys, Sherlock Holmes in Orbit, By Any Other Fame, Dinosaur Fantastic, Down These Dark Spaceways, The Dragon Done It, Alien Crimes*, and *When Diplomacy Fails*, plus the recent *Stars*, coedited with superstar singer Janis Ian.

Mike has always supported the "specialty press," and he has numerous books and collections out in limited editions from such diverse publishers as Phantasia Press, Axolotl Press, Misfit Press, Pulphouse Publishing, Wildside Press, Dark Regions Press, NESFA Press, WSFA Press, Obscura Press, Farthest Star, and others. He recently served a stint as the science fiction editor for BenBella Books, and in 2006 he became the executive editor of *Jim Baen's Universe*.

Mike was never interested in writing short stories early in his career, producing only seven between 1976 and 1986. Then something clicked, and he has written and sold more than 235 stories since 1986, and now spends more time on short fiction than on novels. The writing that has brought him the most acclaim thus far in his career is the Kirinyaga series, which, with sixty-seven major and minor awards and nominations to date, is the most honored series of stories in the history of science fiction.

He also began writing short nonfiction as well. He sold a four-part series, "Forgotten Treasures," to the *Magazine of Fantasy and Science Fiction*, was a regular columnist for *Speculations* ("Ask Bwana") for twelve years, currently appears in every issue of the *SFWA Bulletin* ("The Resnick/Malzberg Dialogues"), and wrote a biweekly column for the late, lamented GalaxyOnline.com.

Carol has always been Mike's uncredited collaborator on his science fiction, but in recent years they have sold two movie scripts—*Santiago* and *The Widowmaker*, both based on Mike's books—and Carol *is* listed as his collaborator on those.

Readers of Mike's works are aware of his fascination with Africa, and the many uses to which he has put it in his science fiction. Mike and Carol have taken numerous safaris, visiting Kenya (four times), Tanzania, Malawi, Zimbabwe, Egypt, Botswana, and Uganda. Mike edited the Library of African Adventure series for St. Martin's Press and is currently editing *The Resnick Library of African Adventure* and, with Carol as coeditor, *The Resnick Library of Worldwide Adventure* for Alexander Books.

Since 1989, Mike has won five Hugo Awards (for "Kirinyaga," "The Manamouki," "Seven Views of Olduvai Gorge," "The 43 Antarean Dynasties," and "Travels with My Cats") and a Nebula Award (for "Seven Views of Olduvai Gorge"), and has been nominated for thirty-three Hugos, eleven Nebulas, a Clarke (British), and six Seiun-sho (Japanese). He has also won a Seiun-sho, a Prix Tour Eiffel (French), two Prix Ozones (French), ten HOMer Awards, an Alexander Award, a Golden Pagoda Award, a Hayakawa SF Award (Japanese), a *Locus* Award, three Ignotus Awards (Spanish), a Xatafi-Cyberdark Award (Spanish), a Futura Award (Croatia), an El Melocoton Mechanico (Spanish), two Sfinks Awards (Polish), and a Fantastyka Award (Polish), and has topped the *Science Fiction Chronicle* Poll six times, the *Scifi Weekly* Hugo Straw Poll three times, and the *Asimov's*

Readers' Poll five times. In 1993 he was awarded the Skylark Award for Lifetime Achievement in Science Fiction, and both in 2001 and in 2004 he was named Fictionwise.com's Author of the Year.

His work has been translated into French, Italian, German, Spanish, Japanese, Korean, Bulgarian, Hungarian, Hebrew, Russian, Latvian, Lithuanian, Polish, Czech, Dutch, Swedish, Romanian, Finnish, Danish, Chinese, Greek, Slovakian, Portuguese, and Croatian.

He was recently the subject of Fiona Kelleghan's massive *Mike Resnick: An Annotated Bibliography and Guide to His Work*. Adrienne Gormley is currently preparing a second edition.